MW00945236

Rainbow Gardens

The Shops on Wolf Creek Square

Gini Athey

Editing: Brittiany Koren/Written Dreams
Cover art design/Layout: Ed Vincent/ENC Graphic Services
Front cover photographs: daisy: © Eireann/Shutterstock.com;
watercolor background: © legrandshow/Shutterstock.com;
storefronts: © LanaN/Shutterstock.com;
wheelbarrow: DeeBoldrick/Bigstock.com;
daisies background: © OJardin/Shutterstock.com

Map illustration by Logan Stefonek

Category: Women's Fiction/Romance

First Print Edition 2015
0 1 2 3 4 5 6 7 8 9

Other Books in
The Shop on Wolf Creek Square series
by Gini Athey

Quilts Galore (Book 1)

Country Law (Book 2)

To Shirley C.—we are married to cousins, but our bond is closer because of words and writing.

To Monica C.—our friendship has brought joy to my life.

Note to Readers

Welcome to Wolf Creek.

In *Rainbow Gardens*, the third book in my Wolf Creek Square series, you'll meet long time resident, Megan Reynolds, and her wonderful flower shop. Other residents and shopkeepers from *Quilts Galore* (Book 1) and *Country Law* (Book 2) are Megan's friends and part of the everyday activity on the Square.

Nestled in rich farm land, Wolf Creek is a small fictional town west of Green Bay, Wisconsin. Unique to the town is Wolf Creek Square, a pedestrian-only area where historical buildings surround a picnic area, a stage used for concerts and festivals, flower gardens and walkways. The Square is a beautiful place during all four seasons.

For many years Megan has entered floral-design contests as an avenue out of town. A requirement of each major contest is that she'd need to leave town and travel for part of the year. She has finally been chosen as a finalist in a prestigious national contest and is now debating her yearning to leave Wolf Creek.

When Clayton Sommers arrives to interview Megan for the final round of judging for the contest and then decides to stay in Wolf Creek, Megan questions her plans to leave. To say nothing about the complications that arise when she agrees to become the wedding planner for two of the Square's women, one of whom will become her sister-in-law.

Snippets of history about the Buchanan and Reynolds' families are intermixed with Megan's story. Many of those living in Wolf Creek and some with shops on the Square can trace their family history to the beginning of the town. (More of the history of the town appears in **Quilts Galore** and **Country Law**.)

So enjoy life on the Square, then visit my website, www.giniathey.com and sign up for my newsletter. You'll want to know what's happening on the Square.

Gini Athey
2015

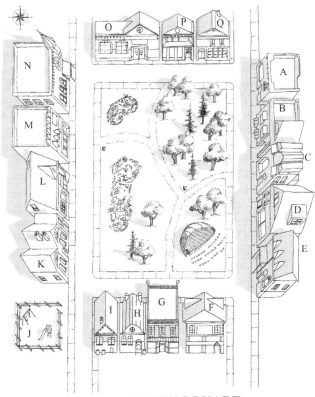

WOLF CREEK SQUARE

A-Farmer Foods
B-Vacant
C-Rainbow Gardens
D-Vacant
E-Country Law
F-Art&Son Jewelry
G-Quilts Galore
H-Vacant
I-Pages and Toys

J-Fenced Playground
K-Styles by Knight and Day
L-Vacant
M-Biscuits and Brew
N-Inn on the Square
O-Museum
P-Mayor's Office
Q-Vacant

From roots to leaves to flower
A palette across the Universe
A seed drops, cocooned by earth
For the cycle to begin again.

—Author Unknown

"If I had a single flower for every time I think of you, I
could walk forever in my garden."

—Claudia Adrienne Grandi

MAY
1

Thud. I opened my eyes wide at the sound. It came from outside, but I tried to ignore it, preferring to hang on to the fringes of the images of the mystery man who'd appeared yet again in my lovely dream.

Sadly, I couldn't manage it. Like so many times before, my dream faded into wispy images and then vanished.

A second thud, followed by the sound of a truck growing fainter, pulling away from the building, I presumed. That got my attention, along with the sunlight streaming through the rooftop sky lights and onto my face. *A truck?* Sunshine? What time *was* it?

I rolled over in my bed toward the nightstand to check the time. *No, impossible.* I checked the clock again—9:52. Reality hit hard. I had exactly eight minutes before another day began at Rainbow Gardens, and yes, it *was* Tuesday. The truck I heard had delivered a fresh supply of flowers on my doorstep at the back of the shop on schedule.

Oh, no. Within minutes a group of tour bus owners were due in Wolf Creek Square. They had a mission, too, namely to take a close look at us as a potential stop for their tours of small towns in Northeastern Wisconsin. Sarah Hutchinson, mayor of Wolf Creek, managed the schedule for the Square as part of her job. Last week, she'd sent an email reminder to all the shop owners about this significant group of tour operators: *Spruce up your shop and make it shine, put out the welcome mat, and be prepared to answer questions about what we offer here at Wolf Creek Square.*

I groaned, thinking about the colossal job I faced. But I threw back the thin quilt and got to my feet, then quickly pulled on my baggy—and raggedy—jeans and the paint-spattered sweatshirt I'd worked in the night before. They'd do long enough to get the door open and drag the boxes of flowers in. I'd find a minute or two before the tour group arrived to change into some decent clothes. But at the moment, I couldn't spare a minute for makeup or hair. Breakfast was out of the question.

Meanwhile, I planned what I could manage to accomplish in, oh, the next five minutes or so. First, give some attention to flowers in the cooler to make sure they looked perky and put on a good color show. Then I'd straighten the display racks and work area before our important "guests" arrived. I grabbed my running shoes and hurried down the spiral staircase that connected my upstairs apartment to the ground level flower shop.

"Megan?" My brother had apparently unlocked the back door and let himself in. He carried a large box.

"Oh, thanks, Eli," I said, nodding toward the carton, "but I could have managed."

"The delivery guy stopped at our store and asked if he should leave your flowers. He said you always meet him at the back door."

"Yeah, I do. But…" Too preoccupied and rushed, I left it at that.

Eli was about to set the box down, but he froze in place, frowning at the display area in the front of the shop. "Want to explain why this place looks like a tornado went through it?"

With cupboard doors open and crystal vases and colored pots scattered about, I grudgingly admitted he'd described it accurately, but I had no time to fill him in with a long-winded explanation.

"I was rummaging around looking for a few things last night."

Eli frowned, but put the box down and left to get another one outside my back door. Over the past few years, my big brother had muttered more than a few disparaging comments about my flower business and they boiled down to two main points: high overhead and minimal profit. He'd also made it clear to me—and anyone else who would listen—what he thought of his baby sister's attempts to mimic large-scale florists in far-flung cities like New York or Dallas. And why would I entertain any notion that I had even a *tiny* chance to win any of the floral arrangement contests I'd been entering for years?

As annoying as Eli could be, I tolerated his remarks. I knew if I ever called on him, he would drop everything to help his kid sister. Both Eli and his twin, Elliot, had always been that kind of brothers. Eli was just a bit gruffer about it.

But as disastrous as Rainbow Gardens looked at the moment, I smiled inside. I had a lovely little secret. At last, my chance to prove myself—at least to some extent—had materialized. What would Eli think when I finally broke the news? After years of disappointment, I'd been selected as a *finalist* in the most prestigious national floral design contest of the year.

I was about to end my silence and blurt my happy announcement when a customer walked in the front door. Had I been so focused last night on arranging a practice piece for the contest that I'd forgotten to lock the door? I glanced around and winced at the mess I'd made in the process of creating something wonderful.

I went to meet the customer, shutting cabinet doors along the way and loading my arms with rolls of ribbon and a couple of pots. "Can I help you?"

The stranger scanned the room, but quickly fixed his gaze on me. "My name is Clayton Rogers. I'm looking for Megan Reynolds."

"That's me." I managed to stick my hand out from under the ribbons and accept his offer of a handshake, suddenly aware of his touch, the pressure of his hand holding mine. Firm and professional, yet warm and friendly.

"Megan?"

The edge of Eli's voice diverted my attention. I let go of Clayton's hand and glanced behind me. Eli had put down another box on my workbench, putting on a show of moving things aside to make room for it. Before I could say anything, he came to my side, giving the impression of support. No, *protection* better described Eli's body language. With ten years difference in our ages, in Eli's eyes, I was still a kid heading off to the big bad world of kindergarten.

I raised my finger in the air, silently asking Clayton for a minute. "Thanks for helping, Eli." *Again.* "But aren't you needed at Farmer Foods?" I put my hand on his upper arm and guided him around the boxes to the back door. "I'll talk to you later."

He raised an eyebrow. "Yes, you will."

I locked the door behind Eli when he left. Why did I do that? I never locked the back door when the shop was open. Maybe I wanted to be sure Eli didn't wander in unannounced again. I shook my head at my own actions and returned to the front of the shop. "Sorry for the interruption, uh, Mr. Rogers."

"Clayton...call me Clayton. And I should be the one apologizing."

"Why is that?" I looked around at the mess I had yet to tackle. Out my front window I could see people walking on the Square. Probably the tour group, along with regular shoppers. They'd be coming in to assess my shop in the one case, or browse or place an order in the other. Both groups would see my shop in shambles. I grabbed a roll of ribbon and began weaving the end through my fingers, making a bow of sorts.

"I was supposed to call ahead and schedule the interview," he said, resting his hand on the workbench, "but I wanted to see your place before I made an official visit."

"Interview?" I didn't remember scheduling an interview. I'd been so preoccupied with the contest and keeping up with my regular business that relatively small things like articles in the local newspaper slipped by me. Besides, I'd never heard of a reporter named Clayton Rogers. Not surprising, since I had no reason to keep anything other than the contest and my business in the forefront of my mind.

Clayton frowned. "Yes, an interview. It's the next step for the finalists in the contest."

Then I saw my reflection in the mirror in the back of the cooler. What would Sarah say if she saw me looking this disheveled? I couldn't let that happen.

I raced up the stairs and peeled off my jeans and sweatshirt, replacing them with my best pair of black ankle pants and a gauze tunic in cranberry red, a color that set off my light brown hair. "Hair," I said out loud, using the brush to fluff up the natural wave in my hair. As I switched to my black flats, I took two seconds to swipe lipstick across my mouth. That was it, and it would have to do. A glance in the mirror confirmed I was new and improved.

Back downstairs, I started with the most eye-catching part of the mess, the vases and pots. Stacking them in piles of three and four, I hid them behind the cupboard doors. I grabbed an empty box and scooped up the spools of ribbons and dumped them inside. They'd have to wait their turn for better organization, with any luck, later that day. If not, tomorrow would be soon enough.

Better, much better. But Rainbow Gardens was a working shop, so maybe a little mess added a special touch. I knew how to hustle on a busy day. Right?

I addressed the heart of the matter next. The fresh flowers that had arrived earlier that morning. *While you were still dreaming away with Mr. Romantic.*

I cut open the first box, my heart soaring in anticipation. Every week I got to experience renewed pleasure as the rush of fragrances rose from the opened box. My babies, I called them, helpless and needing lots of TLC before they withered and died.

I lifted the flowers from the box and spread them around the workbench. They needed to be sorted and watered, but time was short.

A few minutes after eleven, Sarah opened the door and the group of about a dozen men and women trailed in behind her. I exhaled to help me change my focus from the flowers to the people, who arranged themselves to fit the limited space. By the time they were done, the first to enter moved to the back of the shop and the last few filled the remaining room in the display area.

"Okay, everyone," Sarah began when the last to enter closed the door behind him. "Meet Megan Reynolds, owner of the popular shop, Rainbow Gardens. Around here, we also know her as Elliot and Eli Reynolds' sister. You just met the twin brothers at Farmer Foods. The Reynolds family is one of Wolf Creek's oldest."

Grinning, Sarah turned to me. "Your turn, Megan. Tell us about your shop."

I stared at her, suddenly dumbstruck. At the last business association meeting, Sarah had talked about *showcasing* our businesses. No problem, I understood that. The shop owners on the Square were used to groups of three or four tour guides or travel writers coming around. They more or less blended in with the customers and watched us work. We chatted with them casually. But I hadn't adjusted my thinking to the larger group of a dozen people, so I hadn't prepared a presentation. Big mistake on my part, but I had no choice but to wing it.

Sarah cast a pointed smile my way and nodded.

I cleared my throat. "Well, as you can tell from the way you're packed in, this is a small shop..." A scatter of chuckles came from the group standing shoulder to shoulder. *Nothing like stating the obvious.* "But the business is not small in scope. In fact, one of my contracts is with the Inn across the way. I provide the arrangements for their rooms and small vases for the Crossroads' dining room. Other shops, including the newest business on the Square, Country Law, have contracts with me to periodically deliver flower arrangements or decorations." My little speech was even boring me. I glanced at Sarah hoping for some support.

"Go on," she encouraged, absently tugging at the lapels of what looked like a brand new linen jacket in lemon yellow. Perfect for a spring day. She also wore a small multi-colored gemstone brooch, no doubt compliments of Art&Son, the jewelry store on the Square.

Two women in the middle of the pack whispered and nodded toward an arrangement I'd placed on my workbench. That prompted me to add, "Like florists everywhere, I supply flowers for weddings, funerals, birthdays...name an occasion, and I can create arrangements for it."

"Well, then, is this one for sale?" The older of the two women pointed to an arrangement in a vase of robin's egg blue, similar to the color of the blazer she wore. The cheerful white daisies nearly matched her hair.

"Yes, it certainly is." As if I would say no to a customer ready to buy.

"Mark it sold, please, and I'll pick it up after our last stop on the tour. There should be plenty of room for it on the bus." She reached through the front line of visitors and handed me her business card.

"Thank you." I picked up a pen and wrote SOLD on the back of the card and stuck it between the flowers. I made a mental note to add a few stems later to fill out the arrangement. A little bonus.

Another woman thrust her card toward me. "Can you make something for me by the end of the day? It's my mother-in-law's birthday."

My spirits were headed toward the ceiling. "I sure can. What kinds of flowers or colors would you like me to use?"

The woman waved off the question. "I'll leave it up to you. Anything that speaks of spring. I trust your judgment—but I can't take anything too large. She lives in an apartment and I'm carrying it back on the bus."

I quickly made notes on her card and put it in the pocket of my smock.

"Did these just arrive?" A man standing close to the far end of the counter had pulled back the flaps on one of the newly delivered boxes.

"Yes. As a standing order, flowers are delivered every Tuesday. That means I always have a fresh supply."

Another male voice came from the back corner of the room and he leaned sideways so I could see him. "What about artificial flowers for outdoor displays? Do you work with those?"

"If I know far enough in advance, I'm happy to, but I don't have room to keep them in stock."

He nodded, as if storing away the information.

"How about business cards for everyone, Megan," Sarah

interjected.

I grabbed a stack from the counter and passed half to the group at the front of the shop and the rest to those next to me behind the counter. "Take as many as you like."

A young woman just inside the front door sneezed. "Sorry, my allergies are acting up. I'll wait outside... lovely shop, though." She waved, and slipped out the door, the jingle of the bell muffled in the low din of murmuring voices exchanging comments.

"Any other questions before we move on?" Sarah had transitioned back to leader mode, and used the departure of one of the dozen visitors as a cue to head out. I'd seen her manage crowds like this before. She was a great combination of Wolf Creek Square booster and organizer.

A man standing by the glass cooler raised his hand. "I have one. Tell me, do you make *all* the arrangements yourself?" His words came out as a challenge, so much so that most of the others turned to stare at him.

Since I'd been listening to Eli talk to me like that for my entire life, I was used to an edgy tone. My confidence bloomed in response. "Yes, I do. I create all of them."

So there.

He nodded. "I've never seen daisies paired with roses before."

Whoa. This man knew about typical flower pairings. That caught me by surprise.

"You're right," I said. "I created that particular arrangement by gathering extra stems from other arrangements I'd made that same afternoon, the day before yesterday, actually. Rather than discard them, I used as many as would fit in the vase."

"What about employees? How many do you have?" he asked.

The man next to him punched him playfully on the shoulder. "What's the matter, Tom? Tours not enough for you? You looking for a job?"

"I always wanted to have a flower shop or greenhouse," Tom answered in a voice that surprised me with its thoughtfulness.

Sarah looked at her watch. "I see it's almost noon…"

"Excuse me," a woman near the door called out. "What can customers buy from you besides flowers? Beautiful as they are, arrangements like these would be difficult to keep intact on the ride home on the bus or in a van."

I gestured to the shelves near the front windows. "I'm so glad you asked. I always have lots of vases and colorful pottery on display—and a few pieces of garden art. They're popular Christmas gifts. But beyond that, tourists coming from nearby towns will know I'm here when they want personal attention for a wedding or a special shower or anniversary party. I do many events where my flower arrangements or a centerpiece exemplify the theme of a party."

"Well, thanks," Sarah said, grinning. "Time for us to head to Crossroads for a buffet lunch. The chef assured us there would be lots of samples, and they're setting us up in the private dining room. Let's all meet there in fifteen minutes."

Waves and a string of thank-yous followed as the group filed out. Sarah left with a pleasant nod. Somehow, even with the mess and my lack of preparation, I'd done my part. I was pretty proud of myself.

Since Sarah and I were friends, I intended to tell her she needed to warn us about the big difference between the small groups and a fairly large gathering of a dozen people. The way the Square was growing and bringing in greater numbers every year, all the owners would need to up their game. I couldn't be the only one who could have used some warning about the need for a more organized presentation. A little voice inside my head scoffed at that thought. After all these years, did I really need to be told how to string sentences together about Rainbow Gardens?

"Excuse me, Ms. Reynolds." The man the others had called Tom had waited until the rest of the group had left the shop before approaching my workbench.

Irrationally, I bristled inside from what I interpreted as his earlier critique of my daisies and roses combination. "Megan, please. Uh, what can I help you with today?"

"I'm amazed by the work you do here," he said, looking

around him.

Not a trace of challenge came through.

"It's apparent you enjoy your work. I envy you." He paused and stared at the arrangement on the counter that now sported a sold sign. "Like I said, I've always wanted to work with plants."

I kept my voice neutral when I asked, "Is there any particular reason why you haven't?"

He waved his hand nervously. "Oh, the usual reasons, I suppose. Family business. The R word—responsibilities."

I could tell he wanted to say more. "What is it you'd like to know, Tom?"

Again, he hesitated. I waited.

"Can I come and spend a day with you?" he asked.

Instinctively, I took a step back.

He laughed and raised his hands in a show of apologetic surrender. "That came out wrong. What I meant was that I'd like to work in the shop with you for a day. Maybe once I try it, I'll find it isn't the career I want after all—or, maybe I'll find it irresistible."

His offer came out of the blue, but once again, I'd been thinking about hiring a part-time person to help during the summer festivals on the Square. My other secret got in the way of doing that. No one, not even my closest friends or my brothers knew my private thought...wish, I suppose I should call it. If I won the Bartholomew Floral Design contest I'd need to be out of town for extended periods of time. The kind of part-time help I'd taken on in the past wouldn't be enough. I'd either have to hire someone to manage Rainbow Gardens. Or, maybe even...I stopped there. Tom was waiting for an answer.

"How about next Saturday?" I asked, taken in by his sincerity. "That's right before the summer season starts."

Tom frowned. "Could you make it Thursday? I'm taking a group to The Domes in Milwaukee on Saturday."

"Lucky you," I said. "I envy you the trip. I love it there. Where else can you visit the rain forest and the desert in the same half hour?" The Domes was one of Wisconsin's horticultural wonder sites, displaying plants from regions from all over the world—and creating the climate to make it work. "Thursday will be fine. I'll leave a mess for you to pick up."

His look of dismay amused me, but he relaxed a bit when I laughed.

"What time should I be here?" he asked.

"Shop opens at 10:00. I'll unlock the door at 9:30. Bring a lunch."

He looked at his watch and rushed to the door. "See you Thursday."

The bell continued to jingle long after the door closed.

Clayton and Tom. Two new names before noon. Time for lunch, and I hadn't even had breakfast. The shop empty, I ran upstairs to grab the Biscuits and Brew turkey sandwich I'd left in my refrigerator the day before. I poured a glass of chocolate milk, fresh from Farmer Foods, to go with it. I carried my makeshift lunch downstairs to eat while I went back to unpacking and sorting my Tuesday flower order.

Once I dispensed with both lunch and the flowers, I turned my attention to the birthday arrangement for Ms. Collins. She'd asked for something small, but as my mind wandered to Clayton and dinner, and then to my offer to Tom, I kept adding one flower after another until I finally stood back to take a look. I laughed out loud and shook my head. I'd made an arrangement large enough for the lobby of the Inn or the table in Country Law's reception area. I started over and focused, finally finishing a bouquet fit for an apartment.

Just before closing both women came in, talking over each other's words and laughing. Each was carrying a shopping bag filled to the top and then some. They were definite in their promises to return to Wolf Creek Square soon. Each ran a tour company that specialized in vans, not coaches, and they needed new destinations to keep their customers coming back.

The shops on the Square had been on the receiving end of a great day.

"I'll be sure to tell our mayor you enjoyed your tour today," I said.

When they left with their flower arrangements, I locked

the door and pivoted around, resting my back against the door. I gazed into the shop I'd loved for so long. I took in the bright vases and pottery plant pots and the glass case now filled with fresh roses of all sizes and colors, spring irises and daisies, tulips in a dazzling array of vibrant hues, traditional carnations that some people still liked, and white lilies so perfect they looked like pieces of sculpture. For years now, I'd spent most of my life working in the shop and living upstairs.

I used decorative enamel buckets to display bouquets, small and inexpensive enough that almost anyone could afford to pick up one on the way home. The supply was thinned out, so I planned to replenish them the next morning, and then concentrate on arrangements I needed to practice for the contest. Somehow, in the process, I'd figure out how to make the best use of Tom. Other than taking on a part-time employee during peak season weekends, I'd never had many helpers, so I didn't want to waste his enthusiasm.

And then there was dinner. I glanced down at my clothes. The paint-spattered sweatshirt was gone, and I looked pretty good for my shop visitors, but Clayton Rogers' first impression was that of a woman with finger-combed hair and clothes fit for a cleaning crew. I needed a second chance to make a first impression.

2

Once upstairs I changed from the casual tunic and cotton pants to something a little crisper. I thought of the term, business casual. That's what I was going for. I rifled through my collection of jackets and tunics and skirts and pants, finally settling on the most professional looking black slacks I had, often pulled out for deliveries to funeral homes and for meetings with wedding planners. I paired the slacks with a crisp white shirt and a matching pin-stripe blazer. I stepped back from the mirror, evaluating the image I'd gone for. Professional enough to be taken seriously, but casual enough so I wouldn't look like I'd tried too hard.

A sweep of the mascara wand and fresh lip gloss and I was good to go. I gathered cash, keys, and lipstick and put them in a small black clutch rather than in my pockets. Holding the purse would give me something to do with my nervous hands.

As I gave my hair a final pat, I was surprised by the increasingly intense flutters in my stomach. Now that it was time to walk across the Square to Crossroads, the voices urging me not to go grew louder. Well, I had to go. I couldn't leave the guy waiting for me at a table. But I absolutely regretted agreeing to this dinner. What was I thinking having dinner with Clayton Rogers, who, after all, represented the contest? Was it even ethical?

I could just hear Eli's comments when he found out. And he'd be sure to find out, not because I told him, but because some busybody would mention seeing me with a stranger at Crossroads. All the more reason to leave town and strike out on my own somewhere else.

Taking deep breaths, I made my way down my spiral stairway and out the door. It took three minutes tops to make my way to the reception area of Crossroads, where I told the hostess I was meeting someone, Clayton Rogers.

"Oh, of course. He said you'd be joining him. He's already seated with his mother by the window." The hostess, someone I didn't recognize, gestured for me to follow her. "This way, please."

His mother?

Clayton rose from his chair and greeted me when I approached. He casually pulled out a chair for me and nodded to the hostess. The guy had smooth manners, I conceded.

He wasted no time introducing his mother, Sadie Rogers, explaining who I was by adding, "Megan is the finalist I'm here to interview."

I held out my hand across the table. "Nice to meet you, Mrs. Rogers."

"Call me Sadie, please." Three sparkling bracelets clanked against each other when she shook my hand.

I moved the small vase of flowers to an empty space at one corner of the table, giving me an unobstructed view of a woman I guessed to be somewhere near sixty. She looked great, too, with her smartly cut light brown hair and nearly unlined skin.

"Much better," Sadie said, giving me a firm nod. "I never did like looking around a centerpiece."

"I hope you don't mind, but I've already ordered an appetizer for us," Clayton said. "The bruschetta sounded too good to pass up." Clayton lifted an open bottle of wine. "Care to join us for a glass of merlot?"

Merlot. One of my favorites. But was wine a good idea? I still wasn't convinced this dinner made sense.

"A small glass won't hurt," Sadie said, as if she'd read my mind.

"You're right." I nodded to Clayton and slid the wine glass at my place setting in his direction. Since it seemed I'd surrendered to the notion of dinner and wouldn't be making an excuse to run away, I arranged my napkin across my lap.

We put in our entrée orders before the appetizer platter arrived. I stuck with easy-to-eat blackened salmon, with some kind of potato concoction that spared me from the need to chase pasta around my plate. Sadie apparently wasn't worried about that, and even asked for the chef's special meat sauce for her manicotti. Clayton took advantage of the roast chicken, a perpetual Crossroads favorite.

By the time the waitress delivered the platter of bruschetta, Italian bread, and a bowl of olives, Sadie had already asked a million questions about Wolf Creek and the Square. I relaxed because I sensed genuine curiosity, and besides, I knew the answers. Hearing myself talk about the history of the Square and relaying the fact it was almost torn down in favor of a parking deck and an indoor mall brought out my dramatic side. "Sometimes I can't believe how close we came to losing these historic buildings—and the very character of Wolf Creek itself."

I addressed Sadie, but when I paused I glanced at Clayton. His amused smile wasn't lost on me. I'd seen it earlier that day when he was about ready to take my photo. Against my will. My warming cheeks told me I was likely blushing, but maybe it was a reaction to the wine.

It wasn't long before our meals arrived, and between bites of salmon and the house salad, I told Sadie about Sarah, our mayor, and the town history she was working on. "So many of us are direct descendants of the original founders," I added.

When Sadie grinned and commented on my enthusiasm for my hometown, it hit me that I hadn't enjoyed an evening out with new acquaintances in a very long time.

"I think you'd like Sarah," I said. "If you think *I'm* a fan of Wolf Creek, you should hear her talk about our little town, past, present, and future." I'm not sure why I could easily envision the two women becoming friendly, but maybe it was a certain kind of resemblance, not in looks, but in attitude. Open and welcoming.

As the evening passed, my initial impression that there was something familiar about Clayton remained in place. He focused on his dinner, preferring to stay on the fringe of my conversation with his mother, but more than once I caught him staring at me.

Emboldened by Sadie's curiosity—not to mention her hearty appetite—I described another Crossroads special. "No one leaves Wolf Creek without sampling some Crossroads pie. Now, Eli, my brother, likes the chocolate mousse. I prefer the cherry pie, made with cherries from our local orchard and topped off with vanilla ice cream produced at a nearby dairy." I laughed at my own description. "But, that's just my opinion. There are many choices."

"What a wonderful town booster you are, Megan," Sadie said.

Before I had a chance to comment, the waitress came and took our dessert order, followed quickly by Art Carlson and Marianna Spencer approaching our table. I opened my mouth, prepared to introduce them as two more shop owners on the Square, but Art spoke first.

"Clay? Clayton?" Art had surprise etched in every feature. "Marianna, I'd like you to meet an old colleague—and friend—of mine, Clayton Som…"

"Clayton *Rogers*." He'd risen so quickly his chair hovered on two legs before settling back on four. He thrust his hand toward Marianna. "And my mother, Sadie Rogers."

Sadie sighed. "Clayton, really. It's time to stop the masquerade."

Masquerade?

"Please, join us," Sadie said, already shifting her chair to make room for two more.

I moved over as well, while Art took a chair from an empty table next to us. When Marianna and Art were settled, Art couldn't keep his surprise contained. He kept looking from me to Clayton and back again at me. "What masquerade?"

Apparently, I wasn't the only puzzled person at the table.

"Don't look at me, Art," I said, raising my hands in front of me. "I'm not in the know here."

Marianna filled the silence by turning to explain to Sadie that she owned Quilts Galore, the shop next to Art's jewelry store. "Art and I end up coming here just about every night. We just polished off some pie."

Sadie grinned. "Megan told us that sampling Crossroads desserts is a requirement."

With the mood lightened a notch by small talk, Art signaled the waitress and ordered a carafe of decaf coffee. My impatience steadily intensified. What was Art talking about? It had to be important, because in a matter of seconds the energy at the table had immediately shifted from casual and pleasant to awkward, even tense.

I waited for Clayton, or Sadie, to explain, but both seemed self-conscious, unwilling—or unable—to begin. The uncomfortable silence held until the waitress returned with the coffee and unloaded the five desserts from the tray.

"I'll pour the coffee," Clayton said, reaching for the carafe. He stretched his long arms across the table and filled our cups. Finally, he flopped back in his chair. "Okay, Mom, you let the cat out of the bag, you make the explanations."

Sadie rested her hands in her lap. "Oh, this is all so embarrassing, and we weren't ready to talk about it. But here we are, in a place we've never been, far away from New York."

I swallowed a sip of coffee and leaned forward in anticipation. But why was my heart pounding so?

"You see, my—our—old life is long gone now." She picked up her fork, but didn't make a move to cut into her mixed berry pie. "Let me just make a long story short. My second husband and Clayton's stepfather, Albert Winston, was involved in major investment fraud at his brokerage firm."

"Wow," Art said, pulling his head back in obvious surprise.

"I had an art gallery where I sold work from emerging artists, and, of course, I sold Clayton's paintings, too." She shook her head. "But unbeknownst to me, the money to launch my gallery came from profits Albert gained fraudulently. That meant it was seized as part of his assets, ultimately to be liquidated when compensating those whose money was essentially stolen."

"I've heard of that kind of thing," Marianna said, her voice soft, "but I don't think I've ever met anyone it happened to."

"As you can imagine, no other gallery in New York wanted anything to do with us, so Clayton and I packed up and moved to Vermont."

I glanced at Clayton, but he sat still in his chair, his gaze fixed on Sadie.

Sadie filled in the rest of the story quickly, explaining that they decided to use Clayton's middle name, Roger, which became Rogers, and that allowed Clayton to take on a new identity when he looked for work. Sadie sold some family jewelry and Clayton found a job in a seasonal gallery. They'd managed.

"We were prepared to keep up our ruse," Sadie said, "but someone browsing in the gallery recognized Clayton and one of the New York tabloids ran a story about us hiding out in Vermont. We picked up and moved again."

Art and Marianna wore stunned expressions. I imagined I looked the same. Finally, Art cleared his throat. "Why didn't you call me, Clay? You know I'd have helped you. And Wisconsin is a long way from New York."

Clayton frowned in thought. "Before you left, I recall you telling some of us that you wanted to leave to help your son…you know, provide a better environment for him."

The first words he'd spoken, I noted, since the pie arrived.

Art nodded vigorously. "Right, right. And it was the best decision I ever made. Alan is much happier here." Art squeezed Marianna's hand and grinned. "And so am I."

"Wait a minute," I said, meeting Clayton's gaze. "How is it that you're working for Bartholomew Design?" Art and Marianna didn't know that I'd even entered a contest, let alone been named a finalist. I'd kept that a secret from everyone in town, even my brothers. But if Clayton was an artist of some renown, why had he deigned work for the floral design company, doing routine interviews no less?

Clayton shrugged. "No mystery to that. Bartholomew needed impartial interviewers and I needed money. And we also needed to hide. Again."

Sadie lightly slapped the tablecloth with her fingertips, a gesture that accentuated her perfectly shaped oval nails. "But we are *not* going to hide anymore."

I believed her. She didn't seem like a person to make rash statements. This encounter with Art must have shifted something inside her.

"I am still Sadie Winston, but Clayton is no longer a Rogers. He's..."

He held out his hand for me to shake. "Clayton Sommers."

I played along. "Nice to meet you, Mr. Sommers." The earlier warm rush zipping through me from his touch repeated, leaving me unable to add a clever remark. Fortunately, I didn't have to, because Marianna's attempt to stifle a yawn drew everyone's attention.

We laughed as a group when she said, "Trust me, my early start this morning is responsible, not your story." She pushed her chair back and Art did the same. "Best for us to get on home. But it was nice to meet you both." She touched Sadie's arm. "And do stop by Quilts Galore if you have time. I'm at the end of the Square."

"And I expect to see you in my shop soon, Clay." Art flashed a friendly grin. "We've got some catching up to do."

It was as if nothing changed but the atmosphere. And that had definitely improved.

Clayton stood as Art and Marianna rose to leave. "Of course, I'll stop by. I'll come first thing tomorrow, in fact. You were one of my most important mentors, so naturally, I'm eager to see your latest designs. Who knows? They might inspire me to paint again."

I took the last few bites of the pie left on my plate, and took Art and Marianna's quick exit as a signal to depart myself. My fingers itched to type "Clayton Sommers" into the search engine and see what the Internet had to say about him. From what Sadie said, they'd been forced onto a new path, certainly not one they'd chosen. Odd, though, neither appeared broken by what had happened. I pushed away my empty coffee cup and saucer and put my napkin in their place.

"Time for me to head home, too," I said, standing.

"So soon?" Clayton's features showed clear disappointment.

"Like Marianna and Art, I start early—well, usually."

Since Clayton had found me in disarray earlier, I figured an explanation was in order. "Of course, if I'm inspired and work into the wee hours, as I did last night, then my morning is a rush."

Amused, Clayton said, "I see."

I glanced at Sadie. "As a former gallery owner, I'm sure you can understand that I have orders to fill and a front window to change for Memorial Day." I left out the part about Tom Harris coming to the shop on Thursday.

"Thank you for joining us tonight," Sadie said, smiling broadly. "It was a special treat for me. Women talk, you know, is in short supply when there's only one man around. And now I know Marianna, too."

"As the kid sister of two brothers," I said in a matching tongue-in-cheek tone, "I understand you completely."

Despite her teasing, I sensed this mother-son pair shared more than that bond. I sensed mutual admiration, too. A certain amount of pain was inescapable, since both had fallen victim to dishonesty they had no control over, and I wondered how my family would have survived such a far-reaching deception.

"Well, then, good night, Clayton, Sadie. And thanks so much for dinner and good conversation. I always enjoy a meal at Crossroads."

"I'll walk you home."

I waved him off. "No need for that." I pointed out the window. "I'm only going a few steps across the Square."

"You'll have to indulge him, Megan. For all his faults, Albert passed on old-fashioned manners. I'm going to sit tight and have more coffee." As if accentuating her point, she reached for the carafe.

I could see I lost the battle. "There's really no need for this," I said as Clayton and I walked on the winding path across the Square. "But I enjoyed visiting with your mother. And, of course, I never imagined what a difficult few years you've had."

Ignoring my remark, Clayton said, "Yes, I had fun, despite the serious talk. I'm glad you accepted my invitation." He stepped back while I unlocked the door. "Pleasant dreams."

"You, too." I went inside, noting that Clayton stayed in place until I relocked the door.

I raised my hand in a small wave. But when he retraced his steps back to the Inn, an odd awareness washed over me again, as if I had seen him before.

The antique lamp posts in the Square provided enough light for me to navigate to the back of the shop and up the stairs to my apartment without turning on any shop lights. Before turning on the laptop I kept on a desk in my living room, I checked my phone for messages. I'd left it behind on purpose. About a year ago, one too many customers stopped in the middle of a transaction to answer a call or a text. Some days it had seemed like beeps and ringtones and buzzes were a constant in the shop. That's when I'd decided to start leaving my own phone at home when I went out at night. I had to answer calls during the day, but I could go out for dinner without interruption. I had a couple of texts about shop orders, but no voicemail messages. Good.

While I waited for the computer to boot up, I changed into my nightgown and robe, and then poured chocolate milk into a saucepan to heat. My hot chocolate milk had evolved from a now-and-then treat into a nightly ritual. When steam wafted from the pan, I poured it into a mug and headed for my desk.

Okay, girl, time to search. My fingers typed: **Clayton Rogers Sommers** and entries started rolling in. Supposedly several thousand of them, but the first few would provide the key.

"Well, well…my, oh, my." The web search yielded recent headlines first, of course. Search engines love scandals. The articles and wire services filled in some blanks of his bio, from the elite private prep schools to his years at the New York School of Art, where he'd been called a promising artist. This information was mixed into reports of his stepfather's rise and sudden fall into disgrace, including a newspaper photo of Albert Winston being led out of their building on Park Avenue, his hands cuffed. Eventually, he cut a deal and saved the city the cost of a trial, so instead of spending his remaining days in prison, he'd be out in about fifteen years.

Somehow, Clayton's success was linked to the tabloid accounts of his stepfather's fall. Sadie wasn't spared either, and photos of federal agents carrying out computers and art work from her gallery were spread across several newspaper articles. The other artists had their work returned, but not Clayton. The last article I scanned was headlined: *Where Are You Now, Clayton Sommers?* That question was posed by an art critic who apparently felt cheated by not being granted an interview before the bottom fell out of Clayton's career.

"I know where he is, but I'm not telling." I liked saying that out loud. But why? I had no reason to guard his whereabouts. I probably knew less about the real Clayton than the art critic did. But some protective instinct had kicked in and I sure wouldn't reveal anything I knew about him, especially not his location. For reasons I didn't understand, I didn't want people to pass judgment on him, or on Sadie. But at the same time, I didn't care to become involved in Clayton Sommers' personal or professional business.

Clayton. I could hear him saying his name in his crisp, polished voice.

My eyes watered. Maybe it was computer screen fatigue, although I hadn't been staring at it very long.

I forced myself to stop scrolling through more pages of hits about Clayton. Then, I put my laptop into sleep mode and closed the cover. There. I'd spent enough time looking into his past. Besides, Clayton Sommers was here to *interview* me. Nothing more. He—and his mother—would be gone in a few days. Once they left town, I'd never see either of them again.

I swallowed the last of the chocolate milk, cold by now, but still good. As I climbed into bed, it occurred to me that I'd learned more than I needed to know about this artist-turned-interviewer. But all that had nothing to do with the contest and his role with Bartholomew. I had to remember that.

Still, the memory of him staring at me as I told his mother all about the Square made me blush, even while alone in my bed trying to fall asleep. His amused expressions, and the way he stood and watched me lock up the store after walking me home made me wonder if he could be impartial about me. Time would tell, and what I decided to do with the choices and challenges facing me had nothing to do with Clayton Sommers.

3

Early the next morning, I hurried across the Square to join the small group of shop owners at Biscuits and Brew, our café and all around favorite hangout. In the hour or two before opening time, shopkeepers and their employees regularly met to talk about various goings on in the Square. Of course, residents of Wolf Creek and tourists appreciated the great food and legendary coffee, too.

Since I'd launched my flower business in my early twenties, starting with a leased corner of my dad's store, I'd become well-schooled about the importance of our tight knit community on the Square. Long ago, Eli and Elliot had convinced me that Wolf Creek stayed a strong and economically viable town, at least in part, because of relationships—friendships—among the shopkeepers on the Square.

Beyond enjoying each other's company, we brainstormed to come up with new ideas, cross-marketed, and shared in the preparation for the monthly events and festivals that drew locals and tourists alike. May featured a Memorial Day remembrance, followed closely by Founders' Day in June, a time that gave us a chance to tout Wolf Creek's rich history.

But, as much as we enjoyed each other's company, more often than not the women gravitated to one large table while the men gathered at another.

I no sooner got inside the door and inhaled the rich aroma of coffee when I heard a voice call out.

"Hey, Megan, heard you had quite a day yesterday. Want to tell us all about it?" Stephanie, the owner of B and B, grinned as she poured my cup of morning blend.

"Let me get a swallow of caffeine before you start in on me, Steph," I responded, returning her teasing smirk. In truth, I wasn't exactly sure what she was talking about. Had news of my Crossroads dinner with Clayton and Sadie already traveled through the Square? That would be typical—and frustrating. With two brothers and a whole Square of shop owners scrutinizing my every move, no wonder I sometimes fantasized about a life far, far away. But even if word of my dinner had made the rounds, it didn't matter, because I had no intention of mentioning Clayton, or Tom, for that matter. True, I had a lot going on, but I'd kept most of it to myself.

Marianna Spencer had moved her chair over so I could join the group at the women's table. I nodded to her as I slipped into my seat.

"I didn't catch your answer, Megan," Stephanie said, laughing.

"Not a nice way to treat a paying customer," I shot back, a little louder than I'd planned.

Liz Pearson didn't even try to hide her amusement, when she said, "Touchy, touchy." As Marianna's best friend and the wife of Jack Pearson, a partner at Country Law, Liz seemed to know everything about everybody.

"Tom told the whole tour group about coming back to town to work with you on Thursday," Sarah explained, a grin spreading across her face.

Her expression made me wonder just how much pleasure she was getting from watching me squirm. But she and the others could likely see relief on my face. The Tom issue was much more easily handled than explaining to Marianna how I ended up at dinner with Sadie and Clayton. On the other hand, I was beginning to regret joining my friends for coffee. I didn't like being singled out as the topic of the morning. Maybe I *was* being touchy.

"Tom who?" Eli asked from the other table.

Naturally, Eli had his ears open and honed in on Sarah's comment like a laser.

"Should I copy my day planner for everyone?" I quipped. Not in the right frame of mind for this, I had a strong urge to go hide out in my shop. But that wouldn't have been fair. Over the years, I'd done my share of teasing, so I had to prove I could take it as well as dish it out.

"Just tell us who Tom is before your other brother blows a gasket," Elliot said.

When it came to dealing with Eli and me, Elliot, the easier going of my twin brothers, always took on the role of peacemaker.

Wanting to be precise and deflect any innuendo, I took a couple of seconds to gather my thoughts. "His name is Tom Harris. He wants to spend a day with me in the shop to see if he'd rather work with flowers and plants than run a tour bus company."

"You going to teach him all you know in one day?" Eli asked, his voice abrupt and grating.

I knew he didn't mean it in a cutting way, but once again, Eli's remarks and questions were like little jabs at me. And that bad habit of Eli's had steadily grown worse. Something had been bothering him lately, but in gingerly poking around trying to find out what it was, I'd come up empty. A couple of weeks ago, I'd asked Elliot about Eli's perpetual bad mood, but he didn't have any answers either.

Thankfully, Sarah's watch beeped to remind us that morning coffee time was over and business on the Square was about to begin. In unison, we stood and bused our tables, piling our cups and plates into the bins by the kitchen door before filing out.

Stepping out onto the Square again lifted my spirits and erased the edge to my mood the questions and teasing had elicited. The sun warmed my shoulders under my light jacket. Nothing like the day last week when driving rain threatened to mix with snow, which meant the Square was all but dead for the day.

My feeling of wellbeing was fueled by my sense of belonging to the Square, and to the town my parents and grandparents and some great-grandparents, along with an assortment of aunts and uncles had built and loved.

I needed these reminders. Each time I entered a floral design contest I knew that if I won I'd be expected to leave

Wolf Creek periodically to promote the contest, and by association, the industry. The stakes were even higher with the Bartholomew Floral Contest. The rules for that contest clearly stated that the winner would be required to be in New York for three to six months of the year to represent the industry at its various trade shows and other functions. Yes, it was like accepting a PR position, but that's one reason I entered. I didn't talk about it, but for so long I'd been conscious of a nagging voice urging me to consider leaving Wolf Creek, that a fresh start away from people who had known me all my life might be the best thing for me. But then, as the possibility became real, I had to ask myself if I *really* wanted to close the shop I'd spent years building and leave everything familiar behind.

By the time I'd rattled all of that around in my mind, I was across the Square in front of my creation, Rainbow Gardens. It had taken fifteen years of constant effort and focus to first create and then maintain the shop as a successful business on the Square. Yes, my brothers could get a little credit for agreeing to let me launch my small plant and cut flower stand in the old Farmer Foods, when Dad was still running it and grooming the boys to take over. I'd outgrown that space long before Eli and Elliot had outgrown their original store, though. Rainbow Gardens had survived growth pains and economic ups and downs. I'd turned my shop into a full-service florist business with an excellent reputation in Wolf Creek and beyond.

I always said to myself, and to anyone who asked, that I had no regrets about sticking with my dream through the difficult times, even if it meant working seven days a week during the busy months. That's not to say I was completely free of regrets. One was huge and never far from my consciousness, namely that I didn't have a special someone to share the frustrations and joy involved in living my dream. The closest I came was the mystery man who turned up now and again in my nighttime dreams. Great! A man with no flesh, no blood, and who disappeared the minute I opened my eyes.

I stood in front of my shop long enough to critique the

window displays. Definitely outdated. Even one day of neglect was enough to give the spring and Mother's Day arrangements a worn out look. The flowers had wilted, their pale colors faded to almost white, and the greenery had lost their vibrant shades and turned to varying degrees of gray-green.

That was not the image I wanted shoppers to see.

The first order of the day was stripping both windows and replacing the dull displays with Memorial Day decorations fit for the commemoration scheduled on the Square. Last year, we held a solemn ceremony for one of Wolf Creek's local men who'd died overseas. This year, Sarah had arranged a more upbeat weekend, complete with a drum and bugle corps to provide the music and entertainment while they demonstrated their intricate footwork and color guard routines.

At the last business owners' association meeting, Sarah explained a change in policy about vendors that set up on the Square during mid-summer and fall festivals and special events. A few vendors asked Sarah if they could start selling earlier than usual, specifically on Memorial Day weekend. The rest of us agreed this would add some buzz to the opening of the summer season. True, we all pointed out that the vendors were taking their chances with the notoriously unreliable spring weather in Wisconsin, but we wouldn't turn away business either. The more variety we offered on the Square, the better off we were individually.

If all went as we hoped, we'd see an increase of shoppers and visitors, and that meant I needed more small bouquets and festive pottery pieces ready. And I wanted to give each buyer a small American flag as a thank you for shopping on the Square.

I went inside, my head finally off the contest and back on Rainbow Gardens. Preoccupation with the Bartholomew contest had led to giving scant attention to my window display. It was time to challenge myself to be creative with the old and new stock of vases, pots and ribbons. A couple of tri-colored balloons...

No.

I reached into the window and pulled out the greens and wilted flowers. No balloons. I didn't sell balloons and didn't want to give shoppers the impression I did. Besides, as an experienced florist I could surely get more creative in my shop than using balloons as window embellishments.

For some reason, my sunny spring day mood took a nose dive. Standing by the shop window holding a handful of worn out greenery brought it all home. Coming up with ideas and executing them, being upbeat and "happy" seven days a week for the next eight...yikes, could that be right? I counted down the months on my fingers. Yup, eight busy months of displays and round-the-clock work to take me through the summer and the holidays. It all seemed too much—overwhelming.

What was wrong with me? Was I going through a way-too-early mid-life crisis? Was I burned out trying to show my brothers—and myself—that I could successfully run my own business? How much longer would I feel that pressure when I'd already proven myself many times over?

I had to be honest with myself, though. Even the steady flow of orders for arrangements for every kind of occasion hadn't energized me lately. Maybe because I could do them automatically, almost without thinking. Sometimes I feared they looked ho hum, the way I felt making them. Or, at least it seemed that way to me.

Had I identified the problem? Maybe I lived on autopilot way too much.

I wanted to climb my spiral staircase and hide out for the day. Maybe do nothing more than sit and ponder my future. I chided myself for that foolish thought. I would never leave the window half cleared.

The ring of the shop phone interrupted my gloomy thoughts. I hurried to the counter and picked up the call on the third ring. Sure enough, another order. At one time I would have been thrilled to start my day that way. But instead of being happy, my heart sank.

Whoa. That made no sense at all. I put the note on the spindle with a few left over from yesterday. I'd handle it, along with the others, after lunch. For the moment, the window remained the priority.

I smiled wryly to myself. It was so much easier to dismantle a display than create a new one. It took no enthusiasm to dump the wilted flowers and greenery into the composting tub, which was destined for the family farm where Elliot and Eli lived. I added the ribbons to the sales table and washed the containers to use them again when needed. A little sweep over the window floor and I'd call that piece of the project done.

With no plans ready for the next display, I took a roll of white paper and cut off a couple of long sheets. Then I used colored markers to draw some large flowers and leaves, and singlehandedly managed to tape the sheets over the windows. Let the shoppers and my peers in the Square guess what I was doing—or not doing—in my newly constructed cave.

Then the phone rang again and I quickly picked it up. "Good morning, Rainbow Gardens."

"I can see you, Megan."

My heart skittered for a second or two. I'd recognize the crisp voice anywhere now. "Well, hello, Mr. Rog... Sommers."

"Clayton."

"Oops, I remember now," I teased. "What can I do for you today?"

"Lock the door and go on a day-long adventure with me."

Oops. There went my heart again, skipping beats. "Right. Sure thing. When do we leave?"

"Why did you put paper on the windows?" he asked.

"You can see that, huh? So where are you?"

"In my room at the Inn. Directly across the Square. Your lights were on very late last night."

What? He was definitely nosy enough to fit into small town life. No problem.

"Oh, really?" I said. "I guess I was so busy I forgot to turn them off."

That was a fib. Frugal Megan would never forget that, not to mention that I didn't sleep with lights on all over my apartment. But the idea of someone watching me, especially while I was busy researching him, was creepy. What if he used binoculars hoping to get a glimpse of my laptop screen?

Now I was being paranoid. I needed to end this conversation. I also needed to remember to close the blinds on my living room windows in the evening.

"As for your day of adventure, I have orders to fill," I said.

"Okay, have it your way," he said with an exaggerated sigh. "I'll stop by later today to schedule the interview. Bye for now."

The phone clicked. I stared at the receiver in my hand. What was all that about? And had he seriously thought I could close the shop and head off for some kind of adventure? Or was that just a way to make small talk.

The jingling of the bell on the door grabbed my attention. I turned to see one of my regular customers, Georgia Winters, come deeper into the shop and approach the workbench. She worked as a paralegal at Country Law, a firm located in a building down the Square from Rainbow Gardens. But referring to Georgia as a regular customer told only half the story. Georgia was practically family, a sister, sort of. After years of being apart, she and Elliot had renewed their high school romance and were now the latest new couple on the Square. I liked the idea of adding a woman to our family of three and evening up the numbers.

"What's with the paper on the windows?" Georgia asked.

"The new displays are going to be a surprise." *Right. Even to me.*

"Well, that's exciting," she said, fidgeting with her purse. "Well, anyway, I'm here on business, Country Law business. We want to contract for flower arrangements and other decorations for the reception area again this season."

"Okay—I'm happy to hear that." That was true. It lifted my spirits to get the repeat business. On the other hand, Georgia couldn't stop working the strap on her shoulder bag. She seemed nervous, hesitant, like she wanted to say something, but had changed her mind.

"But if I'm not mistaken, didn't I have this conversation with Virgie in January?" I turned to check for the contract printout in my calendar box. I had computer backups, but I liked getting my hands on hard copies. Virgie, Georgia's friend and the new receptionist at Country Law, had stopped by on a cold, snowy day and we'd finalized all the arrangements for upcoming flower arrangements for the office. "Here's the contract."

When I turned back with the copy in my hand, Georgia grinned sheepishly. "Oh, I know, Megan. I'm just fumbling around here. In truth, I'm going to need flowers, lots of flowers."

"When?" I whispered.

"October."

I couldn't help teasing. "And *what's* the occasion?"

She flashed the ring on her left hand and wiggled her fingers. Elliot had given her that ring at the Harvest Festival last October. He'd been the happiest guy in town ever since.

Georgia sent a sidelong glance my way. "You can't say even one word to anyone about the timing of the wedding. Not yet." She checked her watch. "Have to run. But I wanted you to know. You always have lots of good ideas, so start thinking."

She pivoted around and out the door she went, sending the little bell jingling. My heart jingled along with it. After spending so much time apart, Elliot and Georgia were getting married. A love story right in my own family.

My mind took a sharp detour back to my life. If Elliot could find happiness after years of being alone, maybe someone was out there for me, too. We'd always been Eli, Elliot, and Megan, the single siblings. Elliot had married once years before, but it hadn't lasted long. But Eli and I had yet to take the plunge.

I put thoughts of a new window display aside, and instead, took the stack of orders for the day off the spindle and began to make them with new-found enthusiasm. Georgia's news had given me a lift. I dropped my sour mood and gathered my tools and supplies on the workbench. I began my signature combo of whistling and humming to the symphony playing on the CD. Beethoven or Mozart? I didn't know, but the music fed my spirit.

But wait a minute. Why would Georgia issue orders about not telling anyone about the wedding? What was that all about? And how long could she keep her secret? I chuckled to myself. I gave it 48 hours tops.

By noon, the orders were ready for pick-up, and I'd finished the small vases for the tables at Crossroads. While having dinner with Clayton and Sadie, I'd noticed that the tulips and daffodils in some of the displays were beginning to wilt, and I wanted to change them before they looked downright forlorn.

I pulled out my "Back in 10 Minutes" sign and taped it to my front door. Without a regular employee, I'd developed a strategy to allow for quick deliveries to nearby shops. It didn't cost me business, mostly because I could drop off arrangements to any location on the Square and be back in less than ten minutes. I grabbed the box of vases for Crossroads and locked the door behind me. Traffic was slow on the Square, but that was about to change when the summer tourists and day-tour buses arrived. Maybe Tom Harris would like to become a part-time employee and I could leave the shop now and then without rushing so. Maybe I could go on a day-long adventure with Clayton and show him the sights in our corner of Wisconsin. Pleasant thought.

Melanie, the manager at Crossroads, met me at the door and said she'd exchange the vases and return the box with the old ones to me. That gave me time to go to B and B to pick up the roast beef sandwich I'd ordered earlier. My attempt to get out of a rut would start with a different lunch. As much as I loved PB & J, I didn't have to eat it every day, did I?

I was surprised to see Clayton and Sadie at a table by the window. I might have lingered, made conversation, but Stephanie reached around her line of customers and handed me the carry-out bag. I waved to them and left it at that.

At exactly 3:00, Clayton arrived. Since I had no idea how long he and Sadie had planned to stay in Wolf Creek, I had to carve out time for the interview between proms, weddings, graduations, and everything else along the way. Almost nothing took as much time as brides making decisions about flowers for their weddings.

I smiled as I mulled over my family's secret. Although Georgia and Elliot's wedding was months away, I had a growing list of questions. How many guests? Where were they holding it? Were they planning a reception in town? Bridesmaids? Groomsmen? Okay, both were fiftyish, but what did that matter? Small and private or big and showy, I'd be ready. And I had no worries, not even tiny reservations about the match. Georgia Winters was the perfect choice for my easy-going brother.

Okay, Eli, who's the perfect woman for you?
And where, oh where, was the right man for me?

By the time Clayton stood at my workbench and opened his day planner, I'd already decided mid-afternoon on Sunday would be the best time to meet with him. That time offered several advantages, including waning foot traffic, at least this early in the season. I'd put a note on the door about closing early. It also gave me time to break my silence and tell my twin brothers about the Bartholomew contest.

"Well, *Ms*. Reynolds," he started, in full-blown mock formal mode. "Let's schedule an interview and a time I can observe you arranging the new pieces. As you know, past winners of the Bartholomew Floral Design School contest will judge them." He took another breath. "I'll also need you to agree to a portrait style photograph."

Was that a *smile* I saw tugging at the corners of his mouth?

Clayton handed me a copy of the interview questions and an agreement contract for the photographs. "I'll need you to sign them before we begin."

"Begin? Do you mean now?"

"If you'd like," he said. "I don't have any plans for the rest of the day."

"I have an appointment this evening. I was hoping you'd agree to Sunday afternoon. Late afternoon, around 3:00." I looked into his eyes and couldn't stop babbling. "Or, if that won't work for you, then some other time…"

This man's presence turned me upside down, and I knew so little about him. He hadn't even told me his real name in the first place. If Art Carlson hadn't blown Clayton's cover, I might never have learned his story.

I took a step back. Now that the reality of the contest final was here I had to reconsider what it meant for me over the long term. Did I want to, or maybe even *need* to withdraw?

Were fantasies about happily leaving Wolf Creek and traipsing around the country becoming confused with the realities involved? I had to ask myself what would happen to Rainbow Gardens over the next year if winning the contest required me to spend time away. I'd been an early player in bringing the Square back from its years-long decline. Along with Sarah Hutchinson and my brothers and a few others, we implemented the initiatives that turned the Square—and Wolf Creek itself—into a major tourist and shopping destination. I couldn't help but puff out my chest a little. Given all that, could I walk away without regrets?

"Let me put it this way, Clayton. As much as I'd like to have this part of the contest finished, I don't want to be interrupted by customers when doing what's required." I heard resignation in my tone, along with determination to make a stand for what I needed. "But I'm willing to close early Sunday afternoon if you will be in town that long."

"My mother and I have no plans to leave anytime soon."

"Don't you have other interviews to do?"

Clayton shook his head. "Yours is the last one."

"Oh." For some reason that stopped me.

I was saved from further conversation when two women entered the shop. They confirmed my worry about interruptions, but they also showed Clayton that I had a going business.

Clayton smiled and moved to the front door. "I look forward to Sunday."

The bell jingled his leaving.

4

During the slower winter and early spring months on the Square, closing time had a special quality to it. It seemed as if the buildings themselves exhaled and relaxed as we turned off the lights in our shops. Customers and window shoppers and those out for an afternoon stroll ambled toward the parking areas or turned onto the residential streets of Wolf Creek. We needed to bask in this calm because the summer season with its crowds of visitors and shoppers was just around the corner. A mere week away, Memorial Day weekend loomed and the frenzy it began lasted all the way through Christmas. But on that particular night, before the Square changed for the season, I wanted to put all my concerns aside. I was part of the Wolf Creek Square Quilting Bee and I couldn't wait to get there.

In January, Marianna Spencer, relatively new in our group of shop owners, had sent invitations to the women on the Square and others in town who frequented her shop. She'd scheduled a gathering at Quilts Galore for every other Wednesday evening and volunteered to teach us basic quilting techniques. Of course, she intended that we sit around and chat, too, and maybe get to know each other better. On the first night, we'd unanimously agreed to donate the quilts we made to a charity that worked with young mothers. Our small quilts would be gifts to their babies and toddlers.

I hadn't planned to take part, at least not at first. For one thing, I admitted the long, busy days of the holiday season, exhilarating when we had our Halloween festival and moved into the fast-moving November days, had left me wiped out, totally exhausted, by New Year's Eve. All I could think about was going to bed early on snowy January nights and spending some leisurely days reorganizing and cleaning Rainbow Gardens front to back, top to bottom. I used that downtime to experiment with new floral arrangements, along with making plans and creating sales goals for the next season. But, since Marianna had stopped by to issue a personal invitation, I decided to go. It would have been rude to not show up—and no way to treat a colleague on the Square, especially a relative newcomer. I had to at least give her idea a try.

And I'm so glad I changed my mind.

Our laughter started the very first night. Everything seemed to strike us as hilarious. Some of us didn't even know which end of a needle to thread, much less how to run a sewing machine, so mishaps were the rule, not the exception. Marianna had to start at square one before we could grasp the finer points of quilting.

Lucky for us, Marianna was willing to begin with the fundamentals, as in, "Okay everyone, this is fabric." We all groaned, but she got our attention and we'd looked on while she demonstrated how to cut perfect squares, and explained why that was so important. When we tried it ourselves, we'd no doubt wasted more fabric than she'd planned for, but we eventually caught on and managed to cut the pieces correctly.

Each time we met we learned new skills and now, after four months, we each had a small quilt sewn and tied together. Tonight, we'd put the final edging on—the binding, as Marianna called it.

As I walked toward the quilt shop at the end of the Square, I realized that the lightness in my step reflected the anticipation I felt each time our group met. I had deepened my friendship with women I'd known for years, but also made friends with the newer women on the Square and in town.

We jokingly tried to convince Beverly and Virgie, town native and newcomer, respectively, to move to the Square. But instead, they'd hired a local contractor, Charlie

Crawford, to craft a studio in Beverly's house so they could sew Virgie's one-of-a-kind vests. While they had no plans to move their part-time venture, both had connections to the Square through Georgia Winters, Beverly's sister. Georgia also got the credit for bringing her friend, Virgie to town to take a job as Country Law's receptionist-legal secretary. But Virgie was rapidly becoming better known for her colorful vests than her office skills. From what I could tell, Styles by Knight and Day, our clothing store on the Square, couldn't keep the vests stocked.

When I opened the front door of Quilts Galore, the bell jingled, but I doubted anyone could hear it over the din of conversation and laughter coming from Marianna's classroom in the back. I passed racks of new fabrics to join them. I was a few minutes early, but I wasn't alone. Maybe we were all eager to gather for this last session before Memorial Day.

The evening passed quickly, and I'd *almost* completed my first quilt. I still had some edging to hand sew at home. Along with Virgie and Beverly, Georgia, Sarah, Stephanie, and Doris, the owner of the bookstore, we all had either finished our quilts or were nearly done. Marianna sent us home with small bags of supplies and offered to help if we needed more instructions.

"I'm so glad you decided to be part of the bee," Marianna said, handing me a bag.

"It never would have happened if you hadn't dropped by at the shop and invited me in person. It was the push I needed to try something new. I've had a great time. And here's my proof." I held up my small quilt before folding it into a small bundle and packing it away in my tote. "See? I actually learned something. Some baby, maybe one yet to be born, will be snuggly warm in this."

Marianna nodded to me. "A little one certainly will, Megan."

I walked back home under a clear sky and bright stars. Since the evening temperature had cooled, I was glad for my jacket, even for such a short distance. My thoughts turned first to my nightly cup of warmed chocolate milk, and then to tomorrow when Tom would arrive.

Accustomed to working alone, I'd have to change my mindset to be open to answering the inevitable crop of questions he'd likely have. I smiled at the memory of pestering my grandmother, and then my mom, about their flower gardens. I must have asked a million questions. Dad had laughed when I asked if I could set up a small table to sell flowers in our family grocery store. He indulged me, but then admitted his surprise at how well I'd done that first summer. By the time school started, he'd asked me to set up my little in-store shop the following year. So began my career as a florist.

I stopped walking and gazed at the sky. What would my parents think of Rainbow Gardens now?

The small light in my shop I'd left on earlier acted as a beacon, a sign of home. *My home*. I loved it, but did I want it to be my home forever?

Ugh. Back to that question. Lately, it pestered me, the way I'd pestered my grandmother about her flowers.

I was no closer to answering the question than I was last week or the week before that—or last year or the year before. I stepped inside my shop and locked the door behind me and went straight upstairs. I checked my phone for messages, just in case Tom had changed his mind and cancelled. No word from him, which gave me a lift. I would have been disappointed if he'd backed out of his day with me, even if I was a little apprehensive about having someone I didn't know in the shop with me for virtually the whole day. He'd know soon enough if the florist business was right for him.

I changed into my sleep shirt while the chocolate milk heated. After pouring it into my favorite cup, I climbed into bed and turned off the bedside light. I sipped my delicious treat slowly, allowing it to do its job and calm my mind and body. *Rest, Megan, rest*. I put the empty cup on the nightstand, then slid under the covers and stared at the bright stars visible through the sky light. The sight of them, coupled with the warmth of the milk, lulled me into a quiet sleep.

The next morning at precisely 9:30, I unlocked the front door. That's when I spotted Tom walking across the Square with a take-out coffee cup in one hand and a small paper bag in the other. Lunch, I assumed.

Happy to see him, I opened the door wide to let him in. "Morning, Tom."

"Megan." He put his coffee and the bag on the workbench to free his hands and take off his jacket. "I can't tell you how excited I am to be here." He took in a deep breath and released it. "Wonderful. No diesel smell."

Not catching on to what he meant, I gave him a questioning look.

"The buses run on diesel fuel," he said, "so that's all I can smell when I'm around them. There's nothing like the fragrance of flowers and the aroma of plain old dirt."

I laughed. "Not much fragrance with flowers anymore and I don't stock many potted plants."

"No matter. I can dream."

I showed Tom where to store his lunch in the under-the-counter fridge, and I pointed to hooks by the back door where he could hang his jacket. Then I handed him a light green apron with Rainbow Gardens embroidered in a crayon box of colors on the bib. Its design matched the shop's logo, a flower under a rainbow.

Tom followed me from the back of the shop to the front door. I turned to face the interior of the shop. "Let me explain how I arranged the place to entice buyers to come deeper inside." I waved toward the two front windows. "It all starts with getting them in the door, and that begins with the windows, of course. They take up a big bite of time, because the displays change to coincide with holidays or events on the Square. Right now, Memorial Day is on my mind."

A frown briefly made an appearance on Tom's face, making me wonder if the day had special significance for him or maybe, he had an idea for a display. I tucked away a mental note to ask him. Or, maybe he was simply curious about the paper taped over the windows. That would make sense.

I pointed to the glass front display cooler. "I keep the cooler loaded with flowers and greenery. I make a few arrangements ahead, for a customer shopping at the last minute. Mostly, though, I customize them. And I want everything handy."

He followed me to the row of cupboards where I stored vases and pots. Unlike the mess he'd seen the other day, I'd returned those I hadn't used yesterday to the shelves and reordered the spools of ribbon on their rods. So far, Tom hadn't asked any questions, but he'd listened closely and scribbled in his notebook.

The workbench took longer to explain, because I described the tools I used every day to create even small arrangements customers could stop by and pick up on their way home. I also pointed out the way I saved money by using short lengths or spool ends of ribbon to tie on a single flower. "No charge to the customer, of course, but it dresses up that single rose or lily that some people like to bring to the office or have at home."

Tom grinned. "A single flower can be a nice gift."

"You'd be surprised how many people remember that I tied a ribbon around that one stem. I think we all remember small attentions."

I ended the tour at the back door, where I went over the routines involved with the ordering side and the delivery of flowers and other supplies. He'd seen the boxes the day of the bus tour, so he nodded to show me he understood.

"Have I overwhelmed you?"

"Not exactly," he said with a grin, "but would you run through the layout of the shop again. I want to make sure I caught the high points."

Since I'd watched him jotting notes, his request took me back. "Again?" Suddenly, I wanted someone, *anyone*, to come in. I was ready to move on and didn't want to repeat the grand tour.

My wish was granted.

Eli walked in through the back door. Typical Eli, I

thought, as I observed him puffing himself up, acting protective. Well, that's what he'd call it. I'd come to label Eli's blustering as controlling behavior. He brushed past me and right into Tom's personal space. "Ready to start your day?" he barked at him.

"I'm Tom Harris."

I admired Tom's bold tone.

"And you are?" Tom asked, his mouth forming a classic smirk.

"Eli Reynolds." He jabbed his thumb in the air in my direction. *"Her brother."*

"Glad to meet another member of Megan's family." Tom extended his hand and though Eli hesitated, he accepted the gesture and returned the shake. "Your sister is being generous with her time today, showing me the ins and outs of her business."

"Right." Eli shifted his stance to look at me. "Another waste of time."

Another? I suspected he'd heard about the contest and Clayton's reason for being in Wolf Creek.

"With those windows covered, it looks like you're going out of business," Eli said.

As usual, Eli knew how to shift his line of attack. Maybe, though, he hadn't heard about the floral contest and was just fishing for information. It bothered me that Tom was probably unable to read between the lines and see Eli for who he was, an over-protective big brother. I knew enough not to take him too seriously—and not to take offense, either. But I couldn't count on Tom understanding the real Eli.

"Oh, that little detail?" I quipped. "I wanted to create an air of intrigue while I came up with the new display." I wasn't about to admit that I had no idea what the display would be.

I was relieved when the phone rang. While I took an order over the phone, Eli made his exit and Tom wandered to the display cooler. Before I'd finished writing the particulars of the order, Tom opened the cupboard doors and moved a few vases to see what was behind them. He was curious, all right.

Rather than going through a second walk-through, I decided to put him to work on an arrangement. That seemed like the more productive way for him to get an idea of what I did every day in the shop.

"Time for some hands-on work, Tom." I pointed to the spindle. "Four orders on the spindle, and now a fifth. A regular customer just called with a rush order. She's picking it up before lunch."

I took the orders off the spindle and handed them to him. "Take a look," I said, "while I gather some supplies."

We started with the easiest one. I showed him my shorthand notes on the order invoice. "This is an order for '*a small vase, colorful flowers, for a desk.*'"

"And all of it written in code, I see," he said.

His quick smile energized me and I put aside any lingering, troublesome thoughts about Eli's earlier intrusion. For now, anyway.

"That's right. Smv equals small vase, RB—Rainbow, but on an order it always stands for colorful flowers. And 4 a desk is, well, for a desk."

"I do something similar with the tour bus trips, too." Tom grinned. "Guess every business develops its own system."

We moved to the cabinet to select a vase, clear or colored, glass or pottery. It always depended on the flowers. I was more inclined to choose clear or white, but sometimes a colored vase added another dimension to the arrangement. "Go ahead. Your choice."

He debated longer than I would have, but I wasn't going to rush him. Providing we were finished by early afternoon, he could take as much time as he needed to weigh his choices. Later on, I'd tell him that to save time I picked out pots or vases for all the orders at one time, allowing me to work in assembly line fashion.

He held up a hob nail milk glass vase for my approval. It was one of the more expensive types I carried, which I pointed out. "We have to consider the total price of the order," I said. "Since flowers are the focus, a less expensive vase allows more flowers for the money."

Nodding, he studied the order again and exchanged his first choice for another one, checking the price on the bottom.

"Good choice." I led him to the cooler to begin selecting flowers, arranged according to cost. "The least expensive are on the left—the daisies, tulips, mostly the seasonal ones. The specialty varieties, and the more expensive ones, are on the right. This puts them right next to the arrangements I've made earlier. It's a marketing concept that draws people to see, and I hope, want, the more expensive ones."

"Pricing?" Tom was adding notes to his book.

"I don't want you to write that down."

He stopped and raised his head, eyeing me quizzically.

"Two reasons. One, the prices change constantly, depending on the time of year and the availability of the flowers."

"Makes sense," he said.

"And flowers are perishable. They don't last a long time. If I see I'm overstocked with one kind of flower I'll add a few extra stems at no cost."

"Can't see how you'd make any money that way."

I groaned inside. "You sound just like Eli." I couldn't keep the disgust out of my voice. "If you think only about the bottom line, then I doubt you should work with flowers or plants."

Tom shrugged. "Sorry. I think about budgets and profitability all the time."

"Flowers are a luxury. People don't *have* to buy them. I understand that. But they make our lives better, more joyful."

I reached into the cooler and selected an assortment of flowers for the order. "Let's put this one together. I'll show you how I do it."

I carried the flowers to the workbench, and Tom followed, holding the vase. He looked on while I snipped the ends of the stems and chose tall purple irises for the focal point, surrounding them with smaller daisies. I added three perfect yellow tulips and finished it off with sprigs of greenery.

"There. Done." I stepped back. "Check for symmetry and

balance. And then my final step. I ask myself: would I want this on my desk?"

"I sure would," Tom said.

"Me, too." I gathered the throw-away ends and put them into the composting tub. "Okay, Mr. Harris. The next one's yours."

I handed him a simple order. At least, after all these years I thought it was easy.

As Tom deliberated his choice of container and flowers, I remembered when each order brought excitement and a sense of fulfillment to me. Now, so many were routine, admittedly ho hum.

Watching Tom make the arrangement gave me pause. Had I become complacent and stagnant and lost the joy I once had simply from surrounding myself with flowers? My mother and grandmother had grown their flowers for the joy of it. Had the inner challenge of running my own business and proving myself to my brothers distorted the energy that fueled my own love of flowers? While Tom worked, I wandered through the shop, straightening here and rearranging there. I needed to change my attitude. Fast. Maybe changing something in the shop would help. I didn't know.

Tom brought me out of my reverie. "So, Megan, how does this look?"

"Terrific," I said, meaning it. He'd gone with white roses and lilies, using the deepest purple and fuchsia tulips for a stark color contrast. "Such an attractive centerpiece for a table or a reception area, like in the lobby of the Inn or at Country Law. I can honestly say I couldn't have done better myself."

He'd surprised me with his creativity—and it hadn't taken him half the day to assemble the piece. His smile in response to my compliment reminded me of my own pleasure when I began working with flowers. Gram and Mom had taught me well.

"Now, before moving on, figure your cost. You have the container and the stems, so see if you're close to the customer's requested price. I price the labor, too. And then, don't forget to add the markup, a little profit for the shop."

He did a quick count and nodded. "Looks close to the target. I might have added a stem or two extra."

"That's okay—these are the less expensive varieties we're using this time of year for the standard arrangements." I pointed to the daisies filling a pot on a shelf visible from the front door. I've probably made three dozen pots of daisies in the last two weeks. They're impulse items in early spring. Shoppers are drawn to them. That's why I sell so many. People like to bring spring home with them, and not everyone has a garden."

I showed Tom how to fill out the invoice, finishing that ritual by stapling a business card to it. We put the arrangement back inside the cooler and moved on to the next order, which Tom managed to create without a hitch.

With the third arrangement, I needed to translate my code, to get the point across that the arrangement was destined for a coffee table. Illustrating with my hands, I said, "The customer wants it more flat than tall."

I stood at the cooler with Tom, offering a few pointers for a low arrangement. I did many of them, including some for businesses on the Square and nearby offices. The arrangement would be in a shallow dish-like container. I cut a small block of the florist foam to anchor the flowers in place. I described the process of first adding the greenery as a blanket across the container, then adding the flowers. I would cut the stems shorter than I would for a vertical bouquet. "You can be creative with the flowers," I said, "but the smaller carnations, tulips, mums, and baby's breath work well to fill this type of container."

Between helping Tom with the next couple of orders, I fielded calls, wrote down appointments for consultations with shower hostesses and brides, and had a conversation with Georgia. She'd called specifically to thank me for keeping her wedding a secret at Marianna's Quilting Bee meeting. She confided that she and Elliot were going to announce their wedding plans at the business association meeting next week. She sounded giddy, which I found amusing, because it was not a word often used to describe

Georgia.

Tom and I soon stopped for a quick lunch—he'd come prepared with a fat turkey sandwich and half a dozen chocolate chip cookies. My peanut butter and grape jelly appeared extra plain in contrast.

In between bites he fired questions at me, having apparently saved the bulk of his inquiries to go over while we ate. I admired his enthusiasm, and that earlier hint of envy of his fresh energy seeped back again.

Our afternoon passed quickly with customers picking up their orders and casual shoppers browsing the Square. I had a dozen or so bouquets of flowers for sale in cellophane wrapped ready-to-buy packages. Flowers, I'd learned from my days as a young girl selling them in my dad's store, were one of the most common impulse purchases. They were a lot like candy bars that way. Like I'd told Tom, just passing a pot of daisies in a shop often triggered the desire to bring some beauty home.

Tom's natural ease with people, honed through years of bus tours, came through and he had no trouble establishing instant rapport with the shoppers. I answered most of the questions, but he handled the interactions with great skill. He even offered ideas of his own.

Near closing time, Tom and I were busy taking the cupboard doors off their hangers when I heard the back door open and close. Eli had returned.

"Selling the fixtures?" Eli asked when he saw us.

I turned toward him, and being one step up on the ladder, I looked at him at eye level. "Tom is helping me give the shop a new look." I waved at the cupboards. "More open, maybe involving the customer more." Eli didn't know it, but I was parroting Tom's suggestion. "Want to help?"

Eli shook his head, but kept quiet. He stared at me for a second or two, and then turned away. I said nothing at the sound of the back door closing.

Emboldened throughout the day, Tom had engaged me in a couple of fairly lively debates about things I could consider changing. I laughed off some as too expensive or radical, but his idea of changing my custom-designed

Rainbow Garden ribbon was one idea I needed to consider. My ribbon was white, with a rainbow spaced at intervals. It was the same design I'd used for years. Tom wondered why I didn't vary the ribbons, maybe duplicating my logo but adding more variety in background colors. As long as the logo stood out, any of the colors would add something to the look I'd created. Now why hadn't I already done that?

Tom also thought I should order smaller ribbon to use with the small vases of flowers I delivered to Crossroads for their tables. No reason I couldn't use that soft marketing approach in my small vases. But I'd been shy about making it obvious about where the table flowers came from for some reason.

All day, I'd noticed that Tom's energy rubbed off on me. His presence, even for a day, let me see my shop from new angles and with fresh eyes. Ideas tumbled over in my mind faster than I could grasp them. New flower varieties, fresh marketing ideas, taking Rainbow Gardens from doing run-of-the-mill arrangements to being the go-to place for special occasions. I advertised flowers for every event or occasion, but I didn't market specifically to get the baby shower business in town or offer specials for the business luncheons scheduled at Crossroads. I stopped long enough to jot down the brainstorm of ideas in my own shorthand code and put the note in the pocket of my smock.

Tom and I cleaned up the shop before he prepared to leave. When the bell on the door jingled, we both turned to greet another customer. But it wasn't a shopper. It was Clayton. He kept his distance, though, hanging back from the workbench.

"Time for me to go," Tom said, lifting the apron over his head. "I don't want to take advantage of your generosity, but is there any chance I can come back next Thursday?"

Even before I checked my calendar, I knew I wanted him to come back. "Next Thursday works for me."

Tom lowered his voice when he said, "And plan on having dinner with me after closing time. You know, as a way to thank you."

I nodded. Of course, I'd do that.

Tom went around Clayton and opened the door, but before he walked out, I yelled, "Call me with ideas for the window displays."

I didn't have a chance to tell him that I'd enjoyed sharing my day with him. I hoped he realized I liked being a tutor—and learning new ideas from the student.

When the door closed, I turned my attention to Clayton. "Well, hello there. Is it Sunday?" I laughed at my own attempt at humor.

"Not on my calendar," he shot back, his eyes sparkling.

"Is there something I can do for you?" My good day with Tom had brightened my mood and changed my attitude. At least for the moment.

"Yes, as a matter of fact there is. Have dinner with me tonight."

I remembered he'd used those same words his first day in my shop and I'd ended up learning who he really was.

"Wow. Two invitations in one day. That hasn't happened in years."

Oops. That was too personal. Clayton didn't need to know that much about me. On the other hand, why shouldn't I have two dinner invitations? But I needed to keep him at least an arm's length away. As much as I was enjoying the attentions of two men, I needed to be careful. I'd learned almost nothing but an unimportant tidbit or two about Tom's personal life after spending all day with him. As for Clayton, well, I already knew too much.

Was I desperate for male companionship? I didn't like seeing the kernel of truth in the question. After all the years of focusing on Rainbow Gardens and ignoring, or rejecting, the attentions of men, I found myself alone.

That hit hard.

He waved his hand in front of my face. "Clayton to Megan. A single yes or no will do."

"Yes," I blurted.

"Okay, then, I'll pick you up. Like a real date. But…" He looked to the stairway leading up to my apartment. "I…"

Not so fast, I thought. I had things to do. "Uh, I need to talk to Elliot and Eli before dinnertime. So, I'll meet you at

Crossroads. That's where we're going, isn't it?"

"Need permission from your brothers to have dinner with me?" Good thing he winked so I knew for sure he was teasing. Shaking his head and obviously stifling a laugh, he said, "I look forward to dinner. Is 7:00 okay?"

I nodded, trying not to laugh myself, although I couldn't have said what was so funny.

He swatted the bell on the door before he opened it and left. The sound alone made me smile.

I quickly turned the sign on the door, Open to Closed, another business day over. I locked the door and tossed my smock on the workbench. I went out the back, and locked that door, too. Then I walked down to the delivery entrance of Farmer Foods to catch my brothers before they left for the day.

My secret had run its course. I'd been chosen as a finalist in the country's most prestigious floral design contest, but hadn't told either of the two people who were arguably the closest to me, Eli and Elliot. Sooner or later, though, they were bound to cross paths with Clayton or his mother—or both. It would be pretty embarrassing if the contest came up and neither had ever heard of it.

My silence with my brothers was telling in itself. Sure, I understood that my big brothers felt the need to watch out for little Megan, but Eli, far more than easy-going Elliot, had carried it way too far. It had to end. *Now.*

Tom's presence and the respect he showed me gave me a new spirit of independence. Clayton also treated me like an independent person. Both men gave me strength. *Take that, Eli and Elliot. Strength.*

I found Eli turning off the lights and Elliot closing out the last cash register, which, like my rituals, were repeated at the end of every day at Farmer Foods.

"Hi, guys. Done for another day?" I rubbed the white fur of a stuffed bear dressed in patriotic red and blue. They filled a bin near the checkout lanes at the front of the store.

"Heard you've been busy today," Elliot said, not looking up from the roll of receipt paper spewing from the till. Eli wandered over to join us.

"Look, I'll get to the point. I need to tell you about something I've done." I picked up the toy and snuggled it against my chest. "I entered another floral contest."

"We've heard that before, Megan," Elliot said, his tone flat.

Eli snorted and shook his head. "What a waste of money."

"And...I'm a *finalist* in this one." I'd come in prepared with a long-winded explanation, but old insecurities and echoes of Eli's comments snarled my tongue. "Clayton Sommers is in town to watch me put a few arrangements together and ask me questions the judges will use to score this round of the contest."

"Who's Clayton Sommers?" Elliot asked, more interested in my answers now.

"An artist from New York." I decided against telling them more. Still, past experience with the way gossip traveled in Wolf Creek served as a warning to be as honest as possible. "I had dinner with him and his mother on Tuesday."

"His mother?" Elliot raised an eyebrow.

"They're traveling together." I left it at that. Sometimes silence was the best conversation. That amused me. I think I first heard that old saying from our dad, and it had finally come in handy.

I looked at Eli as I was about to leave. "No comment? That's a first. But if you have something to say, as you always do, please get it out of your system now."

"Enough you two," Elliot interjected. "It's your life, Megan, and your money." Elliot went back to feeding a new roll of receipt paper into the checkout register.

Apparently at a loss for words, an unusual development, Eli shrugged.

"I just wanted you to know about the contest. It will be news around town soon enough." I walked to the door, but turned back. "Just so you're up-to-date on my comings and goings, I'm having dinner with Clayton tonight and Tom is coming back next Thursday."

"I'll mark it on my calendar," a raspy voice mumbled.

Eli. Of course he couldn't pass up an opportunity to throw out a sarcastic remark. I resisted the urge to return a sassy retort as I left the store.

It was time, long past time, really, that I kept my personal life to myself, at least to the extent I could in our gossipy little town. My brothers didn't need to know all about me— what I did with my life, and Rainbow Gardens, was none of their concern anyway. My decision to stay or strike out and start over in a new town was my business. I didn't need their permission and I wasn't about to ask for it, either.

5

Slow and awkward. That's the description of the way my dinner with Clayton started. I was cautious, careful not to let it slip that I'd researched his past, nor did I want to ask about his future plans. That might have made me seem too interested in him, or maybe he'd misinterpret simple curiosity as nosiness. I'd also had a cascade of second thoughts about the propriety of having dinner with him the first time, let alone the second, given that the contest interview was still ahead of us.

Nervous and doubting my own judgment, I started with a safe topic—the weather. Fascinating! Rain might come through the region the next afternoon. That was as interesting as it got, except for looking at the wine list and ordering a glass of cabernet when the waitress came by for our drink order. Clayton chose the same thing, which somehow added to my sense of being on a date. It wasn't supposed to be that way.

The break gave me time to come up with another safe topic. At least I hoped Clayton's friendship with Art Carlson was a neutral subject.

"We met in art school in New York," Clayton said, his face reflecting wistfulness in talking about the past. "Art had long since graduated, but he came back to take new classes, and he taught a couple on artisan jewelry, too. We had become friends, but I also thought of him as my informal mentor. Since we worked in different mediums, we were never competitors. Once he married, though, we would end up traveling in different circles. But whenever we saw each other, we always picked up right where we left off."

"You must have had a lot in common," I said.

He looked into the restaurant, and for a second or two seemed far away. I assumed he had traveled into his past when he'd been younger and hanging out with artists already established, like Art.

Clayton smiled, bringing his attention back into the room. "I heard through the grapevine that he moved to Wisconsin, and we exchanged a postcard or two about upcoming openings. I missed knowing he was in the city and available to talk to about things." He shrugged. "As often happens when people leave an area, Art and I lost touch with each other."

I took a chance guess. "You knew he was in Wolf Creek when you accepted the job to do my interview, didn't you?" We both knew the answer.

He relaxed back in his chair when the waitress delivered the wine to our table. I stopped talking, too, not wanting to have anything we said overheard.

Clayton drew the glass across the tablecloth closer to him. "I knew, but I was wary about calling Art to let him know I was coming. He might have agreed with the critics about my success, that somehow it was connected with my stepfather's money."

"But Art's not that kind of person. He's honest, genuine." I leaned in a little closer and grinned slyly. "I always thought of Art as kind of quiet. But lately, I see him as a happy guy. That's Marianna's doing."

"Honest, huh?" Clayton winced as if in pain. "I haven't been honest for almost two years now, Megan."

I heard a combination of regret and longing in his voice, as if the pressures of the deception had weighed heavily on him, along with wanting to live a more normal life, I suspected. "You've had special circumstances, Clayton. No need to be hard on yourself."

Why had I jumped in so quickly to defend him? I couldn't explain it, other than knowing he needed to protect his mother. I gave him a lot of credit for that.

He leaned toward me and held his wine glass up, offering

a toast. "Thank you."

I clinked my glass with his and took my first sip.

The wine sent warmth rushing to my face, and threatened to throw me off my center. I needed a quick shift in topic. The waitress returned to the table to take our order, which saved me from the need to talk. I took the easy way out and ordered the evening special, spring lamb stew with buttered noodles and warm bread. Clayton grinned and ordered the same entree, too.

"So, what are your plans after the interview is over?" I asked when we were alone again. "Where will you and your mother go?"

Clayton shook his head, showing more regret. "Unfortunately, we haven't settled on a plan yet, but Mom is tired of living out of a suitcase. Always on the run. Besides, she's a talented, self-starter kind of woman, so she finds not having work of her own *extremely* annoying."

"I'm not surprised. I can imagine it must be hard—not to mention heartbreaking in the face of what happened." Odd that sticking with unpleasant family business was a safer topic.

Glass in hand, Clayton rested his elbow on the table. "Just last night, Mom casually mentioned that if Art could make a living and be happy in Wolf Creek, far removed from New York and the pressures the city puts on an artist, maybe we should consider staying awhile."

My heart beat just a little bit harder and faster. Interesting. He'd been on the run and now he was thinking of staying put in Wolf Creek. After a lifetime of living here, I was thinking about leaving. Was that the reason I'd entered so many contests that required the winners to travel? Maybe I wanted to avoid a direct decision, and unconsciously chose instead to let the whims of contest judges decide for me. Not a very good way to demonstrate my hard-won independence.

When our stew arrived, I realized how soothing I found the steaming, aromatic plates of homemade food, artistically presented, yet basic. In that moment my discomfort with Clayton receded.

He took a bite of his stew and grinned. "If I could eat like this every day, why would I leave Wolf Creek?"

I gave him the laugh I could tell he was looking for. Besides, like half the town's population, I would have eaten dinner at Crossroads most nights myself, budget permitting.

"So, Megan, what are your plans if you don't win?"

He'd taken us into contest territory, a veer in a direction I considered off limits. "Why wouldn't I win?" I'd spoken without thinking and quickly swatted my hand in the air. "Don't answer that. That sounded ridiculous. What I really meant to say is I'd rather not talk about the contest."

I shuffled the napkin on my lap, resetting it to a perfect square. "Look, Clayton, I don't feel right talking about the contest over a social dinner. And is it really ethical for you to be having dinner with an entrant even before you've conducted the interview?"

His eyes darkened, reminding me of the power of words. Questioning his ethics would bother him, of course it would.

Time to walk that back. "I mean, your evaluation is subjective, but it could become biased in favor, or not, of the contestant. I mean *any* contestant."

Speaking in supposedly non-personal terms fell on deaf ears, even mine. Who was I kidding? We both knew I was talking about the two of us.

He swallowed another bite of stew and rested his fork on his plate before answering. "You forget that I'm not a judge. If I were, I can assure you we wouldn't be having dinner at the same table. But I'm required to answer only one question. Would this finalist be a good representative for the Bartholomew School? Do you think I would answer that question in the negative about *anyone* who successfully made it to the final round?"

When he put it that way, I felt a little foolish worrying about bias, as if I was special in some way. He'd already told me that the judges would use my interview and creativity to arrive at a score. Not his opinion.

"Sorry. I misjudged." Flustered, I stared at my plate of stew, abandoning any thoughts of trying to explain myself. Silently, I vowed to change my mindset and clear the clutter. My job was to do my best work and give honest answers to the questions, and be proud of my small business. In other words, let the chips fall and all that.

"How are the window displays coming along?" Clayton asked, picking up his fork and shifting position in his chair, just as he was shifting topics and tone.

Good. A safer subject.

I laughed. "Here's the truth. Maybe I'll leave the paper on the windows and keep everyone guessing, because I don't even have a hint of an idea about what's next in line for my windows. I have to come up with many different displays year after year. Sometimes, I go stale on myself. Like writer's block, I suppose."

His amused smile and the soft look in his eyes sent a little shiver through me, head to toe. Totally unprepared for my reaction, I laughed again. I pushed my plate away, hoping to calm the slight shaking in my hands.

"My entire livelihood revolves around flowers, ribbons, and vases. It's hard to keep my ideas fresh month after month, year…after…year."

"Do I detect a note of boredom?" he asked. "Or, even burnout?"

"It's hard to admit it, and I've never said it out loud before, but I'm not sure why I don't have the same enthusiasm or get the same joy I once had." I paused and stared into the restaurant like he'd done earlier. "The truth is, good or bad, right or wrong, Rainbow Gardens has been my whole life."

Clayton let out a knowing "Ah ha."

"You get it, don't you?" I blurted the words, pleased to be understood.

"I do, because I was the same way about my painting. Until it was taken away from me. I…"

"But it wasn't." I jumped in to argue, interrupting his thought. I could have backed off, but once I'd blundered in, I kept going. "You can still paint. You still have your talent. What a beautiful gift you've been given." I shook my head, wishing I could erase my words, and the insistent tone that seemed beyond my control.

Clayton became quiet, looking anywhere but at me. Had I made him feel small, as if I were scolding him for being ungrateful?

I swallowed back a gulp of wine. "I'm really sorry, Clayton. I had no right to say those things."

"Maybe not," he said, moving his empty plate to the side, "but that doesn't mean you're wrong. Maybe it's time for me to see what I'm really worth on my own. To paint what *I* want, and not just work to fit the latest trends and even what my own followers wanted a couple of years ago."

Since we'd gone down such a personal road again, I exhaled and with it, quit worrying about the contest. I'd disengaged Clayton from the Bartholomew School and begun to think of him as a casual friend. But being conflicted about the dinner in the first place, plus my long day, had caught up with me. I needed to get home to sort out what was next for me—and for Rainbow Gardens.

"This has been lovely—another delicious Crossroads dinner. But it's time for me to head home. I've got another busy day tomorrow." I put my napkin on the table.

No protests from Clayton, which surprised me. He signaled the waitress and signed the receipt. "I'll walk you home."

I laughed. "Oh, please. No need. It's…"

"Yes, need."

His voice signaled the end of that line of conversation, so I squashed my objections. Besides, I had always wanted to be with someone special and, even though I didn't think of Clayton in romantic terms, he was special.

The next morning I was eager to be downstairs amongst my faithful friends, the flowers. I changed the CD to a medley of upbeat classic oldies—songs I remembered my dad humming along with on the radio. As I changed the water in the flower buckets, I injected my slightly off-key voice to the music, at least where I knew the words. Then I made two fairly large arrangements to replace those I'd sold yesterday. I put so much energy into the showy bouquets that I smiled from happiness when I'd finished.

I started a third arrangement, a little more traditional because I included carnations. When I added the white carnations to contrast with some deep pink ones, a memory popped up in my mind. Years ago, Mom had wanted the boys and me to see that she could change the color of the flower by adding food coloring to the water. One July 4th, we'd each started out with three white carnations, but in no time, we'd ended up with blue and red ones to go with the lone white flower.

Bingo. My window display came into view. I hadn't used that trick in my store for years, so it would be fresh. Besides, I'd never used the food coloring idea in a window for passersby to see. I'd hang a flag as a backdrop and set the flowers in clear vases with the colored water. I'd wind some ribbon through a bed of greenery and it would be done. Simple, colorful, and patriotic—a quiet Memorial Day tribute.

I taped my sign on the door, but knew it wouldn't take me ten minutes to run to Farmer Foods to pick up red and blue food coloring. Once inside the market, I grabbed a bottle of green coloring, too, almost as an afterthought. Since neither brother was in sight, I was spared the need to explain what I was up to, and was back at the shop before my ten minutes were up.

I quickly gathered my supplies, made a new cut at the base of the flower stem and set the carnations in the colored water. I couldn't recall how long it took for the color to appear in the flower, but that would be part of the attraction to the window. I could space out the flower immersions, and include several white carnations in various stages of turning red or blue. Once the flowers fully colored, I'd replace them.

Suddenly, self doubt crept in. Was I kidding myself? I'd entered a floral contest where exotic flowers were often chosen as the winner by the judges. Here I was, delighted over putting together a child's science lesson and calling it a window display. For that matter, who would notice the display or care?

My rebellious side immediately kicked in and pushed aside my negativity. Shoppers mattered—kids passing the windows mattered. My life wasn't about contests. My customers kept my doors open and were the source of my livelihood. I got a kick out of my window idea, and as I assembled it, I had a feeling people on the Square would think it was fun, too.

The jingle of the bell announced my first customer of the day, Sarah.

"Well, hello Mayor Sarah."

She grinned, as she always did when I called her that. "Your shop is the buzz of the Square, Megan." She fingered a vase as she moved toward the workbench.

"Really? Why is that?" *As if I didn't know.*

"The suspense and intrigue about your window displays."

Hyperbolic words for sure. Suspense and intrigue are not exactly words to apply to a window display on the Square. I noticed Sarah was just about to touch one of the carnations in the process of coloring. I playfully slapped her fingertips. "Look, but don't touch. It'll bruise."

"Oops, sorry," she said, injecting a genuinely contrite tone into her voice. "You've told me that before."

"It's just that they're too pretty to risk harming them." My old protective nature had come to the rescue of the white bloom.

"Sadie Winston came to see me today," Sarah said. "Did you know she's looking for a place to rent for the summer? She said she's done running."

I nodded, but in a noncommittal sort of way.

"The chatter on the Square is that you and her son had dinner together last night." She grinned. *"Again."*

There went my heart, thumping a little faster. Silly. Ridiculous, really. "Is that so?" I rolled my eyes just to reinforce the point.

Chatter on the Square. How silly our little group could be sometimes. Still, I wasn't often the object of much gossipy small talk, so it wasn't all bad. Wait until they heard I'd won a major industry contest. It *could* happen.

"Okay, Sarah, what are you really asking?"

"Is he important to you?"

Taking on the challenge of the quickly blurted question,

I willed my voice to be steady and nonchalant. "You bet he is." I paused to consider my decision about the best way to respond. "You see, Clayton is in town to interview me as a finalist in a floral school contest I entered. That's what's important to me."

Sarah's face lit up in surprise. "Oh, Megan, I didn't know about that." She narrowed her eyes. "You're good at keeping secrets, aren't you? But how exciting."

"And it's still my secret," I said, explaining that I'd told my brothers, and now she was the third person to know.

Checking her watch, the same one that beeped at 9:55 each morning, Sarah's expression changed in an instant. "Oops, I want to hear more, but it will have to wait. I have an all day meeting in Green Bay, so I must be on my way."

"Busy woman," I teased, "always on the go." I gave her a once over, head to toe. "And you look every inch the part of a mayor in your stunning pantsuit." She'd set off the warm taupe suit with a bright red silky shell and silver beads.

Grinning, she said, "Hey, are you interested in Chinese for supper? I can pick it up on my way back to Wolf Creek. I could bring it here."

That gave me another lift. I always had fun with Sarah, and we were both fans of takeout Chinese. "Sounds like a plan. You know what I like. If it's after five o'clock, ring the buzzer. I'll let you in and we'll spread out dinner on my table upstairs."

We hadn't shared a takeout meal in a long time, so I welcomed the idea of sharing dinner. As single women, although not particularly close in age, we'd gone to various local events together. Lately, though, her job as mayor had expanded along with the rapid growth of business on the Square. Rainbow Gardens ate up most of my time, so girls' nights out had become increasingly rare.

With our plans made, Sarah hurried through the door, leaving me with my carnations changing color before my eyes.

6

Using Tom's enthusiasm for all things related to gardening and flowers and my renewed interest in my shop, I'd taken an online trip early one morning and extended my stay on a site that featured whimsical garden ornaments and tools. I found the selection exciting, and that triggered a shopping spree much larger than I initially planned—or even imagined. I weighed the shipping options and impulsively clicked on Priority Express. What was I thinking?

But, sure enough, the next morning while I was creating displays and watched as my carnations rapidly changed color, my regular delivery guy showed up at the back and carried in three boxes. The shop was open, but few people had arrived on the Square, so I dove right in. As I pulled packing material from the cartons, I laughed out loud, my mind flooding with ideas on how to sell the irresistible items nested inside.

My regular customers would be surprised by the whimsical large and small whirligigs, ornamental shovels, and a short windmill with a spinning top. The windmill needed some assembly, but I'd save myself some time and put Tom right on it later.

One box held a solar reflecting ball I'd picked out, and another box held the stand. I held the multi-colored globe, loving it as much in hand as I had when I spotted it on the site. I considered taking it to the farmhouse and putting it in one of the flower gardens as a tribute to Mom and Gram. But I quickly changed my mind. Not that I didn't want to honor the people that inspired my love of flowers. No, it was the thought of not seeing it myself that made me want to keep it in my own window.

Window?

Wham. There it was. The display for the second front window of Rainbow Gardens. A flower garden overloaded with the never-seen-before-in-my-shop garden ornaments. The new items would entice the visitors inside to buy easy-to-transport items. No shipping inconvenience or added expense.

I unpacked the third box. It was filled with small garden tools, row markers, and even green hammers for pounding in stakes. *Just what every gardener needed.* I laughed at the memory of Gram using the blade of her shovel to pound the markers in her garden.

Elliot and Eli stocked a small selection of garden seeds, so I decided to stop in at Farmer Foods and pick up a few packets as fillers for the display. I was about to begin pricing each item when a group of three women entered the shop.

"Welcome to Rainbow Gardens," I said, walking toward them from behind the workbench. "Please excuse the mess. I was unpacking a shipment of new items for the shop."

"New? I love being the first to buy *new* items." The woman's smile grew and was as bright as the raspberry fleece vest she wore. She rubbed her hands together and approached the boxes.

I had a sale in the making and returned to the workbench to unpack more small gadgets, holding each one up for the three customers to see.

"Hmm…Father's Day for John—my husband," she said in response to the row markers.

"John doesn't need anything more for his garden," one of her two companions teased. "He already has every garden toy as it is."

From that I surmised these women knew each other well enough to gently mock at least one of the husbands.

"I'll have to tell my daughter-in-law about your shop," the third woman said. "She loves Styles and comes to Wolf Creek often to shop. My son and his father could have matching tools."

A blush traveled over her face. "Sorry. Don't take that the wrong way."

"It's that second glass of wine you had at lunch talking," the woman I dubbed "Miss Raspberry Vest" teased.

It was difficult not to envy the women's obviously close friendship, and their freedom to spend their day in unhurried shopping. Then I remembered Sarah was bringing supper and that reminded me she'd been my friend for years, starting in the lean times when the Square's viability was in question.

So, if—when—I moved away, would Sarah and I continue to be friends? Or would our friendship slowly diminish over time? Like Art's and Clayton's had?

I didn't feel like answering my own question. The third friend of the trio of women shoppers wore a distinctive paisley scarf and asked when my next shipment was due to arrive, and if it would include any garden statuary, perhaps an angel or maybe a gnome. I took Miss Paisley's name and number and promised I would call when the new order arrived.

If garden gadgets were going to be hot items for the summer, then what good businesswoman wouldn't want to be part of it? Ordering would be easy with the account already established with the online vendor. But, in order to keep my options open, I needed to limit my order to a few items at a time.

Talk about indecision. Stay or leave. What did I really want? The answer wasn't entirely dependent on the contest. As much as I loved Rainbow Gardens, for the previous couple of years, I'd been conscious of a strong pull to move away and not just see something new, but create something fresh in my life. Maybe *meet* someone new. I'd take all the experience earned establishing Rainbow Gardens and open a new business where I decided to settle down. Periodically, my mental gymnastics over this decision made for long sleepless nights, not to mention coloring every choice I made for the shop. Especially this year, because the contest could mean such big changes. How could I make long-term plans when the end of the holiday season could mean the end of Rainbow Gardens?

By the time I packaged up the sales of a couple of whirligigs and garden tools for two of the trio of women, the shop had filled up, and the day passed quickly. I held the door open for the last shopper of the day. She needed both hands to carry out the large arrangement she'd ordered. Then I turned the sign to Closed and locked up.

Upstairs, I changed into a pair of baggy jeans and waited for Sarah to arrive. I put in a CD of light classical music, more Sarah's taste than mine, but still pleasant enough to help me wind down from the hectic pace of the day. I took out a couple wine glasses, plates, and napkins, ready to put dinner out.

At loose ends, and oddly restless, I went to the front windows and looked out over the Square. The trees, dormant through the winter, had fully leafed in their various greens, from light celery to dark forest. My favorite trees, the evergreens, had begun to show new growth at the end of each branch. On the ground in garden beds, near the benches that were spaced on the edges of the Square, I could see wisps of the pale colors of tulips and hyacinths and the bright white and intense yellow of daffodils. Breathtaking.

The buzz of the doorbell at the back of the shop announced Sarah's arrival. A rumble in my stomach made me glad she hadn't been delayed.

I bounded down the stairs and opened the door, surprised to see Sadie standing behind Sarah.

"Hope you don't mind. I invited Sadie to join us. She's decided to stay in Wolf Creek for a while—at least the summer. And I thought…"

I couldn't have named the emotion I was certain crossed my face. It had been a long time since Sarah and I had spent an evening alone catching up, and I'd planned to talk with her—for the first time—about the possibility of leaving Wolf Creek. Now I wouldn't, or couldn't, say a word about it.

"Sure, uh, sure." Not my best fake welcome. "Come in, please," I said, filling my voice with sincerity I forced myself to feel. I stood back and held the door so they could enter.

Familiar with my living area above the shop, Sarah went up the circular stairway, a bag of food in each hand. The aroma of onions and garlicky sauce left no doubt we'd be eating Chinese. I'd bet money that one of the containers contained pork-fried rice, one of our favorites. I noticed Sarah was no longer in her crisp professional clothes, but like me, had pulled out her standbys, comfy jeans and a loose sweater.

Carrying a bottle of wine, Sadie stopped before climbing the stairs to look into the shop. Mostly she saw crumpled sheets of packing material on the floor and open cartons sitting atop the workbench.

"New inventory," I explained as I guided her toward the stairs.

"I need to come in the front door like a regular customer soon," Sadie said, "but I wanted to wait until your interview with Clayton was done. You don't need extra pressure."

"We're doing the interview and the arrangements on Sunday afternoon, so wander in anytime after that."

"I'm sure you're anxious to have it done." She went up one spiral turn of the stairway and then stopped to overlook the shop. "You've done a good job, Megan. I'm sure shoppers enjoy coming here."

I assumed she meant Rainbow Gardens, but she might have meant her comment to encompass all of Wolf Creek Square. Sarah, along with the other shopkeepers, had worked hard to make it *the* place to shop.

"I need wine," Sarah declared from the top of the stairs at the entrance to my apartment. Her hands bracketed her hips.

"Uh, oh," I said, "someone must have had a difficult day."

Sadie smiled as we finished going up the stairs.

Sarah had made herself at home by picking up the corkscrew and opening the bottle of wine Sadie had handed her.

I hadn't bothered with clearing any clutter or polishing anything to a shine, so the open kitchen, eating area, and living room were what Sadie saw when she reached the top of the stairs. It was my world and I lived in it. Some clean laundry in one chair, a pile of magazines and newspapers on the couch, this morning's breakfast dishes in the sink. Of course, Sarah had seen my place spotlessly clean, but also so messy she hadn't known where to sit. But with Sadie there, I was pushed to say something.

"I'm sorry…" I stretched my arm out to encompass the room.

"Don't apologize," Sadie said. "I've run a business or two in my day. I know there isn't time to keep everything perfect. Messiness never harmed anyone."

No putting on airs, no preconceived opinions. I decided I liked this lady.

By now, Sarah had opened the plum wine and taken another glass and plate from the cupboard. She poured three glasses and handed one to each of us and held hers high. "To ladies' night out—or in. Doesn't matter. To us—old friends and a new friend."

I didn't know if I'd call Sadie a friend yet, but I wasn't going to spoil the evening by critiquing semantics. We clinked our glasses and tasted the fruity wine.

"Okay, I'm hungry." Sarah put her glass down and began to open the carry-out containers and put them in the center of the table. I'd laid out serving spoons, and she stuck one into each carton. "Nothing fancy tonight. So sit. Dig in."

Sarah pulled out the chair closest to her and sat. Sadie and I followed her directive and began to fill our plates with my favorites: egg rolls, pot stickers, shrimp and pea pods, and a chicken and vegetable dish that was the source of the garlic aroma. And, of course, she hadn't forgotten the large container of pork-fried rice. My apprehension, or maybe just plain disappointment, about Sadie joining us soon became a non-issue, maybe because she was such a curious visitor. She asked one question after another about the town, the Square, and Rainbow Gardens. And Sadie hadn't forgotten our conversation during dinner with Clayton, so it was clear she was genuinely interested in the area and wanted to know more about it.

As we polished off the meal, I divided the last of the wine, and before long, we sat back in our chairs, relaxed and satisfied. Sarah looked especially content, which is why the turn of the conversation took me by surprise.

"Well, here's the bad news," Sarah said. "The Alexander Foundation denied our grant request. It took them all afternoon to decide, too. A total waste of my day. I didn't even have a chance to expound on the Square's enthusiasm for the project."

My surprise sprang mostly from not recalling any mention of a grant. "What grant is that?"

"I mentioned it at one of the association meetings. Probably right after I'd handed out the summer schedule. No one listens to anything after that's announced."

Sadie had leaned forward and settled her elbows on the edge of the table. She held her wine glass in both hands, her wrists covered with the same bangle of bracelets I'd seen before. "I'm interested. What was the grant for? Seems to me the Square is doing rather well."

"Uh, short version, Sarah." I grinned and glanced at Sadie. "We still have dessert coming." I'd heard Sarah before when she'd started talking about a pet project, and Sadie deserved a warning.

Sarah gave me a sly wink as she turned in her chair to focus on Sadie. *Oh, boy.* She had a new audience and would make the most of it.

"The grant was to upgrade the museum by both organizing and cataloguing the contents. Most of the items are from the Hutchinson and Crawford families that worked hard to establish the town of Wolf Creek in the mid- to late 1800s. I suggested we start interviewing older people who have lived here all their lives—or close to it—and establish an archive of oral histories."

"What's not to like about the project? Local historical societies all over the country are gathering and cataloging oral histories," Sadie said. "Everyone, especially historians, know recorded history represents the future. With fewer letters and diaries being created, capturing memories through interviews is about the only way to preserve the past."

As she spoke, I exchanged her dinner plate for a smaller one where I'd placed a wedge of Crossroads chocolate mousse pie.

Agreeing with Sadie, Sarah kept on talking out her frustration, and I got pie for both of us.

Sarah punctuated her points with small waves of her fork. "Few visitors bother going into the museum anymore," she said, "and that's because the displays haven't been changed in years. That made some sense when the Square was on the way out, more or less. The whole place is faded and dusty. A generation or two ago, local women formed a group, The Historical Women of Wolf Creek. They cleaned up a little every spring." Sarah shrugged and looked away. "Those women are gone now or too old to take on that kind of work anymore. People in my generation, and most certainly in Megan's, work full-time now, and don't have time or the inclination to take on thankless cleaning projects for a museum other people in town aren't stepping up to support."

"I'll say," Sadie said, nodding.

Her matter-of-fact tone got a laugh from me, and from Sarah, too.

"I can't even get my own family involved," Sarah said. "What do you think of that?"

"To tell you the truth," Sadie said, holding her pie-filled fork in the air, "I peeked in the windows the other day trying to see what was inside. I was disappointed to find the building closed."

Sarah nodded. "And you've raised another problem. I don't think we can just unlock the door and allow the place to be open unattended. Even if that were safe, it's not good PR. Whoever heard of a museum without a greeter or an information desk?"

"PR aside, it's obvious we need someone to keep an eye on visitors. Some items in the museum are genuine antiques with value," I added. I'd moved back and forth from the counter to the table to stay alert. In my mind it was already the next day, when I'd be busy filling orders, unpacking more supplies, and working on the window display. I also needed to gather supplies for the interview on Sunday.

When I glanced at Sadie, she was covering her mouth to hide a yawn.

Sarah frowned, likely self-conscious about becoming so engrossed in her own concerns.

"Oh, I'm sorry, Sarah. It wasn't your story." Sadie's voice rose for emphasis. "It's just that I've put in a full day looking for a place to live. Clayton and I found a small cottage for rent behind one of the lake homes. The owners' children won't be using it this summer and rather than have it empty, they rented it to us on the spot. Aren't we lucky?"

"Congratulations, Sadie. That's wonderful news," I said. This was the first I'd heard about Sadie and Clayton staying in Wolf Creek, or, at least, locating here for the summer. Maybe Clayton had planned to tell me on Sunday.

"Before we go I have a favor to ask, Megan." Sarah's voice was quieter, more apprehensive than usual. Certainly not reflecting her normal confident self.

We were close, Sarah and I, so I knew whatever she had on her mind was important. "Sure. What do you need?"

Sarah turned to Sadie. "On the subject of preserving the past, I'm writing a history of Wolf Creek and the Square. Each time I get a section done I ask someone connected to that part of the history to read it. Megan and her brothers own the farm that was the Buchanan Horse Farm when the town was no more than a relay station for the stagecoach line that traveled through here."

"Oh, I'd like to read your history," Sadie said, her eyes dancing. "I do enjoy the history of towns and all the people who struggled to help a community survive. Was that your brochure I saw at Biscuits and Brew?"

"Sure is. That was the beginning of this project," Sarah answered.

"Do you have the next section with you, Sarah?" I asked. Sarah had become shy about her writing, but everyone said she did a great job of using the history as part of being an ambassador for the town.

Sarah reached into her large purse and withdrew a manila envelope. "No rush. It will be awhile before I put the parts together in book form."

"What a terrific item to sell in the museum," Sadie remarked.

"I agree." I nodded firmly, looking in Sarah's direction and taking the envelope. "I'll get it back to you as soon as I can."

With that, they stood and gathered their things to leave. I collected the bags and the mostly empty containers. One paper bag didn't feel quite empty, so I gave it a shake and heard the rattle of something at the bottom.

"Hey, fortune cookies," I said, looking inside. I pulled out two and handed one to Sadie and one to Sarah. "I'll open mine later and sleep on it," I said, grinning. "Maybe it will plant the seed for an interesting dream."

"Good idea," Sadie said. "I'm going to do the same thing. Maybe it will give me a hint about a new direction for my life." She slipped the cookie into her handbag.

"Maybe so, Sadie. Who am I to argue?" Sarah said. She put her cookie in her tote bag.

I followed the two down the stairs and locked the front door after they left. Sadie took the path across the Square to the Inn and Sarah headed in the other direction to her home above the mayor's office at the end of the Square. We were neighbors of sorts, not far away from each other at all.

I hurried back upstairs, eager to fix my mug of hot chocolate milk, so I could start reading Sarah's pages. While the mug of chocolate heated, I changed into my sleep shirt and stacked up a pile of pillows so I could sit up and read in bed. Finally, I was settled in, ready to find out what Sarah had written about my family's land when it was a homestead.

But first things first. I pulled the cellophane off the cookie and broke it open. "Okay, fortune cookie, give me a sign."

I read the message and groaned. "Oh, for Pete's sake, you call this a fortune?" *A decision could bring changes in your life.*

As if I didn't know. I bit into a piece of the cookie and picked up Sarah's pages and started reading.

A Pennsylvania Mining Town

Reuben Buchanan held the newspaper with both hands, but the small print was hard to read. If what the paper said was true, he'd finally, after years of searching, found a way out of the dark, dirty mines of Pennsylvania.

He steadied his trembling hands and read each word of the article a second time.

LAND OFFER:
Granted by the Congress of the United States to the State of Wisconsin, homestead land. Ten acres would be deeded free to any man willing to build a house and work the land, as in farming, animal raising, and enterprise.

Rueben didn't know exactly what 'enterprise' meant, but he knew that animal raising included horses. His string of horses were the best in the area. Strong, hardy, dependable.

He folded the paper, tucked it under his arm, and headed for home with a spring in his step. He couldn't believe his good fortune.

Rueben saved his news until his family sat for supper. "We're heading west, Dora."

"How far?" she asked. Dora knew he yearned to leave the mines and be independent.

"To the horizon." Reuben winked at his sons, Harold and Callum. Young men themselves, they, too, no longer wanted to be part of the mining town.

"California?" Callum questioned before filling his fork with stew.

"Wisconsin." Reuben took the folded newspaper from his pocket and passed it to his wife. Everyone ate while she read the article out loud.

She fell silent a moment and busied her

hands, taking a biscuit from the basket and breaking it into pieces she dropped into her bowl. The gravy from the stew was quickly absorbed. Food was expensive and none was wasted in the Buchanan home.

Finally, she looked up and said, "You send a telegram to these people and tell them we're coming."

Reuben reached across the table and grabbed Dora's hand. "We can only take one wagon load. Food, tools, gun, basic house wares."

"That will be enough," she said. "We started with less when we came here."

Reuben thought back to those early days when they'd indentured for a year in order to become established.

He looked down the table to his sons. "You boys coming along?"

"You can't move that string by yourself. I'm coming." Harold enjoyed working with the horses more than his brother did.

Callum swatted his brother's shoulder. "You're not leaving me behind."

Laughter rippled around the table. Reuben looked at his family and lowered his head in prayer.

After sharing the news with friends, other families joined the Buchanans in the wagon train to eastern Wisconsin. They fought through frightening weather, raging rivers, and even a small band of unsavory train robbers. Nothing broke Reuben's vision of a home of his own for his family and a green pasture for his horses.

7

The next morning I opened my eyes, startled. Sarah's papers were scattered across my bed. The reading lamp was still on and the alarm buzzed in its annoying way. I had a pretty good memory for dreams, but I could only conjure up a smattering of images, something about covered wagons crossing a river.

I sat up and scanned my bedroom, my eye catching the tiny fortune cookie paper on the nightstand. I smiled, thinking about life-changing decisions ahead.

Getting to my feet, I stretched my arms over my head and spotted my jeans tossed on top of a pile of laundry on the dresser. It wasn't the only area where I needed to restore order. Fortunately, I'd kept my bedroom simple, basic but wonderful in its own way. A soft, spring-weight comforter covered the bed now and the simple wooden nightstand had room for the lamp and clock and a book or two. I'd added a small comfy chair upholstered in fabric to match the flowered curtains.

Too bad simplicity didn't describe my closet. With the doors open, I couldn't hide the clothes and shoes jammed in every which way. I had a mixture of old and new, the latest fashions from Styles mixed with pieces that would soon fit the definition of vintage. After struggling to keep order in my shop, though, I had little patience left over to sort out my clothes. Besides, didn't fashion always cycle around? Heck, that frilly black blouse I could see sticking out between two lightweight jackets would be in vogue again one day soon. *Right*.

My quick scan of the room left me almost embarrassed by

its bounty, especially after reading about my pioneer family coming to Wisconsin with so little. But they'd had plenty of determination to carve a new life. Even as I observed my own stuffed closet, the aroma of coffee filled the apartment. I gave myself a mental pat on the back for remembering to set the timer before I'd climbed into bed.

Part of the abundance I noted were the four outfits I'd draped over the back of the chair. That's as far as I'd progressed in narrowing down what I'd wear for the interview on Sunday. I'd frittered away a couple of evenings trying on pants and blazers and both frilly and tailored shirts. But why? My clothes weren't being judged, so what was my problem?

As I got ready to head downstairs to open the shop, I smiled at the sunlight already streaming through the skylight and brightening up my apartment. That morning sunshine was a good sign for the Square and boosted my enthusiasm for the day.

I pulled on my slim-legged khaki pants and a cotton top in a deep petunia purple. I shuddered thinking about those awful jeans Clayton had seen me wearing the first time he'd come to the shop. But why did that bother me so much? It kept coming back to haunt me, as if I'd made a fatal mistake and embarrassed myself.

Realizing my mind was filling to the brim with useless tidbits and random nonsense, I grabbed a large mug, filled it with coffee and opened the cupboard where I stashed my energy bars. I chose one with peanuts and coconut coated in dark chocolate. *Take that, Eli.* My brother made no secret of judging so-called energy bars as nothing more than candy bars with some protein powder and a fancy name. Not that he was above stocking a rack of them in Farmer Foods. As Elliot liked to say, "Those bars all but fly off the shelves."

Once I was in the shop with my coffee and breakfast, I had to face facts. My shop was a mess, with packing material everywhere. Still, I wanted to delay tidying up and finish the window display before the shop opened at ten.

A good enough plan, but it was derailed on the spot when Georgia knocked on the front door shortly after I'd washed down the last of the nuts and chocolate and turned on the lights.

I opened the door to let her in. "Hi. You're sure up and out early."

"Can we talk?" She spotted the garden pinwheel on the display stand next to the door. "Oh, I should buy one of those for my front lawn garden before you sell out your stock."

"Don't feel rushed. I'm reordering them—and a couple of dozen statuary pieces, too." I grabbed some packing material off the floor on my way back to the workbench. There was no empty place to put it since I'd not yet emptied a box filled with plant pots painted with animal faces. I dropped it on an already growing pile of bunched up paper on the floor near the bench.

Since Georgia didn't stop in at this time of day unless she had something on her mind, I assumed she wanted to talk about her wedding flowers. "So, are you here to talk about the wedding?"

Georgia stood silent, staring at the arrangements in the cooler. Without looking at me, she said, "No, not today. Uh, I'll just say it. Elliot asked me to find out if you're okay. He's noticed that you seem distracted lately."

Distracted? No. Try totally confused.

"How's that?" I asked instead. "Tell me, what exactly did he say?"

"Nothing specific, but he's noticed you haven't been coming around to B and B for coffee with the group in the morning lately, and he mentioned the papered-over front windows." She pivoted and caught my eye. "And he says you aren't your usual smiling self when he sees you these days."

So, big brother's watchful eye had been near, but unlike Eli, who never held back a blunt remark, Elliot had sent an emissary.

"So?" Georgia asked.

"Okay, he could be right, at least in his observations. But there's nothing actually wrong. I told Eli and Elliot about it the other day." I held my hand in front of me and deliberately made it shake. I explained the situation with the contest and why I'd been so private about it. "The contest interview is *tomorrow* and as the days count down, I'm getting more and more nervous. It is important—*to me*—that I do well. But it also feels like I'm representing the town and the Square and uh…that just piles on more pressure."

"I understand," Georgia said, emphasizing her words with a slow nod, "and once it's over you'll be back to your old self. I'm glad nothing's wrong because I'm so excited about having you as part of my new life with your brother."

"Yes, well, good," I mumbled. "So, you'll tell him I'm preoccupied, but I'll be fine." I grabbed the notebook I'd assembled of photos of bouquets and arrangements from past weddings. "Here, take this with you and browse through it. See if you and Elliot like any of the styles. It's never too early to begin planning."

I slipped the notebook in a Rainbow Gardens bag and handed it to her. "So no one guesses what your announcement next week is all about," I whispered, like it was our own little secret.

Steady-as-they-go-Georgia blushed, but her smile rivaled a mega-watt bulb. "Nope. I've managed to keep a lid on the details."

"So, you'll go back to my brother and explain I'm having contest jitters?" I put that in the form of a question, because I wanted reassurance.

"Agreed," she said, checking her watch. She gave me a quick wave and headed out the door. The jingle sound rose a notch when she pulled the door shut.

Whew. That was close. I'd almost blurted my confused thoughts about leaving Wolf Creek…well, maybe. I often discounted them as only passing thoughts. Sometimes that was an accurate description, because when I got down to the business of picturing myself in another town, establishing another business, or working for someone else, I lost heart in it. How would a major move really improve my situation? On the other side of the argument, sometimes the same scenario seemed bold and adventurous. No more ruts for me!

In spite of my indecision, I needed to give myself more credit. Here I was, not yet forty-years-old, and part of a booming community. Along with my brothers, I was a pioneer in a unique tourist destination.

Sarah's history brought home my heritage. My family had deep roots in the area. And that made playing around with the idea of leaving seem absurd. Sure, I had my reasons. Maybe I was more like my ancestors than I realized. They'd headed out to explore new places. Maybe my explorations would involve the Rocky Mountains or the shores of Lake Superior or an exciting city on one of the coasts.

Uh-huh, sure, Megan. I had to laugh at myself. By the time I finished my fantasy, I had packing boxes filled to the top and professional movers hauling my things around. Not exactly a covered wagon and a couple of cooking pots!

Thankfully the phone rang and stopped my train of thought. It was Sarah.

"Just wanted to thank you for including Sadie in our dinner last night."

"No problem," I answered with a quick laugh, "but I'll be honest and admit it threw me at first."

"And I admit I sprang it on you. I should have called."

"Sadie is charming, though, and probably has many colorful stories to tell—and she's interested in our little neck of the woods."

"That she is," Sarah said. She paused. "Um, are you feeling okay?"

I decided to forgo defensive answers and stick with the truth. "Jitters, I guess. That's as good a word as any for what I'm feeling. Sadie's son is doing my interview for the contest. *Tomorrow.*" None of this was new to Sarah.

"You're sure that's all?" she prodded.

"All? I have a lot riding on this contest."

While Sarah and I talked, I jotted a note to myself to post a sign on the door about closing at 2:30 on Sunday afternoon. I wanted a little time to straighten the shop and lay out the clippers and knives and other supplies I used every day, not to mention finally changing into one of the four outfits I put together. And I'd put on extra makeup for the photo shoot.

"One more question."

Seconds of silence ticked by.

"Okay," I finally said, "ask it."

"Is Clayton *important* to you?"

Sarah had asked that same question before and I'd sidestepped it to avoid answering. Knowing Sarah, if I'd said a quick no, or hedged by saying only that his position with the contest made him important, she'd read past my words and push further into the realm of more personal feelings. Maybe I'd even tell her that I was considering a life change. A big one. To another zip code. I was saved when the bell jingled. "There goes that jingle. Customers are coming in. Gotta run. Talk to you later."

And they kept coming. By the end of another fast-moving day, I'd managed to finish the window display and price the garden gadgets. I was ready for a quiet evening.

As I turned off the shop lights and headed upstairs, I thought ahead to Sunday, wondering if Clayton would be a quiet observer or would he expect me to keep a conversation going as I worked? I didn't think having him nearby would bother me. Over the years, I'd created countless arrangements for customers who stood next to the workbench and watched. I'd handled that proximity, hadn't I? My confidence was surging through me again. I resolved to simply pretend I was making arrangements for some unknown person and the pressure would be gone.

Wrong.

Sarah's question rolled through my mind again, as it had in unguarded moments all day. What did I think, or feel, about Clayton? And why did it matter? What actually *mattered* was that this contest was my avenue out of Wolf Creek, my chance to be in the big league, my chance to shine.

Shine? Didn't I shine already, right in the heart of Wolf Creek Square? Or maybe, I wanted to see how far my dreams could take me? On the other hand, what was it like to shine in a large city? My Internet search of Clayton Sommers had told me he'd once been considered a rising star in the art world. His paintings had sold to important collectors. But here he was, doing an interview for a contest in my little town.

I rambled around my apartment, going from the window in the living room to the kitchen, where I opened a can of soup and pulled out sandwich makings. Then I went into the bedroom and picked up a turquoise tunic from the back of the chair. I held it in front of me and looked into the mirror. But I was going through the motions of fussing with the clothes. My thoughts were stuck elsewhere as I focused on a question. Did Clayton miss shining in the starlight?

8

Before I unlocked the front door, customers had clustered in front of the shop windows. Chatting with each other, they pointed to the white carnations transforming to red and blue. Even through the glass barrier of the door and windows, I heard exclamations of admiration for my garden display in the other window. Customers seldom bought items from the window, but that day was another story. By lunchtime, a good portion of the new inventory was sold, including both of the green hammers. I was almost giddy when I wrote myself a reminder note to order more of those unique items—and soon!

I also stole a few minutes to place a large flower order and pay the extra fee to have it shipped immediately. I sensed a greater than typical need for increased inventory for Memorial Day weekend. What a great start to my day.

As I placed my orders and packed up customer purchases, the morning only got better. For those busy hours I reveled in the feeling of being on top of things, and that brought back the familiar excitement of pulling together all the elements of the welcoming atmosphere I worked hard to create. I'd been so focused on the contest and my ambivalence about staying put in Wolf Creek or bidding it goodbye, I'd forgotten what it felt like to make customers smile. It was particularly rewarding to hear them say that after shopping in my store, they were eager to return to the Square.

That afternoon, a couple around my age entered the shop, but immediately said they were only browsing, so I left them to it. But their meandering was productive and they soon came to the counter with two red, white, and blue pottery bowls, six in all. While I packed their order, the man reached for a business card and studied it a minute.

"Do you ever go to schools and give talks?" he asked.

That came as a surprise. "Well, most of the time I'm a one-woman show here, so it's difficult for me to get away. But is there something in particular you had in mind?"

"I teach science at the Howard-Suamico middle school," he said, "and your flower coloring display would be a great way to begin the school year next September. The students could see science—botany—in a fun way. It might inspire them to learn more about the natural life all around them."

Despite having had such an enjoyable morning, I came dangerously close to blurting something about likely being long gone by September. But after successfully suppressing that impulse, I began to play around with the idea of asking Sadie to fill in for a few hours so I could visit the classroom. Hadn't she said she'd run businesses in the past? True, the flower business had its own unique demands, tending to a store of any kind had common elements.

Sadie? Really? My own idea took me aback.

My mind was a bunch of jumbled thoughts and possible responses to the man, but I managed to engage my brain and say, "Why don't you call me when school starts, and we'll see if we can work something out."

I left the conversation there and the man nodded as they left the shop. I realized my wishy-washy answer probably confused him, though. For the next few minutes I had trouble shaking off a curious let-down feeling. A teacher had presented me with an opportunity to share my love of flowers with young people, but my ambivalence about staying in Wolf Creek got in the way. I had to make a decision soon, so I could finally stop battling the wishy-washy feelings that led to vague "we'll see" answers.

The crowd on the Square reached a peak around noon and eased by the time I posted my "Closed" sign when I locked the door at 2:30. I quickly straightened up the shop before heading upstairs to change. The time had come to decide the biggest question of the day. What should I wear? I had four choices. Which one would it be?

I held up the bright red, tailored blazer. I liked it, but the shop wasn't an office, and the blazer would be great for a business meeting at Country Law. That was the reason I rarely wore it in the shop. The tee with embroidered flowers on the scooped neckline was too ordinary. And the other choice was a loose cotton shift, but much too summery on such a cool day.

Finally, I settled on flared black pants and high wedge shoes and a white-on-white patterned tunic set off with a woven wool belt, distinctive because of its bright colors and bronze clasp. Professional, but a little on the artsy side, too. Best of all, I felt confident in the clothes. I touched up my make-up and hair, and was ready, even relaxed.

Clayton arrived promptly at our appointed time. He'd dressed in slacks, shirt and sport coat, but minus a tie. I assumed he was signaling a professional, but relaxed atmosphere. At least I took it that way.

We sat at the small table and began.

Clayton opened his laptop and brought up the questionnaire. I had my hard copy of the questions, and I'd made notes on the pages for my answers.

The first questions were a repeat of those I'd answered for the initial round of judging. I hesitated, even stumbled, over my availability to leave Wolf Creek for periods of time to represent the Bartholomew School of Floral Design at conferences and regional schools and shows. I'd done the math, and if I was gone for more than six months out of the year, even if only for one year, it would mean closing the shop for good. And, without the income, I'd need to sell the building, too.

"So, Megan, tell me why you want to win?"

That question was more difficult than it should have been. Starting a couple of years ago, I'd gone from a gradual dissatisfaction with my hometown to becoming, only weeks ago, emphatic about leaving. At least that's how I felt in certain solitary moments. I was ready to spread my wings and fly away to explore the world. But then Clayton had arrived. With the end of the contest so near and the realization that I could, after all, win, I discovered my resolve wasn't quite as strong anymore.

My mind muddled with contradictions, so instead I said, "Let's come back to that one later."

From his expression, I suspected Clayton was on the verge of pressing harder for an answer. But he stared at his laptop screen for a few seconds. Nodding, he said, "Okay, but you have to answer it sometime, Megan."

"Not if I withdraw from the contest," I blurted. Foolishly. I sounded like a ten-year-old.

"Withdraw?" He stared at me as if he must have misheard me.

"Well, if I don't finish the questionnaire, then I won't have to answer."

"Come on, Megan." He pursed his lips in disgust.

Would I do that? The words had slid out of my mouth. "Just a thought," I said, keeping my tone light.

"If you did that, you'd always wonder if you could have won. Would you be satisfied with that unfinished piece of business the rest of your life?"

"No." My honesty surprised me. "But what about you?" I asked. "Are you satisfied after being run out of New York?"

I saw a flash in his eyes. Anger? Hurt? Then, as if he hadn't heard the question, he asked me the next one on the questionnaire, which related to my motivation to become a floral designer. I exhaled. That question put me back into familiar territory—my childhood, Mom and Gram, and pestering them to teach me about flowers.

From there, the interview focused on techniques and trends and the debate about traditional versus the more *avant garde*. Easy questions, at least for me, because I could bring the answers back to my market. Finally, Clayton posed the last question. An open-ended one, it challenged me to expound on why flowers are significant, not as a business or just to me, but important in life in general.

I laughed as I said, "Do you have another hour?"

Clayton smiled, but gestured back to me.

"Where to begin? Flowers are the essence of beauty, aren't they? They encompass all the senses. They can feel smooth and soft as velvet, but they also have thorns we need to avoid. Perfumes and other scents start with plants as the reference point. We can add some flower petals to our salads and drinks. They catch our eye and just looking at them brings us endless pleasure."

"Okay, you've covered touch, scent, taste, and sight," Clayton said, a smile tugging at the corners of his mouth. "What about sound?"

"Getting technical on me, are you?" I teased. "Let's just say we can hear their leaves rustle in the breeze."

"Break time," I said, taking in a deep breath. I went to the cooler and pulled out two bottles of water.

"Okay, but not a long one."

"Are you on a timeline?" I asked, surprised he was eager to move along more quickly.

"Not at all," he said, "but I'm curious about what you'll come up with during the next step of this process. You know, the part where I get to see what you can do."

I gulped back some cool water, reversing the dry mouth I'd developed, most likely from my case of nerves.

"I'm ready," I said, a half-fib. Making arrangements with Clayton watching seemed entirely too much like putting on a show rather than creating something for a customer. Yet, with my eyes wide open I had entered this contest, and others much like it. It was part of the deal, the give and take.

Clayton pulled out an envelope and held it up. "Okay, Megan, I haven't opened this envelope. It describes the three arrangements you'll assemble. And remember, I'll be shooting some photos as you work."

Without waiting for me to respond, or work up an even worse case of the jitters, he broke the envelope's seal and withdrew a card. "The first is a small bouquet for a sick child, a girl."

I grinned. Good news, I could handle that. I made arrangements for hospital patients often, and those for kids were the most special. I went to the cupboard where I stored vases and containers. I immediately chose a ceramic standing rabbit, with the ears coming up from either side. I filled it with daisies, baby's breath, and three small pink irises. A few sprigs of greenery added a bit of contrasting color.

Clayton hadn't said a word while I worked, but I was aware of him close by and focused on me, shooting photos as I chose and trimmed the flowers. I stepped back from the workbench to indicate I was done; it had taken only a few minutes to create such a simple display. But that was the essence of my market. My customers expected affordable, yet pretty arrangements. And what I had put together was easily carried into the patient's room. Big and showy wouldn't do at all.

Clayton nodded when I moved away, leaving him with a clear view of the arrangement from every angle. When he was done taking shots, I moved the child's arrangement to a display table.

He withdrew the second card. "The next one is for a business office. They want something large and dynamic to display in their reception area or conference room."

I took out three of my favorite tall pottery vases and let my imagination fill each one. Finally, I chose the ceramic one designed to look like a rectangular woven basket with rounded corners. I smiled to myself. This was a chance to create my signature look—what I'd become known for in my market. I went to the cooler and gathered one flower of each color of every variety I had in stock. I then grabbed some natural dried weeds and grasses I had on display in the corner.

"This is an easy one for me," I said, grinning at Clayton. "I make arrangements like this for Country Law every month. You'll see them in the lobby at the Inn, too, and other places around town."

I gathered all the flowers and dried materials in both hands and shuffled them a bit. Then I put them in the tall vase. No muss, no fuss.

"Done." I stepped back to admire the multi-colored bouquet, eclectic and bold. I moved in to fluff out some of the grasses and move one of the red blooms an inch or two to the side to create space between it and the next one, a bright yellow tulip.

"That's it?" Clayton was surprised, but I saw a twinkle

in his eye. "I wouldn't have believed it if I hadn't watched. Where'd you learn that trick?"

"My grandmother did it all the time with flowers from her garden. She didn't have time to put each stem in the vase separately."

Clayton took more pictures and then turned and snapped a few of me. "Those won't qualify as portraits, Megan."

I laughed, needing those couple of minutes to calm my nerves. I'm sure Clayton had expected more than a grab-and-stuff arrangement, my term for the look that could end up both casual and dramatic. That's why he was taking so many shots from various angles. Over the years, this type of arrangement had become a favorite of mine and of many customers. It reminded me of a field of flowers in their natural setting, free and showing nature's palette. That's why I legitimately called it the signature style of Rainbow Gardens.

I grabbed my bottle of water, twisted the cap and took a couple of huge swallows to drain it. I set it aside to recycle later and enjoyed the surge of energy filling me. I nodded to Clayton. I was ready for the final test.

"Do an arrangement for either a funeral or as a get-well gesture for a man."

I cleared and cleaned the workbench to give myself time to come up with ideas. This held some challenge for me. Arrangements for men were notoriously difficult because flowers had mistakenly been linked with women or with events and businesses, but not individual men. The other day, when I'd thought about this interview and its tests, I had taken an informal inventory of an assortment of artificial birds and feathers stored in one of my lower cupboards, out of sight, but not out of mind. As I'd considered different containers, Clayton followed me and took numerous photographs, first of me and then of several displays that gave my shop its showy look.

I pretended to study the containers, but I was trying to recall where I'd put a particular vase. I wanted to remember its exact location and not appear to be searching for it. Finally, an image of it tucked in a back corner of a seldom used cupboard appeared. It was as if the vase had magic about it and had waited for the exact moment when I could bring it to life. It looked like a short cut of a tree, brown in color with ridges representing bark. A stub of a branch protruded from one side. I lifted it off the shelf and brought it to the workbench.

"Interesting container."

Clayton's comment surprised me. He hadn't remarked on any of my choices with the other two entries.

This arrangement required more time to select flowers and greenery. Since I hadn't known the kinds of arrangements I'd be asked to make, I hadn't ordered specific flowers to use for the contest. I not only wanted to be able to use what I made for the contest in other orders, I wanted to create designs I'd use every day in my shop, which was designed for a small-town community in a fairly rural part of the state.

I chose three giant mums and natural pussy willows I'd cut at the farm, adding one stem of every type of greenery in the cooler. Rather than shuffling and simply putting the whole collection in the vase at one time, with this design I added each stem to the vase individually, making a fresh cut at the bottom of each branch. Several times, I rotated the vase to check for balance. Next I added the willow stems and feathers from my collection, including peacock, pheasant, and wild turkey. I chose the peacock feathers with their circle of turquoise because they added color, whereas the mostly brown hues added to the earthy warmth. The mums added three focal points of color, deep yellow, purple, and red.

I turned the vase again, but from all angles, the arrangement looked dull and drab to me. I wanted to add a few sprigs of baby's breath, but didn't want Clayton to laugh.

Why did I think he might react that way? And where had my confidence gone? I knew perfectly well the arrangement needed those little flowers as highlights.

I squared my shoulders and went to the cooler. Three stems were all it needed and I quickly added them. Satisfied I was done, I backed away from the workbench to make room for Clayton to take a few close up photographs. Realizing his opinion mattered to me, I overcame my reluctance and asked, "What do you think?"

"I like all of them," he said thoughtfully. "I admit I was surprised you used from your inventory of flowers and hadn't ordered any specialty or exotic flowers."

"I know two of the finalists work almost exclusively with exotic flowers, but I don't work with them often enough to be comfortable using them." I shrugged. "They're way too expensive for my clientele. I might have the occasional special order, but most of my customers are more…" I paused, searching for the right word, but not coming up with one that covered what I meant. Finally, I said, "Let's just say my clientele is *hometown*."

Clayton nodded. "Art said the same thing about his work when I talked with him the other day."

"Art's right. I actually prefer the flowers we have in the gardens at the farm, but I've found I can't do both. You know, grow them *and* sell them. So I buy the kinds of flowers my customers prefer."

"That must be very rewarding."

Nice. I heard the sincerity in his voice.

Clayton dragged one of the chairs from the table to the back door. "I want this neutral background for the portrait."

"One minute," I said, holding up my index finger. I rushed upstairs and checked my clothes, adjusting the gathering of the cotton fabric around the woven belt. I considered changing my clothes, but thought better of it. I'd just worked confidently in these clothes, so why question success? But I ran a brush through my hair and freshened my lip gloss before hurrying back down the stairs.

"Ready," I said, giving the sides of my hair a final pat.

I sat in the chair and followed directions. "Sit a little straighter, throw your shoulders back, turn a little to the left, look over my shoulder, turn a little to the right, tilt your head an inch or so…" as Clayton kept clicking the camera.

Suddenly, we were done. What I had worried about for days and weeks was over in a flash of time.

Clayton returned to the table and downloaded the photos

from his camera to his computer. I joined him and looked over his shoulder, surprised at how many dozens of pictures he'd taken.

I leaned in close to him so I could study what he'd done and view the photos up close. *Seriously?* No, what I really wanted was to wrap my arms around him. Surprised by my bold impulse, I shuffled back a couple of inches.

Clayton turned in the chair to face me. "That's all, Megan. Well, almost. You still need to answer that one question. Why do you want to win?" He scrolled through the interview document and stopped on that question.

My mind shuttled back and forth between a made-up answer and the truth. Since Clayton had turned back to stare at the screen, while I stood slightly behind him, it was easier for me to be honest without having him looking directly at me. "I could give you a pat answer about wanting to share my knowledge out of an altruistic impulse, or talk about my urge to travel and meet lots of new people. But none of that's true."

Clayton glanced back at me, the space between his brows creased in curiosity. "Is that so?"

"It is. You see, the real reason I want to win is so I can leave Wolf Creek. I've lived here all my life and I'm not so sure anymore about going through the year-after-year grind of life on the Square."

Wanting to keep my hands busy, I began cleaning up the workbench. I avoided looking at Clayton. What must he think of me? He'd been forced to abandon his home and constantly move around to stay beyond the reach of the tabloids.

"And I don't want you to repeat that to anyone," I said, "not even to your mother."

"All answers for the contest are confidential—between me and the judges. You can trust me on that. We'll simply say you're eager to travel. How about that?" He typed quickly and then closed his laptop and stood.

"Good. That's okay." I found it difficult to talk. His nearness, my honesty, and the thrill of knowing that what I created were three really fine arrangements combined to heighten my awareness of him, my shop, and my longings.

"So, I'm going back to New York tomorrow." He stepped away, opening up more space between us. "I have more interviews to do. One of the interviewers is ill and can't finish his list of finalists, so I'm stepping in. The extra money will help Mom. Good luck, Megan."

A million questions rushed into my mind about *his* life and future—his longings. Instead, I held out my hand to say good-bye.

Clayton took my hand, and then leaned forward and gave me the lightest of kisses. Somehow, I knew he didn't do that with each finalist he'd interviewed. And he walked toward the door without saying anything about coming back to Wolf Creek.

The bell jingled when he closed the door. I stood at the glass and watched him walk across the Square to the Inn. I covered my mouth to keep myself from yelling for him to come back, to come to me. *And kiss me again.*

When he disappeared from sight, I sighed, long and loud. To distract myself, I watered the contest arrangements and put them inside the cooler, and made a plan to take my own pictures the next day. Win or lose, I was proud of my work and wanted to have photos as a personal remembrance. But, I'd likely take them apart in a few days, and like Clayton, they'd be gone forever.

9

I kept to myself the next few days, preoccupied with customers and the growing crowds that spring brought to the Square. But I also wanted to guard my privacy and relive the afternoon with Clayton in my own little world. Still, I was happy to see Sadie when she came in for a visit—through the front door just as she had promised at our dinner with Sarah. She exuded great warmth and friendliness. Her initial reserved attitude toward me, and I suspected, most every new acquaintance, had softened.

She took her time getting a feel for my shop. While I waited on customers, she examined every shelf and picked up pottery and looked at the pots of arrangements for sale in the cooler. "You have a unique shop here, Megan. If you ever need help I'd be happy to step in and lend a hand."

A nice gesture, for sure. And I filed it away. "Do you want to own another business sometime in the future?"

Sadie picked up a turquoise ceramic planter, examining it and brushing her fingers across the smooth surface. "Interesting question. Not many people ask me that anymore. They probably assume I'm too old for new ideas, although that's silly. But, truthfully, I'm not sure what the future holds. My life in New York seems like such a long time ago." She scanned the shop, taking it all in. "Helping out is one thing, owning means you have to deal with all those pesky details."

"No kidding," I said, tying a simple white bow around the stem of a Talisman rose. When I handed it to her, she smiled, immediately reminding me of Clayton. And just like Clayton, after a few minutes passed, Sadie waved and left.

Once again, I was alone in the shop.

⚜   ⚜   ⚜

A couple of days later, I slipped into a chair in the large dining room at Crossroads just as Sarah tapped the microphone and called the Wolf Creek Square Business Association meeting to order.

"We're passing around copies of the agenda," Sarah said, "so we can get started right away."

For the meeting, the tables had been pushed to the edge of the room and the chairs were arranged theater style. I'd been talking with Georgia and Marianna, but when Sarah started the meeting Marianna had taken a seat next to Art, and Elliot had saved a chair for Georgia next to him. I found one of the empty spots at the end of a row, which only emphasized the fact that I had no special person in my life. I touched my lips and remembered Clayton's kiss, but immediately chastised myself for making so much of it. But when I was honest with myself, that kiss had meant something, at least to me.

I forced myself to pay attention to Sarah, who was explaining to the others that the grant application had being denied. "But that doesn't mean I'm giving up. I'll pursue whatever avenue I can find for support for our museum."

Applause rippled through the room, likely because of the resolve in her voice, rather than any inherent confidence that she'd actually be able to get money for our project. We thought Wolf Creek was a special place, historic even, but that didn't mean people who held the purse strings at foundations would agree.

Her expression brightened, showing her pleasure at the crowd's response to her determination. Sarah moved on to Memorial Day weekend. To the surprise of no one, we still had shop owners opposed to having vendors on the Square for the three-day holiday weekend. Their objections were all about change, a change away from what the Square had done in the past. Sarah, open-minded, as most true leaders are, was willing to break with tradition and experiment with various ways to promote the Square and encourage more visitors. We needed dynamic young people with families willing to come from nearby towns. Inviting vendors to participate in the festivals and celebrations was only one of the many ideas she'd championed, not only because of the income it would generate, but also because of the animated atmosphere it would create.

"There's one more announcement tonight," Sarah said. "Elliot? You had something to say?"

I watched my tall brother head to the front of the room with his typical easy gait and bright smile. A sense of emptiness overtook me when I thought about leaving Wolf Creek and not seeing him virtually every day.

"This announcement isn't just about me," he said as he made his way to the front. "Come on up, Georgia. It's about you, too."

The laughter of the crowd didn't surprise me. Elliot and Georgia were hardly a secret couple. I grinned seeing Georgia join him and slide under my brother's arm.

"So, you're all invited to a wedding in the middle of the Square in October—details to follow, folks." He leaned down and kissed Georgia in front of all of us.

Everyone in the room stood and applauded. The second it quieted down, one person after another fired questions at them about the wedding and where they'd live. Mimi, from Styles, asked about Georgia's dress, quickly turning pink and adding that she'd be happy to help pick it out no matter where Georgia bought it. We all laughed our way through a few minutes of handshakes, high fives, and hugs.

When the excitement died down, I saw Eli slip out the door. Eli's life was going to change even more than mine. No longer would my brothers be viewed as "the twins." Although the Reynolds family was gaining a perfect partner for Elliot, it would no longer be the three of us, like a fixture on the Square.

If I were to leave, I'd miss all the excitement in the coming months. Sure, I'd come back for the wedding, but my role would be more like a visitor than a participant. I couldn't even begin to sort through the feelings I'd have about the inevitable tradeoffs involved. I knew that gains came with losses and vice versa, but what would they be? And how would I really feel?

When the dining room door of Crossroads closed behind Eli, I hurried to add my congratulations and left. With all the hoopla, I doubted anyone noticed.

As usual, I'd turned on one of the lamps in the living room before I left for the meeting. As I walked home through the Square, the light became my beacon. Realistically, I didn't need the light to find my way home, but it was a small comfort in my life.

That night I sat with my mug of hot chocolate next to the front window and watched as the shopkeepers and staff left Crossroads in groups of twos and threes and leisurely went off in all directions—to their cars or their homes in town, or to apartments like mine above their shops. Elliot, Georgia, and Sarah were the last to leave the building.

They hadn't thought to ask me about the contest.

I felt a little sorry for myself, lonely up in my front window perch. But why? It had been my decision to be secretive about being a finalist up until almost the last minute. I hadn't gone into detail about the interview or the sample arrangements I'd need to create as part of being a finalist.

I still couldn't explain my silence, other than the dismissive attitude my brothers tended to have toward anything I did that took me out of the Wolf Creek mainstream. They'd always been conservative that way.

Especially Eli. All my life he'd tried to protect me from being hurt, particularly after Mom died, even more so after we lost Dad. But the years had passed, and now it felt like he'd been holding me back. Did they think I couldn't handle the rejection involved in contests? They never commented on Art Carlson's competitive streak. Art sent pieces to New York for judging all the time and made no apologies for it. Win or lose, he received our support.

The little voice in my head also reminded me that Art wasn't about to leave Wolf Creek. He'd figured out how to work in our small town market, but still imbue his work with the sophistication of the larger world of jewelry artists.

As I pondered all this, it dawned on me that Clayton had never mentioned he and Sadie were staying in Wolf Creek—at least for the summer. Only Sadie had mentioned that. He hadn't dropped any hints about his future plans, either.

Reluctantly, I turned off the light and went to bed, feeling low from the confusion and jumble of emotions. It was the first time since Mom died that tears stained my pillow.

10

My shipment of garden ornaments and tools arrived Thursday morning, not long before Tom showed up with his lunch bag and a to-go cup of coffee. We exchanged the usual pleasantries, and then I pulled the windmill out of the box and held it up to show him. "What was that you said about putting one of these together? That it would make for a fun afternoon project?"

Flashing a warm grin, he took it from my hands and pulled out the directions.

"And when you're done with that project, I'll show you a few tricks about tracking the shop's inventory and replenishing the window display."

"Got it," he said.

"I want everything ready for Memorial Day weekend. I imagine in the bus tour business you consider this weekend a kind of kickoff, too. It's as if we're telling the world we're launching the summer season, and people are eager to come out and see what's happening on the Square and what's new to look at and buy."

Tom grinned. "And your shop will look crisp and fresh."

I finalized some arrangements while Tom worked easily with shoppers, helping them buy pottery pieces and three different garden ornaments. I stood back and watched the sales, stepping in to help wrap the pieces and load the shopping bags. Once the customers left, I asked him to unpack the new shipment. Then, working in tandem, we quickly checked the items against the invoice. Fortunately, nothing was missing. Dealing with missing inventory was one of those pesky details Sadie had mentioned. It was the kind of thing that most shop owners tired of. Even if she enjoyed most of the work, I could understand if Sadie didn't feel like actually owning another store. But I had long ago accepted that not every task on my to-do list was great fun.

Since I'd already taught Tom my pricing schedule, we finished pricing the new merchandise, too. Working with him side-by-side, it nagged at me that maybe I really did need a person in the shop part-time. The number of busy days on the Square was increasing. At least on that hectic day, I was more relaxed having him in the shop. Besides, we both had our hands full until lunchtime, when we settled at the table and planned to take quick bites during lulls in traffic.

One customer, for whom the words "harried and tense" were understatements, said she needed a last minute arrangement. She pointed to three in the corner, but they all had SOLD signs on them.

"Sorry, those are spoken for," I said, "but tell me what you need and we'll come up with something fast."

The cooler looked sparse, though. I had another project for Tom's afternoon, to replenish the stock of arrangements.

"Let's see what Tom can come up with for you," I said to the woman, whose face showed immediate relief.

Needing an arrangement for a hostess gift, the customer looked on while Tom chose multi-colored tulips and greenery and whistled as he worked with the flowers to create something wonderful in a bare minimum of minutes. And the woman left delighted.

In between helping other customers, I watched Tom, admiring his eye for color and composition. A natural talent. Some people had it, others didn't. He would make a great flower shop owner. My thoughts drifted in the direction of leasing Rainbow Gardens to him, or even, maybe, possibly offering to sell it to him. If I won the contest, of course. A huge contingency.

I smiled to myself as his one quirk kept reappearing. He loathed throwing out wilted blossoms or broken stems. "Lost profit," I heard him mumble, more than once, but ultimately he managed to dispose of what we could no longer use.

By late afternoon, Tom had finished all the jobs I'd given him and made a turn around the shop, studying each corner. Finally he approached me.

"I've made a decision, Megan. I won't be coming back anymore. As much as I enjoy flowers, I'm too much of a bean counter for this kind of business. I cringe at the wasted overhead. I just don't think it's for me."

Considering how hard he'd worked all day, I was surprised. I had no choice but to accept his conclusion, though. "Sorry as I am to see you go, I understand. Thanks for your ideas and your company. I wish you well."

"Um, about my invitation for supper...perhaps we can still go another time. I would like to thank you for your generosity."

"Sure. Don't worry about it." I had an idea that could ease this parting of ways. "Or, when you're in town with a tour, you can bring lunch to the shop and we can catch up."

"That sounds like a plan," he said with a grin.

Tom shook my hand and grabbed his to-go cup and left. I locked the door and flipped the sign. Officially closed. When I got upstairs I made a PB & J sandwich. Definitely not a Crossroads dinner. And I was fresh out of pie. But that sandwich was comfort food all the same. And I needed a little of that comfort.

The Memorial Day weekend started off with a bang. For real. Thunder tore through the already loud torrents of rain beating on my skylight and woke me from a sound sleep. Just as night was turning into dawn, I was at full alert. Sure I wouldn't fall back to sleep, I made coffee and turned on the TV, where local stations showed maps with locations where the weather service had issued storm watches and warnings.

Later, I went downstairs and unlocked the door, only because we had a rule on the Square that we opened our doors rain or shine. In Wolf Creek's residential neighborhoods a block or so off the Square in each direction, some of our local people often trekked over in bad weather, just because they were so close. They could grab coffee at Biscuits and Brew or have lunch at Crossroads and wander in and out of shops that would likely be crowded on better days. Even in winter, a bad storm gave people a walking destination, so in our shops we often had a chance to visit with people we seldom saw.

The line of strong storms passed through by late-morning, but steady rainfall lasted into the evening. For a Square dependent on foot traffic, this kind of weather spelled a scanty turnout, despite the local people. The majority of outdoor vendors stayed away, too, which I knew only added fuel to Eli's fire.

Early in the dreary day, I'd decided I would clean and restock a few cupboards and make bows from the new custom designed Rainbow Gardens ribbon. It had a light green hue for the background and Rainbow Gardens printed on it to look like embroidery in a variety of colors. I silently thanked Tom for suggesting that my old design, plain and black on a darker green, had grown stale.

I was happily working in the late afternoon when Eli entered through the back door holding a raincoat over his head. As I'd predicted, he had plenty to say.

"Didn't I tell Sarah that contracting with the vendors this weekend and spending that extra advertising money was a waste?"

I shook my head. "Right, Eli. You knew way last winter that we'd have storms this weekend."

What was up with him? Whatever it was, his grouchy ways were even worse than usual.

"Exactly," he said, authority in his voice. "Memorial Day is *always* iffy. Those of us with the commonsense we were born with know it's too early in the year to plan for fishing or picnics. Ha! Even walking and biking around town is usually impossible."

I sent him what I hoped was a withering look. "Maybe the sun will shine tomorrow, *Mr. Gloom.*"

"Dreamer." The disgust in Eli's voice tempted me to ask him to leave. I swallowed back the words, especially when he fingered one of the new bows on the bench.

"Cool, huh? Tom's idea for custom ribbon."

"Is he coming back?" he asked.

"No. He decided he's too practical to run a flower shop—too much risk of spoilage and supplies that go bad in front of our eyes. Like the risk you and Elliot face every day." I paused, thinking about what a contradiction Tom was. "He's quite a creative guy, though."

"I'm glad he won't be coming around. I didn't like him."

"How can you say that?" I asked, incredulous. "You don't know him."

"He…"

Suddenly two women came into the store, both huddled under one giant hot-pink umbrella. That sent Eli turning on his heel and heading for the back exit. Too bad. I wanted to hear his thoughts about Tom. But too late now. I turned my attention to the customers. "Welcome to Rainbow Gardens."

"Whew! Kind of nasty out there." The woman holding the umbrella closed it part way.

"Is there something special that brings you out today? Anything specific you're looking for?" I continued to finish the bow I'd started.

"Since you asked," the same woman said, "my friend was here recently and bought the cutest metal frog for her garden. She said you had a nice selection of garden ornaments."

I smiled and pointed first to a row of display shelves and then to a collection of small arrangements separated by a display of garden ornaments positioned to be eye-catching. "A new shipment came in this week. You'll see they're spread out around the store so take your time and look around."

And so they did, for about one or two minutes. When the rain let up a little, they waved and ducked out without buying anything, but calling out that they'd return another day. Oh, well. Rainy days often brought browsers who had no intention of buying, mostly because they didn't want to haul bags around in the rain.

Thick, pewter clouds kept rolling in from the west throughout the day. A slow drizzle continued after I locked the door and went next door to Farmer Foods and picked up two deli salads and crusty bread for dinner. Afterwards, I went back to my place through the back door and headed upstairs.

I ate half of the salads with a couple of thick slices of buttered bread while I checked the weather on TV and then surfed through the channels looking for something to attract my attention. But other than some forensic TV shows, where solving a murder was the goal, I didn't find anything that captured my attention. So, after the criminal was nabbed and the episode was over, I checked my email and cleaned up the dinner dishes. Then I went to bed with my hot chocolate. After I drained the cup, I let the companionable sound of the rain on the skylight take me back to reading more of Sarah's account of the history of Wolf Creek.

Buchanan Horse Farm

East of Wolf Creek, at the end of Buchanan Road stands a house built by Reuben Buchanan and his sons, Harold and Callum.

In the middle 1800s, the Knight Stagecoach Line served the smaller communities between Wausau and Green Bay. Merlin Knight, of Green Bay, had established a relay station twenty miles west of Green Bay, where an east and west road crossed with a north and south throughway. His daughter, Eleanor, married Asa Hutchinson and became one of the founding families of Wolf Creek, the small town located at the crossroads. The Buchanan family sold the horses needed to draw the coaches. After Asa's death, Eleanor married Sam Crawford.

"It's time for us to be leaving, Eleanor. Harold wants us to be there early to choose the horses before the buyer from the Army arrives."

"I'm ready, Sam. Just have to get my cloak."

As she walked to the buggy the mist swirled about her skirts and dampened the hem. The sun would soon rise above the trees and dry the ground, the warmth so welcomed after the long, cold winter.

"I hope we haven't made a mistake," Eleanor said. She settled on the seat and pulled her cloak closer to her body. "Adding four coach runs will be a lot more work for the station."

"We'll be fine, honey. Town's growing, lots of people moving about. We can get all the help we need."

Two miles east of town, Sam drove the buggy through the archway of the Buchanan Horse Ranch. A group of mares in the west pasture gathered along the fence, steam rising from their backs, vapor from their noses. A foal and its mother stayed close to the east side of the barn gathering warmth in the sunshine.

Harold Buchanan and sons, Jeb and Tanner, stepped from the house. His wife, Mary, and daughter, Etta, followed behind.

"Morning, Sam. Eleanor," Harold called out.

Sam nodded and greeted them. "Saw some mighty nice looking horses driving in. Let's take a closer look."

"Sure 'nough."

Sam and Eleanor left the buggy, and as the group moved to the pasture, business talk began.

Harold talked softly, gently, to the horses as he and Sam entered the pasture and closed the gate. "All of these horses are harness trained. They're all good runners, a couple are better leads. Most won't work on a bridle. Haven't been trained that way."

Sam stood next to Harold, talking in the same low, easy voice. "We need fourteen this year. We need to replace two and want to be able to run the others in sets of four or six. We also need more pasture this summer. We'll need to rotate the teams more often if the weather is as hot as last year."

"Lots of needs, Sam," Harold chuckled, "but we've got plenty—pasture and horses."

"Good. Let's see a couple up close." Sam drew Eleanor to his side. "Well, what do you think, honey? Any you don't want?"

Eleanor turned to Harold, a knowing smile on her face. "This is Sam's way of saying I'm part of the business. For my part, I believe any Buchanan horse will serve us well."

"Well, thank you, Mrs. Crawford," Harold said, returning her smile. He nodded to Jeb, who led Eleanor through the gate out of the pasture. The men followed.

"They all look good, Harold, so I'll get the first set in the next couple of days." Sam looked up at the expanse of blue sky. They hadn't seen such a sky for days. "Weather's broke enough. We can start carrying passengers again."

As they returned to the buggy Harold asked if they had time for coffee. "Mary's made some sweet biscuits. We can give the ladies a chance to catch up on the news. It's been a long winter, not much visiting."

"We'd enjoy that," Sam said, "but I know you're busy. Don't want to be overstepping."

"That won't happen. We're glad you came."

After an hour of talk and laughter, Sam and Eleanor rose to leave. As they approached the buggy, Tanner stepped forward to give a hand to Eleanor, but directed a question to Sam.

"Would you be needing livery help this year, Mr. Crawford? Dad needs me during haying, but I want to work with the horses. Maybe drive one of the coaches."

Sam nodded. "We'll talk when I come for the horses. If your folks say it's okay, then it's fine with me. Always glad to have a man who knows horses."

The next morning, I greeted a different world, one of bright sunshine. The shops opened their doors to let in visitors who'd gotten an early start. Later that day, the scheduled drum and bugle corps from one of the local towns gave their program, bringing everyone outside the shops to clap their hands and tap their feet to the rhythm. They were good all around entertainers, too, and every so often one of the corps members left the formation to teach a few dance steps to the children and adults lining the edge of the Square.

After completing a full round of the Square, the corps stopped at the flag poles for a short service honoring the military men and women from the area.

I put new carnations into the colored water for my window display and noticed how many people stopped to look at the window, some explaining to their kids how these white carnations could turn red and blue.

Thank you, Mom.

I stayed busy all day, eating lunch by taking occasional bites of my PB & J sandwich over a period of about two hours. Then, as the crowd began to thin out late in the afternoon, Sadie stopped in, carrying two cups of coffee from Biscuits and Brew. "Stephanie said the hazelnut is your favorite," she said, handing me a large cup.

"Ooh, thanks so much. How did you know I had visions of steaming hazelnut coffee dancing in my head? Not to mention its luscious aroma." I gestured to my small table and chairs. "Can you stay a minute?"

"Sure. I'm ready for coffee," she said. "I've already walked all the way around the Square, not once, but twice."

"Find anything to buy?"

"Enough to fill a house...if I had one."

"Didn't you say you and Clayton rented a cottage by the

117

lake?" I asked.

"We did, but it's furnished. Besides, right now I don't want to spend any extra money. What I really need is a job."

I didn't have any idea how Clayton was compensated for his role in the contest, nor did I know anything about his expenses, or Sadie's. "Clayton said he was going to be doing more interviews in New York."

Sadie pursed her lips, as if in pain. "True, that's where he went. But what Clayton really needs to do is paint."

I wasn't sure how to respond, but I felt for both Sadie and Clayton and the way their lives had been disrupted so dramatically. "I read what the tabloids said about your husband and the gallery. I'm sorry you had to go through that."

Ignoring my sentiment, Sadie slapped the table and said, "Clayton has enormous talent and he's not using it."

"That's what I told him," I said.

"You did? He didn't tell me that."

Did he usually recount our conversations? It wouldn't seem so. Circumstances had forced Clayton and Sadie to look after each other in various ways, but I imagined he still maintained a zone of privacy with fairly rigid boundaries.

Quickly changing the subject, I described the atmosphere on the Square on any rained-out day. "Except for the people who run through the rain from nearby houses to get here, we're like a baseball game that's been called off because of weather, and the fans disappear."

She laughed at my analogy and asked questions about those living on the streets close by. For the most part, they were like Georgia's sister, Beverly. They had deep connections to Wolf Creek and wanted to live where they could walk to stores like Farmer Foods. Some of the streets behind the Square had service businesses like salons or a day spa. A seamstress owned one shop and did alterations for Styles customers. As I sipped my coffee and chatted with Sadie, I realized how much I enjoyed talking about the town's history.

Still, although Sadie and I avoided any further conversation about Clayton, thinking about him off in New

York only made me want to jump in the car and drive away from Wolf Creek to join him. Was that urge because of Clayton himself? Or was it the thought of him being off in New York, where he'd already had an interesting, probably exciting life?

I didn't completely understand my desire to talk to him, but I yearned to hear him describe the city itself, with its endless restaurants and galleries, shops and fresh markets lining the streets. There was Central Park, bigger than the whole town of Wolf Creek, and a chance to hear every language in the world spoken in one or another corner of that city of boroughs. I could imagine the iconic buildings, each one different from the next. Maybe he'd tell me about his friends, other artists, or maybe chefs and florists or poets and writers. Most of all, I wanted to hear his voice.

But would he want to hear mine?

That evening, I was at loose ends. It took a while, but I finally figured out what was making me so restless. I'd spent so much time preparing for the contest, but now my part was over. Without that to occupy my mind, I didn't know what to do with myself. Clayton had asked me about my plans if I didn't win. As I did with every contest, I hadn't allowed myself to dwell on the notion of not winning. But admittedly, that possibility had begun looping through my mind frequently.

Nothing had fundamentally changed in my world, though. For now, I needed to focus on the immediate future. The summer heat was only beginning to come to Wisconsin, but I had to let go of my indecisiveness and plan for the holiday season. No matter what I decided in the future, being unprepared wasn't an option, because that would reflect badly on all the businesses on the Square.

I slid a frozen pizza into the oven and while I waited for it to heat, I brought out a box filled with old photographs. Years ago I'd taken a picture of each arrangement I'd created. That evening, out of sorts and plagued by my own

119

confusion, I needed a reminder of why I'd worked hard to establish Rainbow Gardens.

But what had that focus cost me? Not in terms of money, but for my life? What had I missed? I considered my family, the current generation, and those of the past. Everyone, except Eli and me, had found a special person. It had taken Elliot years to reconnect with his love, and now he and Georgia were going to spend the rest of their years together.

That thought only added another layer to my dissatisfaction. For the longest time I'd thought about two things, leaving Wolf Creek for greener pastures and wanting a partner—for life. Okay, I'd ruminated and grumbled about those things so long even I was bored with my train of thought.

Megan, either leave or stay, but stop whining about it.

Yes, Mom.

I wrestled with my dilemma most of the night. Before sunrise I made coffee and started with a fortifying breakfast, an omelet with bacon and thick slices of toast. I hoped it would give me the stamina to handle a steady stream of customers. By the time I went downstairs to open, it was with renewed, well, sort of, enthusiasm.

Once again, though, the sun didn't shine that day. Another slow moving system of steady rain had arrived and blanketed northeastern Wisconsin. I'd managed Rainbow Gardens through years of good sales and a few sluggish seasons. I didn't label any of them bad years because I'd always been able to pay the bills and save a little money. So, I took a philosophical approach to this weather as another bump in the road I couldn't control.

I finished cleaning the buckets of flowers in the cooler, removing wilted or broken stems and filling them with fresh water. Flowers were my first love, and I suspected they always would be. Maybe my only love.

Clayton's face crossed my mind. He'd occupied a good portion of my thoughts lately. Did he take up too much space in my head? I didn't know, but this wasn't like other predicaments, the kind I could casually bring up with Sarah or one of my other friends. Wanting to keep my complicated feelings about Clayton private, I couldn't ask anyone else for advice about it, especially not Sarah.

I wiped down the cooler's glass doors and switched on the window lights. Their brightness contrasted with the dreary grey day outside. It didn't matter that it was 10:00 in the morning. Time to unlock the door.

And it was 11:00 in New York.

What? I'd begun keeping track of the time zones now?

Clayton Sommers was gone and he wasn't coming back. Deal with the reality, girl, I told myself over and over. Maybe he'd come back to check on Sadie, but that had nothing to do with me.

The ringing phone startled me, and then made me anxious. Who would call so early on a holiday unless it was an emergency of some sort? But long ago, I'd tried to change my attitude and remind myself that a ringing phone could be a sale.

"Hello, Rainbow Gardens," I said in a cheerful voice.

"Megan, hello." His voice seemed far away.

"Clayton? Where are you? How are you?" The questions tumbled out, making me sound like a school girl.

"I'm in New York. I've finished the interviews. I have a favor to ask."

Come to me... my mind heard him say. I cleared my throat. "Uh, sure. If I can."

"I'm shipping my painting supplies to Wolf Creek. Can I have them delivered to Rainbow Gardens?"

"Did I hear you right?" Oops, I hadn't exactly played it cool and hidden my surprise.

"Yes." He chuckled. His voice had taken on a lighter tone. Perhaps he'd initially been unsure of how I'd react to his request and was relieved by my willingness to help.

"So, you're coming back?"

"Yes. Soon. About the boxes..."

"Of course. We can put them in the building next door until you get here. Does Sadie know you've planned to return?"

"I'm calling her next." His voice sounded garbled, as if the connection wasn't clear.

121

I heard voices in the background. Women's voices? His mumbled words left me thinking he'd covered the mouthpiece.

"So, Megan," his crisp voice had returned, "bye for now."

"Travel safe."

I hung up the phone and replayed the call in my mind. He'd called me first, even before calling his mother. I took that as significant, admittedly for no particular reason. He was only calling about a shipment, after all. How important could that be? And his plan to return to Wolf Creek? Maybe I'd read more into that, too? I wondered about the women's voices, feeling a bit hurt. Oh, right…that made a lot of sense. I laughed out loud at my own foolish thinking.

Well, I certainly had my answer to Sarah's question. Yes, Clayton was important to me. But what did that mean? I didn't really know Clayton the man at all.

I'd just slid down the crest of the rollercoaster I'd been on for days. And those up and down feelings lasted most of the workday. A few customers ventured in, but with the rain, they'd bought only a few garden ornaments.

The hours ticked by and the day lasted forever. Liz Pearson, the wife of one of lawyers at Country Law, called around 3:00 to cancel the after-work picnic she'd planned to host at her house. She'd heard that severe storms were predicted for the evening, so she suggested we reschedule for another night.

Truthfully, I didn't care.

When I went up my stairs after closing it occurred to me that I truly lived in a cave. Yes, the front and back doors led to the outside world, but the spiral staircase, which everyone agreed was gorgeous, was the only entrance to my apartment. If I invited a man to my apartment, he had to be immersed in my business first.

A few years back, Charlie Crawford had first suggested the circular stairs as a space saver, because I'd needed to remodel to gain as much room as possible in the shop. I also thought the stairs were cool, somehow. Weren't spiral staircases always a conversation point? For some goofy reason, Charlie thought the stairs were safer—more time to

ward off intruders. What a silly notion, but Elliot and Eli
agreed with him. I hadn't stood up for myself and said no.

But what difference did any of that make now? None.
Zero. Besides, the stairs *were* kind of cool. They did add to
the resale value. At least, that's what I told myself.

June
11

The rest of the week Mother Earth laughed at the world with bright sunshine and temperatures in the seventies, perfect for shoppers and visitors on our pedestrian only Square. As Sarah reminded us in her regular news-updates-reminder emails and texts, the first tour bus would be arriving next week.

The weekly order of flowers arrived on Tuesday and Clayton's three large boxes on Friday. I'd already asked my brothers to help move them into the old Farmer Foods store. It had been a while since the three of us had talked about the fate of that building. We'd inherited it from our parents, but Elliot and Eli had bought the new Farmer Foods building at the end of the Square and I owned the Rainbow Gardens building. That left the now empty building sitting between us like an elephant. Once a busy store, but at the moment large and silent.

Sarah had asked us not to rush to either lease or sell it. She had a few ideas that would keep us as owners, but so far, nothing was pending. As often happens with empty spaces, it had become a handy storage place for the three of us. I'd gotten lazy about taking my seasonal decorations to the basement where Charlie had built sturdy shelving. The Es, as my brothers were called, had purchased new display shelves so the old ones were left there in disarray. The plain paper covering the windows hid the mess. At least I'd drawn flowers on the paper I'd used to cover my windows. It occurred to me they should paint the windows or put arrows to our respective stores. At least make it look less empty and, well, useless.

Vacant buildings on the Square complicated Sarah's job as mayor. One of her main tasks was encouraging new shops to our Square, but they had to follow the guidelines set up by the owners in partnership with the town. And that meant retail shops, but no service businesses. Tourists and locals didn't come to the Square to get a manicure or to drop off dry cleaning or to meet with their tax accountant. We had plenty of those small businesses in town, but they were located on side streets behind the Square. So far, Country Law had been the sole exception to the Square's rule. It seemed that Sarah was always on the lookout for new shops, owned by people willing to make a commitment to our town.

And why was all this milling about in my head? Clayton was returning to Wolf Creek. Good for him. But as far as I knew that had nothing to do with me. I needed to quit acting like an indecisive teenager and get down to the serious business of planning my life. The contest figured in, because I'd need one set of plans if I won, and another set if I lost.

I sighed to myself. If this, then that…an exhausting proposition.

Marianna had sent an email inviting the women from our quilting bee to an evening update party. Although we weren't meeting regularly, she'd promised a surprise to entice us to this evening meeting, along with the usual snacks and wine.

I looked forward to going, mainly because I needed the distraction. I'd been spending too many evenings alone.

When I arrived across the Square and let myself inside the store, I found Marianna back in her classroom. She'd set up the chairs in a circle, one for each of us, and a few extras. I wondered who else would be filling them.

I sat next to Doris Parker, who owned the bookstore. She'd recently partnered with Lily Winters, who had leased a corner of the store to carry handmade toys and books for kids. For years, Doris had been known as the Square's chief complainer, but lately, working with a young person like Lily was seemed to have softened her hard edges.

Others from the bee arrived, singly and in pairs, laughing, chatting, smiling.

During a momentary lull in the conversation, I heard a baby cry. Rachel, Marianna's stepdaughter and Thomas' mom, had stopped in earlier to say hi before heading upstairs to be with her son. But Thomas was an older toddler now, not an infant. The cry sounded again right outside the classroom door.

Before any of us had time to react, in walked six very young women, girls, really. Four carried infants and two were very pregnant. A woman about my age was the seventh person. She introduced herself as Eileen Sawyer.

"Welcome, welcome," Marianna said. "Please, take a chair." She pointed to those of us sitting together. "Move apart, so one of these girls can sit between you."

Surprised at mild-mannered Marianna giving such pointed directions, we did as she asked. She was a great quilting teacher, but she would have been equally good with a bunch of fifth graders.

Doris and I opened two folding chairs and put them between us. Two girls, one with a baby and one pregnant, claimed the chairs. I was next to the mom, and before I had the chance to say yes or no, the girl plunked her baby in my lap.

"Her name's Laura. She smiles if you tickle her tummy. I'm Susan." The girl reached into her tote bag, diaper bag, or miniature suitcase, whatever it was called. Based on its size, I could have packed for a weekend.

As the last child in the family, what would I know about babies? I was taught about the care and propagating of flowers, not people. *Oh, get off it, Megan.* A baby's a baby, whether it's a flower or a person. So I tickled Laura's tummy and was rewarded with a toothless smile.

"Juice?" Susan held the bottle for Laura to see. "It's her bedtime snack and she loves it." Susan handed the bottle to me. "Go ahead, she's easy to feed."

I nestled Laura into the crook of my elbow and proceeded

to feed the hungry baby. I wasn't alone in suddenly tending to the babies. When I glanced around the room, I saw that Stephanie was cradling a baby, and Doris was grinning at a little face smiling back.

Susan reached into her bag again and brought out one of the quilts we'd made.

At that point, Marianna softly clapped her hands to get our attention.

It worked. I was all ears.

"The whole point of this evening is for you to see that the quilts we made have been given as special gifts for these young mothers, and mothers-to-be, and their babies."

"We're here to say thank you," said Eileen, the apparent housemother of sorts. "There were more girls than quilts, so we did a lottery drawing. These girls are a few of the lucky ones."

I glanced at Marianna. Two years ago she'd come to the Square as a new shopkeeper. A widow, she'd also dealt with a step-daughter and a grandson she'd never met, yet the three had forged a family. And she'd found Art Carlson, too, and the Square had a new romance. As usual, she looked happy being among these young mothers and babies.

Marianna asked each of the girls to say a little bit about themselves. Most were shy and a little embarrassed about their situation. But I'd also noticed a hint of fortitude and resolve in their words, which spoke of hope. Regardless of where they were now, they said in so many words, they'd do better in the future.

As I walked home, I was conscious of feeling almost ashamed of myself. I'd spent weeks droning on, at least internally, about my decision to leave a well established business and home in a building I owned. Poor me? Seriously? It was past time for me to shift my thinking and move on.

Sarah tapped the microphone to get the meeting started. "Our agenda is short tonight, so let's begin."

The association had gathered for its monthly meeting, and while most of the shop owners showed up, the season had started for real and we all looked a little harried—already, and it was only June. This meeting ended up being one more item on our to-do lists for the day. A woman with a long task list herself, Sarah ran through some news, including her announcement about an extra tour bus stop the following week.

"Tom Harris has been spreading the word about the Square," Sarah said, "and because of him, I'm getting calls every day. We'll be seeing more tour groups coming through this summer and fall. And let's hear it for Megan. She let Tom spend a few days in her shop, and in the process of observing the flower business, he got to know us a bit better."

I chuckled at the unexpected mention of my store and waved in response to the round of applause and whistles. After all his grouching about Tom, even Eli gave me a thumbs up.

"Enough now," Sarah said, laughing. There was nothing casual about the way she took back control of the meeting. "Because of his continued opposition to the vendors for Memorial Day weekend, which, I admit was pretty much a washout, pardon the pun, I'm appointing Eli Reynolds to be the coordinator for the vendors for the rest of the year. The Square has gotten far too busy for me to handle all the details myself. Any concerns or problems will be directed your way, Eli."

Again the room erupted into applause, more as a way to cheer him on, and maybe tease him a bit, I mused, than to congratulate him. We all knew Eli too well. Sure enough, I watched his smile quickly dissolve. I could only imagine Sarah's inner imp making that decision. *Good for you, my friend.* But I hoped Sarah was prepared to see my brother planting himself in front of her desk the next morning.

"The last item tonight is a reminder about the Founders' Day weekend. The lunch tent will be put up in the center of the Square on Thursday," Sarah explained. "Vendor tents will be allowed in the Square on Friday. Eli, I have notes here for you from the last few years."

Sarah passed a thick expandable folder back to him and began to gather her notes.

"Any announcements from the wedding couple?" Art Carlson asked.

Elliot held up Georgia's hand. "We're still together."

A laugh rippled through the group as we began to cluster and walk out together, but neither Elliot nor Georgia offered any details about their wedding plans.

A few days later, my brother's wedding was already on my mind when a couple around my age, late thirties or so, came into the shop shortly after I'd unlocked the door. The woman walked with a cane, but a slight limp slowed her otherwise easy gait. A simple flower brooch on her lapel and matching earrings complemented the colorful floral print blouse she wore with a tan pantsuit. The brooch looked like an Art Carlson creation to me.

Maybe I was especially attuned to weddings, because of Elliot and Georgia's, but I immediately guessed the couple as a bride-and-groom-to-be. Through the years, I'd noticed women about to be married had a particular kind of glow surrounding them. This woman had it in spades, and a smile a mile wide. It was obvious she was happy.

The tall, slim man at her side reminded me of Clayton, maybe because of the khakis and navy blazer and light blue oxford shirt. He looked pretty happy, too.

As I finished the last button on my Rainbow Gardens smock, I welcomed them and asked if they needed help.

The man pointed to the small table by the workbench before turning his attention to me. "Yes, we need some help, but I'm leaving it to the two of you."

"Okay." I wasn't exactly sure what he meant, but I had an even stronger feeling a wedding was involved.

"Good. I'll be on my way," he said, smiling at the woman, who'd settled in one of the chairs. "My appointment is at 10:30, so you enjoy yourself here. I won't be gone long."

The bell jingled as he left.

"I'm Nora Grayson," the woman said, extending her hand.

"Nice to meet you," I said, shaking her hand. "Megan Reynolds. I own the shop."

Taking the chair across from her, I noted she put her purse on her lap and then on the floor and then she picked it up again. Something was making her nervous. Maybe she wasn't planning a wedding after all. Maybe she'd come about flowers for a funeral and was concerned about doing a good job. But something in her radiant smile didn't signal a sad occasion.

She inhaled deeply. "So, Megan, how quickly can you put together some flowers for a small wedding?"

A wedding? Much better than a funeral.

"That depends on a few details, of course, as in what, where, and when. What kind of flowers, where the wedding will be, and when it's taking place?"

"I don't need anything elaborate." She hesitated, but the smile remained.

"But you want it to be special, I assume…I mean, for the bride." I tried to infuse an upbeat tone into our conversation. I wasn't completely sure she was the bride, or the sister of the bride…or someone else involved. I needed more information.

"They're for me." She shifted her purse to the side of the table, which is when I saw the glitter from the huge diamond ring dancing under the spotlights over the bench. She saw that I noticed, and the smile grew even brighter.

I laughed, making an elaborate show of examining the ring. "So, exciting, huh?"

"When I think about marrying Matt, it just takes my breath away."

"Lucky man, I'd say." I grabbed my notepad and pen. "But tell me, when and where?"

Still smiling, she said, "The Saturday after the Fourth of July, in the small private dining room at Crossroads."

"Good choice. I've done flowers for many weddings there, big and small. And what is your flower preference?"

Brides always wanted flowers, lots of them. Sometimes way too many. The room at Crossroads was fairly small, so I'd keep the arrangements appropriate in size.

"Let's start with happy but small," Nora said.

Okay, we were getting somewhere. "What color is your dress?"

Nora's face brightened even more. "It's a blush pink sheath. I'll wear a raspberry silk shawl if the room is cold."

"Well, then, how about white tulips, a white lily, and maybe a few white or pink tea roses. We could add some baby's breath and tie the bouquet together with pink and white ribbons—and a ribbon streamer." In my mind's eye I pictured the bouquet done and in her hand.

Nora nodded. "Sounds beautiful."

"And for the groom?" As I spoke and thought about the flowers, I twisted a small ribbon into a bow from a spool that had been left on the table. Sometimes my brain seemed sharper if my hands kept busy.

"We'd want that small, too."

Over the next few minutes, we settled on tea rose boutonnieres and shuffled around the flowers for her bouquet, and then we dealt with her attendants, JoAnn and David, who would have smaller versions of the bride and groom's flowers.

It took only a few more minutes to choose a complementary centerpiece arrangement using the same kind of flowers. I mentioned checking with Melanie at Crossroads so we could coordinate all the details.

Nora grinned. "Melanie has been as easy to work with as you are."

"We aim to please." I grinned and turned the page in my notebook to write up the order. I confirmed the spelling of her full name, and then asked for the groom's full name.

"Matthew Alexander."

My pencil hovered over the paper. Huh? Had I heard her correctly? I looked up to see a soft smile cross her face. I'd seen pictures of Matthew Alexander, but none had done justice to the man I'd just seen.

She nodded slowly.

"Wow. He's only the most eligible bachelor in all of northeast Wisconsin—or he was. And now you want me to do your flowers." I put my hand to my heart. "You could have hired one of the larger shops in Green Bay, but you want me?"

As excited as I was, I was conscious of a dozen questions pressing on my brain. For one thing, why was such a well-known man having such a small wedding? Of course, if they wanted to keep a lid on the news, all the more reason to use local businesses and ask for discretion.

Nora stared at her tightly clasped hands. "Matt's parents don't approve of our marriage. They never did, but since my accident they see me as being really flawed—imperfect." She patted her leg. "That means I'm not *suitable* for their high-status family. Like I said, I didn't fit the bill of the sort of person they imagined for Matt."

I waved that thought away. "Their loss, I'm sure. But good for you for not letting them ruin your wedding."

"But their disapproval is why Matt and I want such a small wedding. *Elegant* is the word I like to use. Besides, I was married before," Nora said, "but my husband died."

"Well, you're entitled to whatever kind of day you want," I said.

Brides often disclosed personal information, sometimes more than they planned to. But early on, I made it my business to file these conversations away as confidential. Keeping a zone of privacy wasn't always easy in this fishbowl kind of town, so all the more reason to keep secrets…no exceptions.

"If you haven't told anyone else about your plans, then only Melanie and a few people at Crossroads and I will know anything about it," I said, closing the notebook. "I can make a sample bouquet for your approval, if you'd like."

"Oh, no need," Nora said. "I saw the flowers you did for my friend, Maddi Brown—Maddi Powell now."

"I remember her. She loved daisies, lots of daisies." Nora laughed along with me when I held my arms out from my sides to indicate a huge armful of flowers.

"Did you know she named her daughter Daisy?"

I laughed, glad we'd gone back to happier subjects and

Nora was once again a radiant bride-to-be. "No, I hadn't heard that. But appropriate—and predictable."

As we finished up, another shopper came inside.

"Quick question before I leave," Nora said. "Can you tell me where I might find Nathan Connor? Or, I suppose I should say, Country Law?"

"Sure, take a left out the door, it's only two buildings down. Do you know Nathan?" It wasn't my place to ask Nora about her business, but Nathan was a relative newcomer on the Square and he was in the midst of his own love story.

"Nathan is a good friend of Matt's. I know him, too. We were kids together in the same neighborhood." Nora stood and slung her handbag over her shoulder and used her cane for support as she turned toward the door.

"Thanks for coming to Rainbow Gardens," I said. "I'll send you a picture of a sample bouquet."

"No need. I'll stop by next week." She looked around and sighed. "I've always wanted to work in a flower shop."

She maneuvered through the shop, stopping to admire a piece of hand-painted pottery. When I approached the new shopper, Nora waved and left with the bell jingling.

Of course, I'd be tightlipped about Nora and Matt's wedding, small by any standards, but I couldn't deny my curiosity about the couple. Odd, too, Nora didn't seem reticent about admitting his family's disapproval, although maybe that was a momentary letting down of her guard. I wondered where her family stood about the marriage.

I'd lost count of how many people told me they'd like to work in a flower shop, but most were like Tom, in that once they found out what was involved, it lost some of its appeal. Maybe being a florist sounded glamorous in some way. But like any other business, the day-to-day work could get routine.

There was something about the ease of creating the bouquet for the wedding that made me even more eager for the contest to be over and done with now. Since Clayton had said he'd finished with the interviews, it couldn't be long.

Later that day, when I had a lull in traffic, I checked the website, but no update appeared.

No matter what happened, I could move forward…win-leave, not-win-leave, or not-win-stay. I chuckled to myself. In eight words, I'd defined my options.

I glanced around the shop. Years ago I'd moaned about not having enough stuff for people to buy at Rainbow Gardens. Yes, back when I was barely out of school, but already in business, I'd called everything stuff, from clothes in the closet to food in the fridge, but then I realized that "stuff" kept Rainbow Gardens going.

Now the shop exploded with stuff, old stock, new stock, and my twenty years' worth of embellishments. The walls and cabinets overflowed with items I ordered and stowed away to use for that one special arrangement. On the other hand, I'd have bet a week's worth of profit that a few of the items I bought would fly off the shelves, only to reluctantly put them in a cupboard to gather dust later. What had I been thinking when I'd ordered some planters shaped like donkeys—pastel donkeys at that? I should have sent them off to the thrift store years ago, but maybe if I dragged them out, a few people would see them as campy. I smiled to myself. That might be one way to get rid of them.

When I took the flower coloring display down, I could fill the window with old stock and feature a two-for-one sale, buy a regularly priced item and get another priced with a yellow dot at half price. It would be a quick way to reduce stock instead of having to pack it all up and store it away.

I sighed, thinking about all I had stashed in the basement—I'd been hauling boxes down there for years. The only reason there wasn't more was the unappealing idea of trying to haul boxes down there. And what would happen if I left?

I'd not carefully considered the fate of my shop itself. Impulsive behavior drove me to prove, to Dad first, then Mom, then Eli and Elliot, that I could succeed. And I'd prevailed. With nothing left to prove, I was free.

That afternoon, between waiting on customers, creating special orders, and refilling the cooler, I'd also managed to redo the window. Nathan Connor tapped on the window pane when I was nearly done. Surprised to see him, and his little boy, Toby, I motioned for them to come inside.

"Excuse the mess, Nathan. Changing window displays is never a neat job." I began to gather the vases still filled with colored water. Nathan grabbed a few, too.

"Careful. There's food coloring in the water. It might stain your fingers or your clothes."

"Toby and I stopped by for a closer look. He kept telling me about those flowers that changed color. Seems we came in just in time."

"My mom taught me this science experiment—I call it a trick," I said, grinning at Toby.

"And here you are teaching it to other people," Nathan said. He put the vases on the bench, but made no move to leave.

"Was there something else I can help you with today," I asked.

"Actually, yes, there is," he said. "My friend, Matt Alexander, stopped by with an invitation to his wedding. I don't see many of my old friends since I moved here with Toby, but that's not why I stopped by. I would like to give Matt and Nora their flowers as a wedding gift."

"Terrific gift. I can show you the order, so you know what they've planned."

Did Nathan know Matthew's parents weren't happy about the wedding? They were, after all, a prominent family in the area. Virtually everyone in our region knew about the Alexander family—only a few actually knew them personally. I wanted to ask Nathan about it, but swallowed back the words. All that was none of my business.

And it didn't matter anyway. I'd liked Nora immediately, enough to imagine her helping me in Rainbow Gardens, just as I'd been able to see Sadie in my shop. I tucked away the idea that I could approach her the next time she stopped in, maybe probe a little more deeply into her desire to work in a flower shop.

I pulled out the order and held it out to Nathan. "Have you known Matthew long? And Nora?" I wanted to steer my own thoughts away from Matthew's family and my near nosy blunder.

"Matt and I grew up together—and Nora was on the same

block. Our three houses were fairly close together. Then, when my mom got sick Matthew couldn't come around anymore. It was like we weren't perfect enough for his mother any longer. Appearances were her specialty—to an extreme." He looked away, biting his lower lip, as if he regretted what he'd said.

"And Nora?"

"Her family moved away shortly after Mom's illness became known in the neighborhood."

It was hard to miss how often Nathan referred to his mother, and her illness itself seemed to be the dividing line in his life, a kind of before and after. How sad. I'd lost my mother, too, but not at such a young age. My mother had lived long enough for me to having clear memories of being with her—learning from her—when the two of us spent time together in the garden, her favorite spot on the farm. Nathan hadn't been that lucky.

Toby pulled on Nathan's sleeve. "Daddy, we'll be late."

Nathan looked down, lost in his past and staring into his future.

"Right you are." He grinned and tousled the boy's hair. Then he gave the order sheet a quick glance and handed it back to me. "This looks fine. It's going to be a nice wedding. But it's time for us to go. Sally's having a puppet show and ice cream today. Okay, Toby, let's say good-bye to Megan."

A very short "bye" was all he managed. But then the little boy gave me a wink and a smile.

"Bye to you, too, Toby."

I'd already heard about his infamous winks. One morning over coffee at B and B, Georgia, Toby's great-aunt, had told us that Toby had taken to offering a little wink to certain people he favored. "He's quite the charmer," Georgia had said, shaking her head. "I can only imagine the hearts he'll break in a few years."

I suppose everyone on the Square had a soft spot for Toby. Adopted into the Connor family, he'd been born with a congenital kidney disease. After his kidneys failed, his birth mother, Lily, had turned out to be a match and donated one of her kidneys. Right in front of our eyes, the mystery of

Toby's origins was revealed, and a love story developed that met all the conditions of a magical fairytale. As I watched Toby skipping down the Square with Nathan at his side, it was easy to see why he'd become such a special child in our little community.

12

Later that week, I started hauling the years' old stock from the basement to use in my yellow dot sale window display. I was standing in the midst of boxes and piles, when Elliot and Sarah brought two young women and a man into my shop through the back door.

Sarah stepped forward, bringing the women with her. "Maybe you remember Katie and Tracie Peterson? They're Katie Brent and Tracie McDonald, now. And their brother, Shawn."

"Peterson? From out by the farmhouse? Sure," I said, nodding to my three visitors. "It was a long time ago, but as I recall, I babysat for you a time or two." I'd lost track of them after they no longer needed a sitter and I began selling flowers, but they had long roots in the community. And a sad story.

"As you probably know, our folks are gone now," Katie said with a sigh. "Shawn built his own home a few years ago on the opposite side of the pasture." Katie looked at her brother with pride.

"Katie and I live in the old house now," Tracie said, finishing the family rundown. "Perhaps you heard that we both lost our husbands in Afghanistan several years ago."

"Yes," I said. "I was sorry to hear that." I glanced at Elliot to fill in some kind of explanation for their visit on that particular day.

Shawn broke in before Elliot could speak and explained that he'd bought his sisters some sheep for their farm. "When I brought them those sheep and a couple of lambs, I thought of it as some kind of project that could help them deal with their grief…"

"But, instead we built a business while we rebuilt ourselves," Katie interjected, adjusting the royal purple shawl she wore around her shoulders.

"Now we want to expand," Tracie said. "You know the old phrase, take our business to the next level. And for that, we need a storefront."

"My store?" I asked, incredulous, as if my secret about *possibly* leaving Wolf Creek had been exposed. "You want my store?"

"No, Megan, nothing like that." Elliot's calm voice drew my attention, but he looked taken aback at my reaction. "They'd like to rent our old store. Since you're part owner of that building, we need you to agree to their offer."

"Oh, I see," I said, flushing. Wow, I'd sure overreacted. What was that all about? I knew Elliot dreamed of having every storefront on the Square turned into a viable business. That was exactly what Sarah and all the rest of us wanted, too.

"And this offer would be?" I grinned at Katie and Tracie.

"A guaranteed three-year lease," Elliot said. "They want to use some of the shelving and display racks we left until they get their own."

"Guess I'll have to move my boxes then, huh?" I couldn't be happier, for Sarah, for the Square, and for my brothers and me. That empty building had become an eyesore. "When do you plan to open?"

"We're aiming for Founders' Day weekend—if we can round up enough people. Some veterans groups have offered to help us."

"And what will you sell?" My curiosity was getting the best of me.

"Wool from the sheep. Yarn. Supplies. Mittens. Throws. Scarves." Tracie ticked the items off on her fingers.

"And shawls like mine." Katie held out the soft fringe of the wrap.

I reached out to touch it, as if testing my hunch that I'd find it soft enough for a newborn. I wasn't disappointed. "You made this?"

"With wool from our own sheep," Katie said. "You must come for a visit and see."

Tracie nodded in agreement to Katie's invitation. Their brother grinned at both of them in obvious pride.

Elliot moved toward the back door. "I need to get back, but if you're okay with them being next door, I'll have Nathan or Jack write up a lease and we can all sign it later. They'll probably put Georgia on it."

Just as they gathered to leave through the back, Eli walked in the front door, with Clayton following closely behind.

Eli? Clayton? Together? And when had Clayton come back to Wolf Creek?

Eli's presence stopped Elliot from leaving.

"Sorry. Didn't know there was a meeting going on here," Eli said studying the group of us.

"Katie and Tracie are renting our old store building," Elliot said, putting his hand on Eli's shoulder.

"Oh, I see," Clayton said with a shrug. "I guess I'm too late."

"Too late for what?" Sarah stepped forward.

"I stopped into Farmer Foods to ask Elliot and Eli if I could rent the building for a studio and storefront. I was going to open a gallery for my paintings and ask local artists to add their works, too."

Well, well, Clayton would stay on in Wolf Creek, at least for awhile. I couldn't keep the butterflies in my stomach quiet. I realized in that moment that I had missed him more than I wanted to admit. Even to myself.

"Let me see if I can offer a solution," Sarah said.

Amused, I watched Sarah gather her thoughts. As mayor, she was known as a deal maker and a problem solver. I could see the wheels turning in her sharp mind.

"Charlie Crawford bought the building on the other side of Rainbow Gardens. He called the other day to let me know he'd finished the renovations, so now that building's available."

Clayton cleared his throat. "Uh, I'm not in a position to buy the building, Sarah."

I winced inside, not so much at his admission, but his

obvious embarrassment. But Sarah wouldn't be deterred. She pulled out her cell and called Charlie, and there in the back of Rainbow Gardens, a brief conversation resulted in an agreement to meet with Sarah, Clayton, and Charlie at noon in Sarah's office.

"Great...I'm gone." Elliot waved and opened the door. Eli followed him out and pulled the door closed behind him.

Sarah made the rest of the introductions, including Shawn, although he'd stepped back, almost as if he was getting out of the way.

"So, Katie and Tracie," Sarah said, "you and Clayton are almost next-door neighbors."

Sarah's phone rang and she waved to us as she headed to the front door and answered it on her way out.

That left me feeling like the hostess by default. "New neighbors on both sides. I don't think I've ever had that before."

I couldn't believe how quickly life on the Square was about to change again. And for the good, too. I turned to the sisters, while Clayton hung back, looking pleased with what had just transpired. "What are you going to call your store?"

"The Fiber Barn." They answered in unison and laughed. "We do that all the time, you know, say the same thing at the same time."

"Perfect." I reached out and gestured to Clayton, trying to bring him into our circle. "These women raise sheep and turn the wool into yarn to make mittens and shawls."

"Other things, too," Tracie said, "and sometimes we sell the fleece for people to use in their own projects."

Clayton grinned. "I'll be sure to stop by when you open, but beware of my mother. She'll buy your whole stock if she likes it."

I wondered if that had been Sadie's way of shopping in New York before her gallery was shut down.

Tracie was quick to reply. "I don't think that could *ever* happen. We have whole rooms at home filled with wool and yarn, and organized by type and color."

Good for them. She'd made it clear the idea of a retail store had not been some spur-of-the-moment lark.

"What are you going to name your store?" Katie asked Clayton.

"For lack of anything more creative at the moment, I think 'Clayton's' will do. That is, if I get the building." He smiled, careful to include Shawn in the conversation.

I knew that his paintings had been seized by federal agents, along with everything else in Sadie's gallery, but I had no way of knowing if Clayton had other paintings to sell. Or, maybe he'd have to start from scratch.

"Why wouldn't Charlie want to rent to you?" I blurted.

Clayton raised an eyebrow to me. That gesture alone spoke of his entire past. I could have kicked myself for asking that question in front of three people who were virtually strangers to him.

"For one thing, he might have an interested buyer," Clayton said, as if stating the obvious. "For another, he might want a longer-term agreement than I can guarantee."

The bell on the door jingled with Rainbow Garden's first customer of the day. The time for clean up had passed, and I was opening for the day with a mess on my hands, namely the old stock scattered about. But since my morning plans had been lost to filling two buildings on the Square, I was happy, almost buoyant to be privy to the new development. Why was I even considering leaving this place?

Katie took the start of the day as the end of their visit. "We need to get home. It was nice meeting both of you. This is so exciting." Both Katie and Tracie, and Shawn, too, shook my hand and Clayton's before going out the back door.

"After my meeting at noon, I have to go hunt up Mom and tell her the news. But I promise I'll call you later and fill you in about this new development."

"I'm sure she'll be happy."

"And it will be wonderful being so close to you." Then he left before I could respond.

Flustered by Clayton's words, I stepped forward to greet my customer and the day.

That evening, long after I'd locked the door and had finally brought some order to the old stock and the new window display, I went upstairs, a little on the disheartened side. Clayton said he would call after his meeting with Sarah and Charlie, but he hadn't. So much for his sweet sentiments about being close to me.

I went through my nighttime routine and began to warm the chocolate milk, but even that bedtime snack wasn't appealing. I shut the burner off.

And shut my mind off to Clayton Sommers. Then I heard the buzzer on the back door. I hurried to answer it. My heart got there first.

"Who's there?" I called.

"Clayton. Can I talk to you? I'm sorry I didn't call earlier? I'd like to tell you why."

There was something in his tone that surprised me. He sounded lonely behind the door.

I turned the dead bolt and opened the door wide. My heart beat faster to see his soft, gray eyes looking at me.

"It must be important if it can't wait for tomorrow." I couldn't help but have a little edge in my voice.

"I'd rather not stand outside and talk. Can I come in?"

It was his turn to sound annoyed. I opened the door wider and with a small sweep of my hand invited him in.

The shop was encased in a glow from the antique lamp post in the Square and the light in the cooler. It was a peaceful atmosphere. Sensual, too, if I'd let my mind go there, which it did all on its own. I could have turned on the store lights and we could have talked there, but that's not what I wanted. Besides, when Clayton was around I didn't think all that clearly.

"Come on up," I said, gesturing to the spiral stairs. I led the way.

"Wow. This is a nice place, Megan," he said, when we reached the top.

I stepped back and he led the way deeper into the apartment. I grabbed a few items, a token of straightening up, but more to keep my hands occupied. When he suddenly turned around, I found myself within inches of him.

"I'm sorry I didn't call, like I said I would, but it took a while to get all the pieces in place."

"You could have called anyway," I said, feeling irrationally petty. I turned away and meandered to the front window overlooking the Square.

"Maybe so, Megan, but in any case, we're going to be neighbors. Charlie understood that I didn't have enough money to buy the building outright, and then Sarah suggested a rent-to-buy option. We called Jack Pearson— you probably know him—and he and the paralegal…"

"Georgia Winters," I said.

"Right. Georgia…anyway, they came over to get the information and Georgia drafted an agreement."

By then, I'd sat on the sofa and motioned to the easy chair, where Clayton settled. His excited energy filled the room, making me eager to hear more of his story.

"So, while all that was going on, I called Mom and she came by to look at the building. She has a good eye and knows how a gallery should look. I'll live and paint upstairs," Clayton said, his words tumbling out. "And Charlie had no problem with building some interior walls to create separate gallery spaces."

His enthusiasm was infectious, making me almost giddy. "How about a drink? Soda? Tea? Coffee?" I almost offered him chocolate milk, but that would require some explanation. I needed something to drink myself, especially because having him in my apartment made me nervous— and thirsty.

"Some kind of soda, whatever you have, sounds good. I don't need any more caffeine today."

I fished out two bottles of caffeine free soda from the back of my fridge. "Do you want ice in a glass?" I asked from the kitchen.

"Nope, straight from the bottle is fine. No fussing with anything. I have more to tell you."

I twisted the cap off the bottles and handed one to him before nestling in the corner of my sofa and pulling my legs up under me.

"So, as soon as Mom saw the place, she insisted we get

some furniture, so we went to Green Bay and I picked up a futon couch I can convert into a bed for now. We got a chest and a reading chair, so she has a place to sit when she visits. I bought a table and four chairs for the kitchen. It's all open though, kind of like your space here."

He stopped and laughed. "Such progress. Charlie gave me a set of keys, even though the contract isn't finished. But we have an understanding. The furniture is coming tomorrow, and Charlie got right on ordering appliances. He's having them installed by the end of the week."

"Wow. You *have* had quite a day. You're putting down roots."

But you still could have called and shared the excitement. A quick call from the car on the way to Green Bay would have been enough.

"Mom said she'd help me set up a scaled-down version of the gallery we had in New York and we'll be open for Founders' Day. Then I'll get the studio set up."

"Founders' Day? Really?" That was a big event on the Square, and coming up fast, too.

"You may not have seen her in action yet, but you've probably guessed that my mother can be a powerhouse. After all that's happened, I need to make sure she's okay, though. But now that things have settled down, and she likes it here, I can begin building my own life again." He paused. "And that includes painting."

Hearing him say that warmed my heart. "She's quite a woman, your mother. And it was hard for her when you couldn't paint. That's the last thing she wanted."

"She's been through a lot." Clayton absently brushed his fingers through his hair. "It's good that we can settle down here."

"I like her attitude, too," I said. "It's as if she knows she's got a life to pull together and she intends to do it."

"That's my mom," he said, grinning.

He took a long gulp from the soda bottle, and then scanned my apartment, as if studying it with a purpose. "My upstairs only has the bathroom walled off now. It's more like a loft, without a separate bedroom. I can use screens and other dividers for that. And I'm glad I have both inside and outside stairs. It'll make hauling everything upstairs easier. Yours is a little smaller, I think, but so is the building."

"When I renovated, I wanted a bedroom separate from the living area, and Charlie suggested keeping the kitchen small and open to all the rest of the living space."

Clayton nodded his approval. "Nice. I like it. Charlie told me about the various options people had in these old buildings, and how each one is different. My studio will overlook the Square, where the north light from the large windows is perfect."

His stared off into the distance, not looking at anything in particular. I assumed his imagination was busy picturing himself painting in his studio.

He stood up and walked to the front window. "It feels good to be settled in one place again."

"I imagine so," I said, staying put.

He bent to look at the antique clock on the table by the sofa. "It's late. Time for me to go, but it was great sharing my news with you."

We walked to the spiral stairs. I needed to follow him down to lock the door, but I really didn't want him to go.

"There are so many things to do tomorrow," he said, making the final spiral to the first floor. "And I can't wait to begin. First thing in the morning I have to call Gretchen."

Who was Gretchen? I decided not to ask, because I didn't want to hear the answer. Maybe I was too tired for more information.

I held the door open for him to leave, never expecting him to lean forward and give me a kiss, light and friendly. Like the last time he'd left me.

"Good night, honey. I'm glad you're my neighbor."

I didn't step outside to see which direction he went. Absently I locked the door and went upstairs.

Honey? His mother called me dear, but that wasn't the same.

Did these endearments mean anything or were they just words, thrown around casually?

And Gretchen?

Questions whirled around in my mind. Including the results of the contest. There it was again, nagging under the surface, never leaving my mind. I logged onto the school's website to see if the winners had been posted. Nope, nothing yet. I was getting tired of reading the same line: *Final placements will be announced soon. Thanks for your patience.*

Ha! What a joke. Patience was not a virtue I could claim as my own.

I gave into another long night of questions with no answers. Katie and Tracie kept coming to mind, too. They reminded me of myself years ago when I'd been nervous and excited about opening my new venture. They were anticipating their opening day, the same way I'd looked forward to the morning I opened my front door and introduced the new Rainbow Gardens to the Square. I had a twinge of *something* go through me. Seemed to me it felt a lot like envy.

13

A few days later, I ran across the Square to Biscuits and Brew for early coffee with the other shopkeepers. The tables were full, women at one, as usual, and men at another. The only difference was that Clayton was sitting with the Es, along with Nathan and Jack. Toby was there, too, focused on an egg sandwich and milk.

Jessica from Styles rarely came in this early, but she scooted her chair closer to Doris to open a place for me. Marianna and Liz were on the opposite side of the table. Sarah sat at one end, Sadie on the corner near her.

It seemed that everyone was talking at the same time. Stephanie handed me my favorite blend of coffee and I wedged in next to Jessica to hear the latest news.

Then, when Nathan's dad, Richard Connor, came through the door all conversation stopped, replaced by an uneasy silence that soon filled the room. Nathan had left Richard's law firm in Green Bay last year and struck out on his own with Country Law. I had no idea what happened between the two men, and no one else in my group on the Square seemed to know, either. Or if they did, they weren't talking. Richard had been seen around town when Toby's condition worsened, and then when he was recovering from the kidney transplant.

I was becoming more familiar with Richard because a few months ago he'd begun stopping by to pick up flowers for Lily, Nathan's fiancé. Usually, he left my shop and crossed to the other end of the Square to deliver the flowers to Lily at her toy business inside Doris's bookstore.

Today, Richard looked comfortable in jeans and sneakers,

definitely not the clothes of a top-tier lawyer in northeast Wisconsin.

Tension or not, Nathan stood to greet him with a friendly, "Morning, Dad."

Toby was off his chair and chicken-walked under the table to get to his grandfather. Richard bent down and gave the young boy a big hug. "What are we doing today, Grandpa?"

"It's Grandparents' Day at Bay Beach Park today," Richard said. "Would you like to go there?"

"And ride the train? Eat hot dogs?" Toby asked.

Apparently, Toby already had been to the Brown County Amusement Park and knew what wonders awaited him.

"You bet." Richard looked for an okay from Nathan. "Grandma Beverly's coming with us."

"Then let's go!" Toby took Richard's hand and pulled him to the door. "Bye, Dad."

We all laughed when Richard waved at Nathan, and off they went. When the door closed the conversation returned, but before she lost the opportunity, Sarah stood and began talking loud enough to get our attention. "As long as just about everyone's here now I'll pass on a few announcements."

Grinning, Sarah told the group about the women opening The Fiber Barn, and in time for Founders' Day. Lots of loud clapping followed over hearing about a new business, especially one that would complement Quilts Galore. That was good for everyone.

Sarah held up her hand. "Wait, there's more. Clayton Sommers is going to open an art gallery, simply called Clayton's. His mother, who is an experienced gallery owner and manager will be helping out there." Sarah put her hand on Sadie's shoulder and waved her other hand toward Clayton. "Thanks to you both for deciding to stay in Wolf Creek. We're glad to welcome you."

More applause. But right on schedule, Sarah's watch beeped, reminding us another day on the Square was about to begin.

I put my nearly empty mug on the counter and followed my colleagues out to the Square and under a cloudy sky I headed to my waiting shop.

Founders' Day preparations began early. One sure sign was the rumble of a truck inside the Square, unusual because the Square is a pedestrian-only area. In order to maintain that image, maintenance and event vehicles entered and left before the shops opened. That worked most of the time. From the front window of my apartment, I saw an army of workers erecting an enormous white tent and unloading tables and chairs. This type of open-air dining was another of Sarah's new ideas. No seasonal event was ever a mere replica of the year before.

One of the area's pioneer-days reenactment groups would be cooking biscuits and beans over wood-fired grills to serve to the public. According to Sarah, the group would ask only for donations, and half of whatever they took in would be shared with our owners' association.

As I stood watching, I could almost taste the buttery biscuits. I only hoped they'd have food left by the end of the day when I'd be free to get out to the Square myself.

Once I was downstairs and had opened for the day, small groups of customers wandered in, but they were mostly window shopping. I overheard them talking about coming back over the weekend for the festival, when they'd actually open their wallets and do their real shopping.

When I first opened, that pre-festival browsing puzzled me. I assumed most people wanted to shop when fewer people were crowding the stores and the Square. That revealed how little I knew about the kind of people who never missed our weekend events and waited to buy until the festival special sales were up and running.

This year, my special was my yellow dot sale, and nearly everyone asked if the sale would last both Saturday and Sunday.

"Yup. That's the plan," I repeated again and again.

Despite the lack of sales, window shopping day had its amusing moments. One woman handled quite a few items, and casually put a garden ornament behind another one propped in a corner. Not exactly out of sight, but close to it. I'd seen that type of harmless subterfuge before. I'd keep an eye on it to see if another customer discovered the piece before she returned. I wasn't going to move it, but simply enjoyed seeing the ruse play out.

On Friday morning, trucks once again returned with vendor canopies. Some of the vendors returned year after year to be part of our town's festivities. Others were people from the town who sold their arts and crafts only on the Square during the summer. I watched Eli, clipboard tucked under his arm, as he placed a sign with the vendor's name on each tent. And surprise, surprise, he wasn't scowling. No, from where I stood watching, he seemed to be enjoying his new job.

By noon, Sarah officially opened the Wolf Creek's Founders' Day Celebration with a short, welcoming speech. I stood outside the door to listen to her speak from the stage. This year, she announced that those interested in the actual history could visit the museum because it would be open all weekend. She understood that most of the people weren't interested in a trek through the past, but this particular weekend still had the potential to reinforce the fact that Wolf Creek had endured for nearly 150 years. Somehow, though, I'd missed the memo about the museum.

Sarah's welcome over, I returned to the workbench to price a few more sale items, but Sadie came in with another woman in tow and said she had a favor to ask. She grabbed the woman's arm when she stopped at the sale table. "I'm going to be working at the museum this weekend, and Gretchen's going to help Clayton."

I suppressed a laugh. So this was Gretchen. The joke was on me. She was old enough to be Clayton's mother. I smiled to myself.

Sadie did quick introductions. "Megan has been instrumental in our decision to stay in Wolf Creek," she explained. Sadie spoke quickly, too, like she had little time to spare. "And for her part, Gretchen taught me everything I needed to know about running a successful gallery."

I reached across the workbench to shake her hand and say hello, but a large group of visitors entered Rainbow Gardens and distracted me. "So, Sadie, what was that about a favor?"

But it was Gretchen who answered. "I hope people will like the selection of Clayton's paintings I brought to fill the gallery. Would you stop by and have a look?"

I glanced around my crowded shop. "When I can, sure, I'd enjoy seeing what you have. But by the number of people I see already on the Square, it may be later this afternoon before I come by."

"No problem. Stop in when you can." Gretchen paused. "I'm just afraid you might be the only person who stops in."

"Trust me," I said, lowering my voice as if confiding a secret, "I can promise you that won't be the case. People who come into the Square, especially during these special weekends, tend to stop in *almost* every shop. They browse, buy, have coffee, lunch, and maybe even stay for dinner. They'll stop in, especially because it's new."

I enjoyed watching Gretchen's face light up.

By the time Sadie and Gretchen left, other shoppers had entered the shop. These shoppers knew a bargain when they saw it, and buy they did—my yellow dot items were more popular than I'd imagined.

Finally, after closing time, I hastily assembled one of my arrangements that used one of every flower I had in the cooler. Then holding the vase with both hands, I dashed next door.

The door to Clayton's was locked, but through the glass door I saw him and Gretchen and Sadie walking among the displays. I knocked, hard, to get their attention.

Clayton almost ran to the door when he saw me.

"Come in, come in." Grinning, he coaxed me inside and lifted the arrangement out of my hands. "I can't believe the day we've had. At times, the people were standing shoulder-to-shoulder in the gallery. Oh, and Sarah stopped in to congratulate me."

He held the arrangement out in front of him. "It's one of your signature arrangements. Thanks so much." He stared at it another few seconds and then said, "Come with me to the back. We're celebrating with a glass of wine."

Sadie gave me a one-arm hug while balancing a wine

glass. "Clayton, wine for Megan."

"Of course. I'm getting her a glass." He put the arrangement on the table where Sadie and Gretchen could see it. Then he took a wine glass off a tray and brought the bottle with him. "We settled back here where Gretchen could sit. Her feet hurt from standing so long."

"Now, Clayton, I told you that was a good hurt." She didn't try to hide the fact that she'd slipped off her high wedge shoes. She nodded to the flowers. "How beautiful—and unusual. I've never seen anything like it."

"That's because it's Megan's concept," Clayton said.

"I'm really happy for you," I said, aware I was flushing from the compliments. "From experience, I can tell you that if the weather holds, we'll be even busier tomorrow. As she does every year, Sarah created an extensive advertising campaign for this weekend." I shrugged. "And it appears to be working."

Sadie gave me another hug. "You young folks relax and enjoy the moment. Gretchen and I are going home for a hot soak and sleep. I think we're both too tired to eat."

"Always time for food, my friend," Gretchen said, sliding her feet back into her shoes.

Clayton and I laughed as they left out the back door.

"I think they have the right idea, Clayton. It's been a long day and the season's just begun."

I walked to a display area so I could look, really look, at Clayton's still life paintings filling the walls. In one after another, the crystal bowls he painted jumped out against their varying backgrounds. Wow, I knew how difficult those were to paint, especially because the objects reached a degree of realism unusual for any painter. His bowls showed the most subtle light and shadow and intricate cuts in the glass.

"These are incredible," I said, shaking my head in wonder. Some of the articles I'd found on the Internet talked about the unique nature of his work. The writers weren't exaggerating. He painted landscapes, too, from skyscrapers to deep forest glens, using bold colors. No wonder he'd received such acclaim.

I noticed three of the four paintings had sold signs on

them. "Are they really sold, or is that a New York trick to make shoppers think they should buy now?"

Instantly, the happiness faded from Clayton's face. Rather than seeing it as teasing, he obviously saw my remark as insensitive, and as a result, I'd discredited his talent.

"Oops, I'm sorry. That didn't come out right." I put my glass down. "Maybe I better go before I say anything else."

The silence hurt. I'd been upset over a missed phone call, and now I could tell that he was taken aback by my insensitive remark. I wanted to go hide. The wine was even making me dizzy.

"Megan, sweetheart, they *are* sold," Clayton finally said. "I asked the buyers to pick them up after Sunday so I wouldn't have bare walls the rest of the weekend."

"Well, I'm sorry anyway. Good night." I went out the front door and closed it behind me. There was no jingle from a bell. It felt so wrong to leave. But I couldn't bring myself to look back.

As I locked my door and navigated through my shop, which was in disarray, the sound of his voice calling me sweetheart looped through my brain. Did he mean that? Was he one of those guys who threw around terms of endearment without meaning anything by it? Somehow, he hadn't struck me that way. The bigger question was whether I could have a future with Clayton. If that's what I wanted, I had a weird way of showing it. I'd just run out of his gallery. On the other hand, if he became a big time success in Wolf Creek would that provide the nudge for him to leave and return to New York?

And what about me? Did I need to wait for the results of a contest to figure out what I wanted to do with my life? In less than a month, Clayton Sommers had nicked my heart and made me want more. Of him.

14

It was Founders' Day weekend all right. On Saturday morning, after a restless night, I came down before 10:00 and saw shoppers waiting outside the door. So much for my fantasy about reorganizing the sales items strewn about. But, I rationalized, with the crowd we'd see that day, I doubted they'd stay in my neat displays for long anyway.

Browsers and serious shoppers came and went all day. I handed out my new business cards to everyone. It was one of Tom's ideas to spend extra money for a folding card, and I silently thanked him. I'd always kept cards in a small box at the counter, but I hadn't always remembered to slip one into every bag, nor had I put them in the pocket of my smock so I could hand them to customers as I circulated through the shop. I had to laugh at my revitalized promotion campaign. Did I look like a business owner getting ready to close her shop and leave town?

Around noon, Sarah walked in balancing three carryout boxes of pioneer food. "Clayton called Sadie and asked her to bring lunch for you, and for Gretchen and him. But she was way too busy with visitors at the museum, so I picked up the slack." She waved at the window. "Besides, it gave me a chance to check out the action on this side of the Square."

"Thanks, I'll pay you later." I spoke quickly, because I was busy multi-tasking. Packing up a shopping bag for one woman, while waiting for her credit card approval, I was also answering a man's questions about my groups of single flowers. He wanted a deal on a dozen of them, one for every sister and niece in his family. Well, fair enough.

Still, whether I was talking to people or pulling yellow-dot stock out of the window, Clayton was never far from my thoughts. He'd had a great first day, so I wondered how his second day in the gallery was going.

When Sarah's phone rang, she quickly left the shop.

Then as the bell jingled a couple of seconds after she left, I burst out laughing at the sight of Tom Harris. He nodded, but quietly went to the back of the shop and grabbed an apron from the hook by the door. "Need a little help here? I know the owner and she said I could come back anytime."

"You have a bus here?" I asked, as I finished tying a piece of Rainbow Garden's ribbon on a shopping bag.

"Not on Saturdays," Tom said. "Not a great day for this kind of tour. It's more of a family day."

Before I could ask how he was doing, he offered to help a woman interested in the garden reflecting ball. It would be a major sale for the day if she bought it, but I knew that if the woman was debating over taking that piece home with her, Tom's knowledge and charm would convince her she had to have it.

Sure enough. He even boxed it up and wrapped the stand. I moved in next to him just in time to thank the woman for coming in. As soon as she was out of sight, Tom and I managed a brief high-five and then I hurried away to help others in the shop.

The traffic flow was steady enough that I used the brick door stop to keep the front door open and traffic flowing in and out. The twang of electric guitars and drums and the blended voices of a country music group filtered into the shop, singing clear and plenty loud. The fast beat seemed to make me light on my feet, and a shot or two of extra energy surged through me as I carried myself a little taller. It made me wish I'd added a vendor booth to sell my one-flower pieces and wilder bouquets. I'd said that aloud to Eli, but he'd shot it down fast, pointing out that I couldn't cover both places at once. He was right, of course, but I still wished I'd hired on a college student or some kind of temp to help out, so I could be in the middle of the festival. Today, though, with the door wide open, I was.

As the day wound down, the number of shoppers dropped

to a slow trickle. Without fanfare, Tom took off his apron and put it back on the hook. Then he handed me his tour company card. "Here's my new cell phone number. Call if you ever need help. For anything."

"Thank you so much. I'm really glad you stopped in—and stayed. This traffic on the Square was almost double what I expected. Overwhelming, really. These are the best crowds we've ever had."

"I'm glad to help, Megan, and bring the busloads in, too. But, I'm sorry I can't come back tomorrow."

He didn't wait for an answer, but stepped aside for a woman entering the shop. Then he left.

I recognized the woman. Nora Grayson.

"Well, well, Nora," I said, "I'm surprised to see you in the middle of our madhouse here in the Square."

She made her way past a couple debating whether to buy two garden ornaments or one. She leaned toward them, "You need to buy both. Then you can each laugh about the other's funny face."

When she got to the center of the shop where I was standing, she couldn't contain her joy any longer. "Oh, isn't this exciting? I'd give anything to be part of it."

"You just were." Then an idea hit me. "Do you know how to use a register and credit machine?"

"Sure. I worked retail before the accident."

"Want to work here at Rainbow Gardens tomorrow?" I asked.

Her eyes grew as big as her smile. "Are you sure?"

"I am. The man who stood to the side when you came in is a friend who helped me out today, but he can't be here tomorrow. If it's anything like today, we'll be very busy."

"I'm sure I can, but I'll double check with Matt." She pulled her phone out of her handbag. "He's busy with some project for the foundation, and I think he's tied up with that all day tomorrow, too."

I gestured toward the rear door of the shop. "Sure, go on to the back—it's quieter there."

She walked toward the back door and I packed ceramic pots into a shopping bag for another customer. Meanwhile, the couple held the two ornaments and kept browsing.

I was still at the register when she came up behind me. "Give me a quick lesson now and I'll be ready to go tomorrow." Her smile danced on her face. She looked like she was right in her element.

One time through the register keys and screen and I knew she'd be fine. Besides, I'd still be around if we had glitches. I smiled at a woman approaching the counter. "Okay, Nora, first customer. You check her out while I wrap her pottery bowls."

Nora knew what she was doing, and she was pleasant and gracious to boot. A gift.

"Thank you for shopping at Rainbow Gardens," she said. "Please, come again."

Matt walked in a little before our 6:00 PM closing time. I stood back and listened to Nora describe her afternoon of waiting on customers, right in her element. She ended up thanking me twice for the opportunity before she left with Matt. But I was grateful for her.

I'd barely noticed the time as the hours passed, but as I closed and locked the door behind the last customer I realized how hungry I was. Just as I turned away, I heard loud knocking. There was Clayton waving his arms so wildly, I thought he must have an emergency of some kind.

I unlocked and opened the door and he walked through it, talking away at breakneck speed.

"Is it like this every day? How do you manage alone? When do you sleep? How am I going to paint and run the gallery? You're experienced with this madness. Help me, please."

"Calm down." I tried to swallow a chuckle. No luck. I went ahead and laughed. "Relax, it's not like this every day. Winter comes soon enough. And then even in the summer, *most* people stay away on rainy days. But, you make your summer income on these sunny days and during our festivals."

His features relaxed, but he still needed a little coaching on the ways of the Square.

"But just wait 'til the tour buses come rolling in." I raised my hands and wiggled my fingers for emphasis. "It's pure madness for a few hours and then they're gone just as quickly as they arrive."

Seeing him frown, I said, "Come in, have a seat." I went to the fridge and pulled out two bottles of water. I was pretty exhausted myself, but in an exhilarated kind of way. My sales for the last many weeks had significantly exceeded my expectations. That meant I had a bigger cushion for the times business slowed down and money to invest in new and different stock. In the meantime, old stock from the basement would fill the open spaces around the shop.

Clayton and I sat at my table near the workbench. His face showed a mixture of fatigue and excitement. "Mom and Gretchen haven't had this much fun since they set up the gallery in New York. Gretchen's been on the phone with some of her favorite artists, urging them to send paintings. She's complaining that we don't have nearly enough stock, and she's desperately, as she puts it, 'trying to fill in the holes'."

I laughed at his fairly lame imitation of Gretchen's proper voice.

"Not bad, huh?" he smiled. "I sound almost like her."

I took a long swig of water while I thought about what I wanted to say. "Apology time," I said, raising my hand to stop the objections I saw coming. "I need to say this. My comment about the 'sold' signs was childish, even petty. You didn't deserve that. And—"

"How could you know?" he interrupted.

I waved him off. "Not the point. You've been honest with me from the beginning. Well, from a few hours after we met." I grinned and tried to lighten the tone. "And, when you said you needed to call Gretchen, I thought she was a friend...um, a special friend."

He rolled his eyes and reached for my hand. "There is no special friend, Megan."

I had no response, so I stood up, breaking free of his grip in the process. "If I don't eat soon and think about getting some sleep, I'll pass out right here in my shop." Suddenly, I remembered the lunch and stood to go to the register. "Ah,

I owe you for the box lunch."

"My treat. I wanted to taste the fire-cooked food and Sarah said they were going to be sold out soon, so I ordered for all of us."

I nodded, thanking him. "I wanted to try it, too, but the beans were bland and the biscuit was hard. I'm glad I don't have to eat that every day."

"Not the best fare I've eaten either, but it kind of made me feel like one of those hardy pioneers who settled this land and this town."

"It did, huh?" I laughed. "Maybe you'd have been better at pioneering than I'd have been. Call me a spoiled princess, but I like my hot running water. But speaking of settling a town, I wonder how the women did next door."

"I tried to stop in around mid-afternoon," Clayton said, "but I couldn't jam myself into the place. It looked like customers were grabbing everything off the shelves."

"Bet the new owners were a little overwhelmed, too." Hmm...he'd taken the time to visit the other new business on the Square. I hadn't, and that didn't sit well with me. I wasn't raised to ignore newcomers. Mom and Dad would have pointed that out, too, if they'd been around to comment.

Clayton got to his feet and headed to the back door. "I'll go out this way. You lock yourself in and sleep well." He unlocked the door, but then bent over and kissed me.

My body moved forward, responding, engaging. But he pulled back, out of reach.

"Later." He ducked out the door before I could even say goodbye.

What was that all about? He'd kissed me, but then pulled away when I kissed him back.

I shook my head, a gesture to reinforce my resolve to leave it alone and shut that part of my mind down. I climbed the stairs, stopping only long enough to view the mess my shop had become after a busy day. I'd take time in the morning to give it some order. I threw together some snack food and called it supper—crackers, cheese, an orange, my favorite honey-roasted peanuts, and a chocolate bar. Good enough, I told myself, since I had most food groups covered. It was as close to a balanced meal I was going to get. I shoved the last bite into my mouth and headed to the shower. Tomorrow was another day of many to come. And what little surprises would Clayton have for me tomorrow?

15

It was an artist-perfect day, with a blue sky and puffy white clouds washed with sunshine. Observing the sun lighting up the front of the shop made me wonder about the subjects of Clayton's paintings, his bigger vision. The paintings I'd seen in his gallery used light, whether that was to show the detail of a glittering bowl or a dense forest, all were created with acrylics. What new themes would come up now?

As I began to bring order to the chaos in the front of the shop, I noticed a familiar garden ornament, a sunburst with a happy face. It was the piece the shopper had carefully tucked away in the corner. Her little trick worked, too. The garden art was still there waiting for her to claim it.

I organized areas of the shop that I assumed would be difficult for Nora, who appeared to rely on her cane at least some of the time. I didn't know enough about her injury to predict which movements would be difficult.

When Nora arrived shortly before opening time, I grinned at her Founders' Day get-up, a peasant dress and bonnet.

"Have you been next door to the Fiber Barn?" she asked, her features animated and bright. "I'm going to shop there a lot come fall. I've decided to try my hand at knitting. And I'll be bold and start with making Matt a sweater for Christmas."

I smiled at her, then checked my watch. "I still have a few minutes. I can go next door now, but I won't be gone long. You don't have to do anything, except help a customer if one should come in right at opening time."

"Good. I'll be fine here."

I grabbed a small arrangement from the cooler.

"Everyone's talking about the new shop and I want to see it—and I always bring new owners some kind of welcome gift."

"You'll be fighting crowds already," Nora said with a grin.

True enough, women were in line waiting for opening time. I scooted to the front of the line and knocked. "I'm not butting ahead," I explained. "I'm from Rainbow Gardens next door and I need to make a delivery." I told my small fib with a smile, so no one looked too suspicious.

Katie unlocked and opened the door and immediately stepped aside, as I was carried inside by a surge of women. The newcomers might have been overwhelmed yesterday, but I glanced around and saw full baskets of yarn and orderly shelves.

"Wow, I'm impressed." I handed Tracie the flowers. "Just wanted to say welcome to the Square. But I'll come back and have a look around when it's quieter."

"Please do," Tracie said, moisture making her eyes glisten. "We owe you so much for letting us rent the building."

"My pleasure," I said, wanting to talk a minute or two more, but she turned to catch skeined yarn tumbling out of a woman's hands.

I worked my way back through the crowd and out the door only to see a large group enter Rainbow Gardens. I hurried to join Nora. Before I could get back to the counter, a woman saw my Rainbow Garden smock and grabbed my arm. "Is there a limit on the number of sale items I can buy?"

"No limit, but each sale item needs to be paired with a regular priced item. One plus one."

"Darn. That's what my friend said. But they're so cute." She held up a handful of miniature birdhouses on a stick.

"I know...I couldn't resist ordering them when I saw them," I agreed.

"Okay then," she said, "I'll look around some more."

I found Nora behind the workbench at the register, with a pile of garden pots to package. Seeing a line form there, I knew that if we didn't get them checked out soon some would put their items down and leave.

"You check them out, Nora, and I'll wrap and package."

Nora and I both kept up the small talk with the customers, and ended each encounter with a quick, "Thanks for coming by," or "Please come again."

About an hour later, a woman approached the counter holding the metal sunburst. She winked when she met my eye, almost as if she was acknowledging me as her silent co-conspirator. "Never in a million years did I think it would still be here."

While Nora counted the change from the sale, I wrapped the oddly shaped piece in white paper and tape, finished off with ribbon tied to make a handle so she could easily carry it while she visited other stores. Sometimes, wrapping the packages was half the fun.

By mid-afternoon the vendors in the Square began to pack their goods and head out to trucks and vans waiting in the parking areas behind the shops. The annual Founders' Day weekend was winding down. Without going out on a limb, I could predict that chatter at B and B the next morning was going to revolve around the record number of people on the Square, along with happy sales reports. And sure, we'd also grumble about being tired, especially because it was only June, still early in our long busy season.

During the occasional lulls, Nora began straightening the display area. She moved pretty well, but I wondered if her injury still caused her pain.

"You don't have to do that," I told her. "Mondays are usually slow and I'll have lots of time to decide where to put things I bring up from the basement."

Nora hesitated in front of the cooler, an empty cavern, temporarily. I'd need to fill it with arrangements. Only a few buckets of loose flowers sat in the corner.

"You sold all your arrangements. But I'm not surprised. They were beautiful." She touched the glass as if wanting to touch the loose flowers.

"I don't know how to repay you for your help today, Nora. You know, beyond the compensation we agreed on. But you've gone way beyond what anyone could expect."

She turned around and with her back to the glass walked

toward me, her limp more exaggerated now, from fatigue, I presumed.

"Since you asked," she said with a grin, "I'd like to make my wedding bouquet and the other flowers for the wedding."

That was a first. Never, in all the years I'd owned Rainbow Gardens, had a bride asked to help put her flowers together. "Okay, then, flowers arrive on Tuesdays. I usually begin putting arrangements and wedding bouquets together on Thursday, and then I add the final details either on Friday or right before the ceremony."

"So, is that a yes?" She was tentative, probably because I hadn't been particularly clear.

The bell jingled behind her, so someone had just come in and would soon need attention. "Sure." I squeezed her arm. "It will be fun."

"What will be fun?" Matt was the person at the door.

"Megan's agreed to let me help her put the flowers together for our wedding," Nora said, her excitement showing on her face. He put his arm around her shoulders and she rested her head against him. The two seemed completely at ease in their mutual affection.

"This woman has worked very hard today," I said, pointing to Nora. "So, she deserves big-time pampering tonight."

"I'm too tired for pampering," Nora said with a chuckle. "A quick bath will have to do. Besides, I'll probably be asleep before we get to Green Bay."

"Hey, I'm glad you had such a good day." He turned to me. "She's a natural to work in a flower shop, don't you think?"

"Yes, I do."

Nora lifted her head. "How can you say that? I never touched a flower all day."

"Hey, arrangements I can teach you," I pointed out. "Being savvy about customers is something you have a feel for or you don't. I can't pass that on. But it's obvious you enjoyed working with people."

"I do," Nora said. "And I can't wait to help out again. Call me when you need me."

I handed Nora her purse from the corner under the workbench where she'd stashed it. Then, I stood at the door and watched Nora and Matt walk hand in hand across the Square cloaked in the early evening shadows.

I started the next day with more than an energy bar, preferring to scramble a couple of eggs and slather thick slices of toast with grape jelly. For my breakfast dessert, I polished off the lone apple in a bowl on the counter—rescuing it before it shriveled. As I ate, I jotted notes about everything I wanted to accomplish. Since, as usual, I ended up with far more to pack into my day than was realistic, I had to set priorities.

Clearing out the cooler and using the remaining flowers topped the list at the beginning of every week, because I always needed the room for Tuesday's flower delivery. And the order I was waiting for was huge, my biggest ever.

As soon as I got downstairs, I started with the cooler, noting that the glass doors were so smudged with fingerprints, it looked like a group of preschoolers had been playing in the shop. As tolerant as I was of clutter and the messes I created making arrangements, I liked the glass and chrome to sparkle and the wooden shelves to glisten, as if I'd just given them a lemon oil bath and buffed them to a shine.

Around noon, Sam Benson, the mailman who served the Square, and cousin to Stu Benson, the funeral director I worked with regularly, came through the front door. I smiled to myself when I saw him giving the door a little shake to make sure the bell announced his arrival.

Such tradition around here. Sam's father, George, had been Wolf Creek's mailman before he retired and Sam was reassigned to become his replacement. George had been a quiet, old-school kind of man, using the back door for delivery and putting the letters and magazines on a small table by the door. He'd arranged the letters by size and then tied them all together with string.

No one described Sam as quiet, like his dad had been. On the contrary, Sam used the front door and whistled or hummed all the time—sometimes he sang old pop songs softly to himself. I also looked forward to seeing him since he never failed to admire my window displays or the arrangements. Small price to pay for his idiosyncrasies, which included his haphazard way of banding the mail. I always shook out the catalog pages just in case a stray letter was hidden inside. And regardless of what was on the workbench, damp stems or fresh blossoms, he dropped the mail in the middle of it.

When Sam came in, I was still bringing the outside chrome of the cooler to a shine, my hands encased in rubber gloves. As busy as we'd been all weekend, the pendulum had quickly shifted to the other side. I'd had only a trickle of customers since I'd unlocked the door. Sam and I exchanged pleasantries and he put the mail on the workbench and went back to whistling "Baby, You're the One." When he left, he swatted the bell to make it jingle, and right on schedule, I laughed out loud.

I pushed the mail aside to deal with it upstairs after closing, choosing instead to keep scratching items off my to-do list. I put a bucket of single flowers with a ribbon outside my front door, priced to move because my fresh batch was soon arriving. The day passed, not as quickly as the previous two, but there was something satisfying about bringing order back to the shop and having a clean cooler to fill with newcomers the next morning.

After locking the door, I grabbed the mail and went to the stairs. About midway up the spiral, I stopped and gazed down at my day's work. Perfection, and ready for another day.

When I reached the top of the stairs and shuffled through the envelopes, I saw the bold Victorian letter "B" in the corner of one letter. Tossing the other envelopes on the table, I stared at the letter from the Bartholomew School of Floral Design.

Afraid to actually open it, I second guessed the contents. Wouldn't they have called me if I'd won? What about an email? Okay, I hadn't checked email since early that morning. But wouldn't it have come in before, win or lose?

They had a website and Facebook page and Twitter. Before that day, I'd checked my computer and cell every day. Somehow, I couldn't believe they'd send a letter through the mail.

Since I'd never won any contest before, the procedure was all new to me. I'd waited weeks for this day and now that it arrived I avoided the answer. But I still had to find out what was in the envelope. I ripped the envelope open and took out the letter.

Dear Ms. Reynolds,

I read on. I didn't win.

Not even close. *Fourth runner-up.* A long way from first.

I dropped the letter onto the table. It was a *confirmation* letter anyway, sent Friday. The actual announcement had been made online that morning. I wandered over to my computer and watched emails scroll in, all the while wondering why I had been so naïve as to think I could compete with nationally known designers from the largest and most upscale floral businesses in the country. There it was, the big announcement email, and there was my name at the bottom. I picked up the letter and scanned the first through third placements. Sure enough, I knew those names. But did they know mine? No.

Foolish me. Eli had been right all along. I'd wasted time and money.

I reread the letter, formal in style, but with a hint of personalization. And a thank you from Keith Evans, the contest chairman.

In the bottom left-hand corner was a handwritten note from David Bartholomew: *Thank you for entering our contest. Clayton was enthusiastic about your arrangements, your confidence with balance and style. However, our judges leaned toward the use of exotic flowers and dramatic arrangements. Keep true to yourself and your future.* He'd signed his note with his signature combined lowercase *d* and *b.*

Those words helped me make my decision. Perhaps it was the part about being true to myself. Maybe I'd come to the realization myself before this, but staying in Wolf Creek was the way I'd be true to myself and my style. I knew that now. Never, in all my thoughts about leaving my hometown, had I ever imagined myself working with so-called exotic flowers. No, my thoughts had always run closer to using the plants and flowers that already dotted my landscape.

To satisfy my curiosity, I went to the Facebook page, and since the other finalists had congratulated the winner, I added my note, too.

Then, with my confidence strangely renewed, I called Clayton.

"Hi, Megan." His voice sounded far away. "Talk loud. I'm on speaker while I paint."

"A letter came—then I checked my email."

"I see? And?"

I didn't have to explain. He knew what I was talking about. "Fourth runner up. Not even close."

"I know."

"I was still hoping for 'The Call'."

"I know."

What was up with these lame answers from him? "What do you mean 'you know'? How?"

"David called on Friday and told me the results they'd announce this morning."

"What?" I asked. "You're telling me you knew *before* the weekend? And you didn't tell me?" My voice had gone higher with every word. I couldn't believe Clayton would treat me like a young child who needed protection. I hung up without so much as a hasty goodbye. Okay, that *was* childish.

My phone rang and when I saw it was Clayton calling back, I turned off the phone. I needed to be alone with my thoughts, my disappointment, but even more important, my plans.

Then and there, I realized for certain that I'd learned an important lesson. No more contests for me. They were *not* my way out of Wolf Creek. If I ever decided to leave, it was going to be my clear-headed choice, driven by my needs, and not some judge in New York or San Francisco—or wherever.

169

I gathered the books I had studied for the contest and piled them on the kitchen table. I'd add them to the sale table downstairs. *Out with the old.* Isn't that what I was doing with the old stock of unsold items? Then I stretched out on the couch and felt sorry for myself.

I gave it about twenty minutes. Sick to death of batting around my future, I finally got off the couch and went to bed. Sleep, when it arrived, came in spurts with caricature dreams and disjointed memories. I hauled myself out of bed the next morning, not exactly rested, certainly not overjoyed, but not destroyed either.

Clayton came in just after I unlocked the door.

He stood near it, and I took a few steps back to widen the space between us.

"I could say I'm sorry, Megan. Sorry for you and what this means for your plan to leave Wolf Creek." He ran his fingers through his hair, staring into the room, but not at me. "But, really, I'm not. You're here and I'm here. I don't know why, but whatever the reason is, we'll live with it. I've found a place where I feel like myself, where I'm comfortable. It's been a long time since I felt that way. If the past comes knocking on my door, I'll face it. But I'm not going to be pushed around anymore."

Yeah, well, good for you. "It's over, Clayton. I did my best, and I was a finalist, something that will always mean something to me," I said, my voice strong and my chin lifted a notch or two. "Meanwhile, I'm going to keep Rainbow Gardens and enjoy working with the flowers, as I always have. I'm not talking about it again, and I'd appreciate it if you didn't either."

With his one hand resting on his hip, he said, "You women have strength. You and Mom, I mean." He extended his arm toward me, but I inched back again.

"Not today." I couldn't tell him I was too fragile for a comforting hug, almost shaky, not to mention unsure of myself.

"I understand." He turned to hold the door open for my first customer and then left.

She was a browser, and declined my offer of help. I

was grateful for that, because I didn't care to engage with anyone. When she left, I turned my attention to the flower delivery that arrived at the back. Fresh and crisp, the lilies and daisies, irises and dahlias, roses and mums of all colors and sizes brought me back into my comfort zone. As I sorted and restocked the cooler, possible combinations for Matt and Nora's wedding drifted through my mind.

I stopped to call Nathan to talk about the wedding.

Nathan was his typically cheerful self when he asked, "So, what can I do for you, Megan?"

"Just an update," I said, going on to explain that Nora asked to help put together their flowers for the wedding. "I've never been asked that before by any bride," I said, "but depending on what she chooses, there could be a slight difference from the quote I gave you. Once she starts to assemble what she wants, she might want to add more flowers or change her mind about the type she wants."

"No problem. It won't matter a bit. I don't want her skimping or thinking she has to be careful, knowing I'm paying for them. Actually I feel honored to be invited. Lily, too."

"I'll try not to let anything slip out, but you know how that goes." I waved my hand in the air, but I don't know why. Nathan couldn't see me, anyway.

He was interrupted by someone talking in the background. "Gotta run, Megan. Thanks for checking in with me, but the bride should have exactly what she wants."

I predicted Nathan would say exactly what he had, but I was still glad I called to check with him anyway.

The day was slow, which gave me a chance to spruce things up for the bus tour scheduled for the next day. I noticed the compost tub was almost full, so with little afternoon traffic I decided to close early and head to the family farmhouse. Every now and then I found I longed to spend a few hours weeding the gardens Gram and Mom had planted years ago, and today was one of those days.

I drove my van close to the back door. The full tub was heavy and cumbersome. I'd obviously waited too long. But I was stubborn enough not to call my brothers for help.

171

Instead, huffing and puffing, I pulled it to the doorway. When I stopped to straighten up and stretch my back, I saw Clayton standing by the door.

"I'd like to lend a hand." His voice rippled through me.

Still being childishly stubborn, I shook my head, not wanting to argue or debate.

Ignoring me, he reached in to take one handle. "I like to help my friends."

I could feel a smile coming on, but I hid it. He didn't need to see what I was feeling.

With two of us working together, it took little effort to put the tub in the back of the van. I closed the hatch door.

"Where are you going with that?" he asked.

"To the farmhouse," I said. "I'll add it to the compost piles we have out there."

"Uh, would you mind if I went along? I'd like to see the house and the gardens, and I can help you empty it." He gestured toward the tub.

In order to keep myself from shouting, "Yes, yes, come with me," I swept my hand toward the passenger seat of my van.

Clayton ducked back into his gallery long enough to grab a portfolio. He locked his door and slid into the passenger seat. We drove the few miles outside of Wolf Creek, avoiding the main highway and going down the back roads. The silence in the van became tense, but despite that, having Clayton close was more comforting than being alone.

I started telling him about Gram planting flowers near the house to bring a little color to the acres of crops—the hay and corn for the animals. Mostly, she kept her garden going because she loved flowers, and passed on that love—and her knowledge—to her daughter and, in turn, to me.

"You're lucky to have this heritage and family roots to come to whenever you want. That is something to be proud of."

There was a wistfulness in his voice. I could only imagine how lost he must have felt in the years following his stepfather's betrayal.

We quickly emptied the tub, and then when I started to

pull weeds from between the flowers, Clayton took a seat on the granite bench at the edge of the garden and began sketching. We worked in silence until dusk. When the mosquitoes began their nightly attack, we ran to the van and kept swatting those that had gotten inside. I laughed at his attempt to shoo them away.

Once back home, I got ready for bed and let the events of the day wash over me, allowing my protective guard to relax. The cycle of emotions that I experienced that day had broken my negative feelings. "So," I said out loud to the empty room, "it's over. I didn't win the contest. Yes, I was disappointed. No, I will not let it break me."

I sat down on my bed and started reading another section of Sarah's pages.

Wolf Creek, Wisconsin

Jasper French had worked for the Buchanan family for years. He'd come to them as an orphan and, although much younger, he worked alongside Harold and Callum, man to man. Reuben and Dora had treated him no different from their own.

But Jasper saw the world changing. He predicted stagecoaches and horses would be replaced by the trains and motorcars people were talking about. The more Jasper talked about it, the more Reuben shook his head and called him a fool.

Then one summer day Reuben sat in his rocking chair and gazed at his land, even laughing at the spring foals frolicking near their mothers in the near corral. Dora had died during the past harsh winter and Reuben hadn't recovered from the loss. By the time the sun fell and closed the day, Reuben had joined his wife.

Sadly, neither Dora nor Reuben had lived

long enough to see the love blooming between Etta and Jasper.

Reuben and Dora had a will that divided their property so each of their children received an equal share, including Jasper. Harold and Callum gave Etta and Jasper the family home as a wedding gift. Each of the boys built homes nearby and Harold took the horses.

With the town of Wolf Creek continuing to grow, Jasper saw the need to provide local food to the townspeople. He plowed under the pasture and planted peas, corn, and potatoes. He extended his garden to included carrots, beans, and cabbage the following year.

Etta worked a smaller garden near the house, and everyone in town enjoyed the lettuce and onions she grew. While the food crops were their mainstay, Etta added small areas of color with zinnias, hollyhocks, and marigolds. She allowed chicory, wild daisies, and native roses to mix freely in the far corner of the patch.

The town supported Jasper when he opened a small store in Wolf Creek to sell his vegetables, and slowly through the years, his business flourished and became the main food store in the town.

Etta's daughter, Martha, loved the flowers as much as her mother and they worked side by side in the gardens. They expanded the natural garden by adding perennials and seasonal bulbs.

As a young wife, Martha started her own herb garden. It was a compliment to her mother's love of growing and harvesting.

Ten years after the birth of their twin sons, Martha and Albert welcomed a daughter into their home. Martha wasted no time bringing Megan into the gardens and started schooling her in the care of the flowers.

Megan was an eager student, and as a third generation Reynolds'woman, Megan maintains the gardens at the farmhouse and established her florist shop, Rainbow Gardens, in the tight-knit community of Wolf Creek Square.

JULY
16

The end of the contest also coincided with turning the calendar page. Half the year was behind us. I didn't see Clayton the rest of the week. Sadie dropped by, but only mentioned that Clayton had finished setting up his studio and was spending long hours painting. She talked more about the museum and how it was a shame to have it neglected by the townsfolk.

Meanwhile, every time I thought of the 4th of July, the date reminded me that I was the *fourth* runner-up in the contest. Nowhere near the top. Of course, the holiday passed quickly for me. The Square was open for business and shoppers liked the holiday discount specials. I gave each customer a small American flag—I had hundreds left over from our slow Memorial Day weekend.

I politely thanked Liz Pearson for inviting me to join her and the others from the Square out at the lake for the annual fireworks display at dusk. I didn't lie when I said I had other plans.

And I did. For real.

An evening spent working in Gram's and Mom's gardens would be the best thing I could do for myself, especially after reading about my family's connection with the town. Although I adored the Square, my roots in this town were put down on that land and in those gardens I grew up. And Wolf Creek is where I would stay.

I packed a PB & J sandwich and a soda and some water in the cooler. Then I tossed in a chocolate power bar for good measure. I grabbed my ring of keys for the farmhouse and went on my way.

I'd filled one tub with weeds from the perennial patch and had started another tub when I heard a car drive in.

Clayton stepped out of his car and brought his sketch book with him. He sat on the bench, like he'd done before, and I watched his hand dance across the page.

"Secrets?" I pointed to his book as I walked toward him.

"No. Never from you." He gave the book to me. I sat next to him on the bench and opened the cover. Each page had the drawing of a flower from the garden. They were beautiful. "You did these the other day, didn't you?"

He nodded.

"What a gift you have," I said. "Why aren't you painting all the time?"

He hesitated, starting to answer but then abruptly stopped. Then he found his voice. "As you can see, this is a different kind of painting than I did in New York. I'm learning how to blend color differently, which gives the pieces a new look, unique for me."

"These flowers look real. Like in the cooler at my shop." I touched the page, forgetting my hands were dirty from weeding. "Oh, no. I'm so sorry." I tried rubbing the dirt off and only made the smear larger.

"It's only a sketch. Don't worry. I can do another." He turned the page and with a few strokes of his pencil the basic design of the flower immerged.

And the mosquitoes returned—in full force.

"I'm heading home. I need all the blood I have." I swatted the one on my forearm. I grabbed the cooler and ran to my van.

Clayton followed. Halfway to the van, I stopped and hollered to him. "Let's grab a burger at the Creekside Pub—it's on the corner of the turn onto the county road into town."

"Are you sure it's open?" he asked.

"No, but we'll soon find out. Follow me."

A few minutes later he pulled into the nearly empty parking lot behind me. The pub's neon sign was on, so it looked promising.

"We need our night vision in here," Clayton joked when we went inside the dimly lit room. Pool tables filled one end, and a bar and tables sat at the other.

"This doesn't look like much," I said, "but trust me, the food is good." At least it had been the last time Eli, Elliot, and I had driven out this way for dinner. "Every now and then my brothers and I crave a pub burger, and this is where we come."

The bartender, who recognized me, nodded and waved. "Sit wherever you like," he said. A few minute later he took our order for two beers, two burgers.

"We stayed open, but for now most everyone is down at the lake for the fireworks," he said when he came back with the beer. "I expect a few people will wander in later."

Clayton looked around and grinned. "A great way to spend the 4th. No crowds, except for mosquitoes."

Over our burgers, Clayton gave me an abbreviated version of his history as an artist, and the journey from working in charcoal to oils, a detour to acrylics, where he'd found success, and now another trip into watercolor.

"By the way," he said, "you'd be amazed by the comments I've had about your arrangement. You describe it as simple, but to people wandering in, it's unusual. Noteworthy, which is exactly why they comment."

"I'm glad you like it," I said with a grin.

"I want an arrangement every Friday," he said, "to dress up the gallery for the weekend."

I nodded, pleased beyond words. "You've got it. I'll write up a work order in the morning for you to sign."

Clayton agreed that the Creekside special was one of the best burgers he'd ever had. I could tell he was trying to hide his surprise, too. Granted, the pub itself looked a bit rundown, but it was also one of the oldest businesses in Wolf Creek.

Later, we stood by the back door of our shops and extended our conversation about how much Sadie liked the town. I was reluctant to call it a night, but was unsure of what came next.

Finally, Clayton took a step toward me. "You're a

beautiful woman, Megan." He rested his hands on my shoulders. "From the minute I saw you, dressed like an orphan, you've been on my mind."

The butterflies began to move in my midsection. My heart beat faster.

He leaned forward and wrapped his arms around me. I molded to his body and my world tilted when he kissed me.

I didn't want to leave the strength of his body and the promise for a future with him, but he pulled away and stepped back. "Good night, my love. Pleasant dreams."

With that, he was gone.

I went inside and locked the door. That was no light kiss, no mere brush of his lips across mine. My imagination took me into the next day, the next week. But I had no idea what his sweet words or his kiss meant. And he hadn't hung around to tell me.

As I climbed into bed with my hot chocolate milk, I reminded myself that Clayton lived and worked right next door—whatever I wanted our dinner, our evening, our kiss to mean, I needed to be very careful.

On Monday, my mood was better than it had been in weeks. What a relief! I'd put aside my hidden so-called scheme to leave Wolf Creek. What kind of scheme was it, anyway? It was only half-formed, and I'd never done any research about other regions or towns. Even my daydreaming had changed from one week to the next. It didn't even feel odd to wash my hands of the whole thing, maybe because I hadn't confided my roller-coaster ride of "stay-leave-stay-leave" to anyone. And I'd keep it my secret forever.

Maybe my evening with Clayton had lifted my mood, too. A little…or a lot.

The familiar—even comforting—routine of sorting flowers and renewing the water in the buckets in the cooler gave me time to think ahead to Nora, who was due to come in later in the week to work another day. There were so many things I wanted to show her.

When the box from the ribbon company arrived, I was eager to open it, so much so I forgot all about the next job on my to-do list. I'd ordered special ribbon for Nora, white satin on one side and a pale pink satin on the other. I ordered three different widths not knowing which would work the best for her. Since the ribbon had no right or wrong side, it would be easier for her to make a professional looking bow. I hadn't specifically asked her about the ribbons, but if she didn't like this new double-sided style I'd use it later with someone else. But I had a feeling that Nora would like most any ribbon I suggested. She was what anyone would call a positive kind of person. Traditional, and open-minded.

I closed the box and put it under the workbench. It would be my surprise on Thursday.

Between visitors and shoppers, my day left little time for my mind to wander. Although I wasn't pulling up my roots, I still needed to figure out what I wanted for my life. When I tried to think it out, Clayton would worm his way into my mind, making me struggle to push thoughts of him aside. I couldn't count on anyone—not Clayton or my brothers or my friends—to create a future for me.

I'd just finished a quick lunch when Tracie came over from the Fiber Barn carrying a large tote bag stuffed to the top with skeins of deep charcoal heather yarn. "So, Megan, not so many people on the Square today, huh?"

I couldn't tell if she was simply making an observation or expressing apprehension, but I said, "Mondays often give us a little break to get ready for the next surge."

"Katie and I go home exhausted each night," she said, grinning, "but, at the same time, we haven't had this much fun and met so many wonderful people in a long time."

We were chatting about which hours of the day were the best for cleaning up our shops when a group of three women filed into Rainbow Gardens. One immediately spotted the yarn in the bag Tracie was carrying.

"A friend of mine was here on the Fourth of July and was impressed by how many new shops there are to see." She pointed to the tote, with the Fiber Barn logo printed on it. "Her description was good enough to get me out here. I haven't been to the Square for two years and, boy, how it's changed. More shops, more fun stuff to see. And I saw that the museum's open for visitors now, too. I'll have to tell my husband about that."

"We all think these are good changes." I came out from behind the workbench and stood at Tracie's side. "As a matter of fact, Tracie is one of the owners of The Fiber Barn, the new shop next door."

"That'll be our next stop," the woman said, smiling at Tracie, "but right now I see a whimsical frog that would look terrific on my back porch steps." She moved to the table where I'd assembled a collection of ceramic frogs in various colors and sizes.

"I've restocked the table two or three times just this week." I'd added some larger pieces on the floor around the display. "Let me know if I can help you."

Tracie had put her tote down next to the workbench and leaned forward to continue our conversation. "Nora Grayson stopped in the other day and asked me to put together the supplies she needed for a sweater she's making for her husband for Christmas. We didn't have everything at the shop, so I needed to search through our inventory at home."

When she started laughing, I assumed it was about their house, but wasn't sure until she added, "What a mess. Our neatly organized rooms are no longer neat *or* organized."

More laughter. "And do we care? Not a bit."

She picked up the tote and handed it to me. "Now for the real reason I'm here. Nora said she'd be here on Thursday, but if it's an inconvenience for you to keep it, I can hide it somewhere next door. She wants to keep it a secret from Matt. If he saw her going in and out of our shop, he might ask her what she was up to."

"No problem at all." I took the bag and went to the staircase and put it on a stair about halfway up, past the "Employees Only" sign. A few years back, I finally put the sign up to keep shoppers from assuming I had more merchandise on the second floor. But I also chuckled to myself, since plural "employees" was a bit of an exaggeration, after all.

"Thanks," Tracie said. "Gotta run. We haven't figured out

a good way for one of us to be gone for very long." She stopped and peered at me. "How do you manage? You're here alone most of the time."

"I grew into the business, and somehow came up with a few tricks, like a fridge down here to keep food and cold drinks. And I don't worry too much anymore if the place isn't exactly pristine." I lowered my voice and added, "I'd rather look breathlessly busy than have everything in perfect order."

Tracie's phone signaled an incoming text. "Oops. Katie's asking for help."

She dashed out, leaving the door open. I left it that way and turned my attention to the women who were discussing the ceramic frogs. Somehow, the day kept getting better and better. I turned the CD player on, starting up the collection of lively Irish songs.

All three women bought a frog; different sizes, colors, and expressions. "I love this orange one," I said, wrapping it in paper and placing it carefully in a shopping bag. I repeated the routine two more times and tied the handles of each bag with short lengths of my custom Rainbow Gardens ribbon.

When I looked around the display area after the women left, I was struck by how many of Tom's suggestions I'd used in the last few weeks. Maybe I'd been in a rut and hadn't been aware of it. But his ideas, even the one about using floor space more effectively, had helped give the shop a new look, but without changing my style. Vases, pottery bowls, and flowers had long been mainstays, but this year the garden and lawn ornaments added a festive look. More than a flower shop, Rainbow Gardens gave customers a reason to consider adding beauty to their gardens.

The three frogs were important sales, and having the women wandering around the Square carrying my distinctive shopping bags was all too good. By the time I locked the door and headed upstairs, retrieving Nora's bag of yarn on the way up, I was hungry. Long ago, Eli and Elliot had taught me all about Dagwood sandwiches, and I happened to have the fixings for one, thanks to my brothers' well stocked deli counter. I piled turkey and ham and three kinds of cheeses on a giant roll, and then added mustard, homemade pickles, tomatoes, lettuce, sliced black olives, onions, and sprouts. *Thank you, guys.*

Somehow, I managed to get the sandwich in my mouth, but I laughed at my own expense doing it. Taking my time with my Dagwood dinner, I began to review my day planner for the upcoming months. Wow, so preoccupied with the contest, I hadn't focused on it before. Fortunately, nothing caught my eye that needed immediate attention, as in that minute. This gave me a chance to grab one of the knitting books Tracie had left for Nora. I paged through it, but what was up with me, anyway? I found myself putting Clayton's face on the models and then imagined knitting a sweater for him. I even started evaluating what color might look best on him.

Ridiculous. I knew nothing about yarn and knitting needles, and had never much cared to learn.

Restless, I cleaned up the kitchen and took a shower, letting the hot water cascade down my back as I massaged shampoo into my hair. It had been such a good day, and winding down was just as pleasant. I toweled dry my hair and slipped my terry robe on, feeling ready to end my day.

When I'd brushed out my hair, an easy job since I'd gone for a short pixie-ish cut, I changed into my nightgown and made my hot chocolate and sat in the chair by the window. It was almost dark, and with the exception of a few people wandering back and forth, most likely going to Crossroads or to one of the restaurants outside the Square, it looked like it was buttoned up for the night.

I finally wandered off to bed, and although I was worn out, sleep didn't come easy. Even when I'd drifted off, I had dreams of Clayton wearing a sweater I'd made. Even more confusing, I was walking toward him carrying a bouquet of white roses. He definitely reminded me of the man who had visited my dreams before.

Restless anyway, I gave up on sleep, and dressed before the alarm rang or the coffee brewed. It was Tuesday, flower delivery day, and a pleasantly cool morning. Taking my coffee down to the shop with me, I straightened up, focusing on rearranging the ceramic planters. An email from Sarah reminded me that a tour bus would be arriving on the Square right around 10:00.

I opened the door in time to say hello to the driver, who carried the boxes inside my door. Over the years I'd been approached by a number of competitive flower distributors. Somewhat better prices, reduced delivery rates, and lower minimum orders were always the selling points. But loyalty kept me with the company that had accommodated me back when my orders were quite small, always giving me good prices, including me in special sales often reserved for larger stores. And, they were great at delivering special orders in a timely way.

And with great care. When I opened the box of Nora's wedding flowers, they were both chosen and packaged carefully. I lifted the white roses from the box and placed them in the cooler. My reflection in the glass holding the roses reminded me of my dream, and I blushed.

I'd thought I would hide Nora's flowers in the back, but seeing them in the cooler, I grabbed an index card and wrote "SOLD" on it and propped it in front of the vases. Hmm...a little free marketing.

I finished sorting the flowers and greenery and was just about to add a few pieces to the front window when two women wearing Harris Bus Tours name tags entered.

"Welcome to Rainbow Gardens—your tour got here right on time I see."

"Tom told us to come in and say hello," the first woman said. "He's on a trip to Wausau today, but said he'd much rather be heading this way."

"Thanks for mentioning it. And be sure to say hello back." I pointed to the sale table. "Fourth of July sales are still on this week."

I left them to browse while I answered the phone.

"Sorry to bother you, Megan, but have my flowers come in yet?"

I smiled when I realized Nora couldn't keep the excitement from her voice. "They're in the cooler as we speak."

"Can I stop in and look?" Nora asked.

"Sure. Where are you?"

"Biscuits and Brew."

I let out a hoot. "Steps from my door. If you were any closer, I could see you sitting at a table talking to me on your phone. So, bring me a cup of coffee. Steph knows my favorite."

"Will do," she said before ending the call.

I hadn't had a bride so excited about her flowers in a long time. Or, had it been that with my focus all over the place, I simply hadn't noticed.

In the five minutes it took Nora to get my coffee and cross the Square, the shop filled with more people from the tour. Mostly women, but two couples were examining garden art.

Nora went directly to the back and put my coffee on a table by the door. She got her apron on fast and stashed her purse under the workbench. She was ready to go and positioned herself to help the first woman in line. I needed a picture of her smile on my bathroom mirror to remind me what happiness looked like.

The next two hours passed quickly, and I was on the phone taking an order when I saw Nora finally looking through the cooler doors at her flowers. After the call ended I stayed quiet, not wanting to interrupt what seemed to me like a private moment.

"I don't believe it's really happening, Megan," she said, looking away from the flowers and at me. "After my first husband died, I never believed another dream would—or could—come true. Now, here it is. In four days we'll be married."

"You'll be a beautiful bride," I said, meaning it.

She beamed, and even turned a little pink as she pushed her shoulder-length, brown hair away from her face.

We had a lull shortly before noon, exactly when I imagined B and B and Crossroads were rushing around serving lunch to the tourists we'd waited on all morning. Nora sat at the table to get off her feet. I noted that she hadn't used her cane, and had seldom even rested her hip on the stool when she operated the register.

I asked if she had plans for the afternoon; she said she

185

hadn't made any and had planned to go on home.

"Then why don't you stay for lunch. After that, I can put you to work. I have orders to fill, and I can show you how I put the arrangements together. Meanwhile, we'll take care of the customers together."

Nora grinned. "Sounds like a plan."

"Good. I'll call Steph at B and B for to-go salads," I said, reaching for my phone, "and I'll go pick them up."

I gave Steph a few minutes to get the salads ready and then out the door I went. Later, I realized it had never occurred to me to worry about my shop while Nora was there alone.

During our uninterrupted lunch, Nora talked about the upcoming ceremony and mentioned a Unity candle as part of it.

"Do you have plans for the candle after the service?" I asked. An idea came to me as she was describing the flowers on the side of the candle.

"I don't know. Take it home, I suppose, and display it on a shelf."

"I was thinking that you should use it as part of the centerpiece for the table. We could make three low trays of flowers to surround it." I used my hands to depict a make-shift triangle.

"Oh, I like that," Nora said with a grin. "Better than just a bowl of flowers."

When we were done eating, I cleared away the salad bowls and wiped off the table. "Okay, let's move to the workbench. Have a seat on a stool. Lesson One is about to begin."

Nora grinned. "I have a feeling you're going to reveal the tools of the trade."

"Exactly." We got started, and in between customers, I gathered knives, clippers, and cutters to create arrangements for the special orders for the day. They were fairly typical and included a wedding anniversary arrangement, one for a grandmother's birthday, and two for a baby shower. As I made them, I asked Nora what she'd add or take away, and she offered her opinions and ideas. She had a natural eye for symmetry and balance.

With the orders done, I went to my regular supply of vases and picked out three. "The cooler still looks bare, so why don't you put three small arrangements together in these vases and I'll show you how to price them. Use the flowers on the right to keep the cost down."

My teaching techniques—more hands-on than explanation—had worked with Tom and I imagined they'd work with Nora, too.

Leaving Nora to the arrangement, I went to greet a woman who had entered the shop. She held her purse close to her chest, as if trying not to touch anything.

"Is there something you are looking for today?" I asked.

She looked at Nora, then back to me. "My daughter mentioned a woman named Megan Reynolds from Rainbow Gardens."

"I'm Megan. Uh, who is your daughter?"

"Susan. She was part of the group of young mothers that came to say thank you for making quilts for their babies." She stopped to take a breath, to calm what appeared to be nervousness. "Susan mentioned that you gave her daughter, Laura…my granddaughter…a bottle one evening."

"Yes, I do remember that." I still didn't understand her reason for being in my shop.

"I stopped in because you and the other women who were part of that group really helped Susan and the other girls. My daughter began to think more about her future, so she's finishing high school and plans to go to the technical college."

"That's terrific." I looked in Nora's direction to try to include her in the conversation, or at least not ignore her. "Marianna, the owner of Quilts Galore, is responsible for asking us to make the quilts and for finding the girls."

"Maybe so, but Susan mentioned you directly. And she and I are talking again now. It's been a long time. I didn't handle the news about her pregnancy especially well. She's actually asked for my help." Moisture gathered in her eyes and she reached into her purse for a tissue. "She sees a better life for herself, for us, and I wanted to thank you."

We had slowly moved further into the shop and were

close to Nora, who was busy with flowers and ribbons.

"I'm sure your daughter, with your help, will be successful, too," I said.

"Susan mentioned a girl who lives on the Square. I think her name is Rachel. She has a little boy, who visits the house with Rachel. It helps the girls fight for their future—for their kids' sake, if for no other reason. She's quite the role model for them."

Were it not for the ringing phone and shoppers coming in, we might have talked longer. But, I didn't have much more to say. The afternoon rush had started in earnest. I reached across the workbench and handed one of Nora's arrangements to the woman. "I'm sorry. I didn't get your name, but I'd like you to have this." I put the vase in her hand. "You and Susan will be fine—and you have a lovely grandchild. Congratulations."

"Claire, my name is Claire Just." She took the vase and tried to speak, but no words came. Eventually, she said, "Thanks for being kind to my daughter."

"We all make mistakes," I said with a shrug. "It's what we do to fix them that matters. At least that's what my mom always told me."

Claire squeezed my arm and smiled. As more women came through the door, she quickly slipped out.

Nora walked past me on her way to complete a sale. "Wow. Someday you'll have to tell me *that* whole story." She finished the transaction and never stopped smiling.

"Didn't you like the arrangement?" Nora asked when she came back to the workbench and started clearing the space and wiping off the tools.

"Are you kidding? I liked it a lot. You have an eye for putting flowers together to make them appealing. That's why I gave it to Claire. I wanted her to have something nice."

"Well, thank you." Nora turned her attention to help another customer with her purchase.

After she completed the sale, she added the last of the flower scraps to the compost tub. She washed her hands and checked her watch. "I have to go. I only came to look at my flowers, but I'm happy I was useful this afternoon."

I noticed that she carried her cane, rather than using it, as she walked to the front of the shop. She turned and waved before closing the door. Her smile would charm any man. Lucky Matt.

I didn't allow myself even a minute to dwell on the lack of a man in my life, but noted that I hadn't heard from Clayton in a few days. I planned to call him—eventually— and I wasn't going to be hesitant about my intent. Yes, I wanted a man in my life.

No. I wanted Clayton Sommers in my life.

Later that evening I called Clayton, and when he picked up, I said, "Hey there, I haven't heard from you lately. Are you settling in?"

His soft, smooth chuckle made my ear tingle. "You won't believe this, but I was going to call you tonight. Great minds and all that, huh?"

Even that exchange sounded a bit hollow, unlike the easy way we had talked at the farmhouse.

"So, are you busy tonight?" he asked.

I heard in his voice a degree of insecurity, or maybe it was uncharacteristic shyness. "No plans. Why?"

"I have something to show you. I'll unlock the upstairs door. Just walk in."

"Now?" I asked.

"Uh huh? Now."

"I'm on my way."

I gave myself a once over in the mirror. Not bad, considering I'd worked all day. I brushed my hair and added a sweep of lip gloss. Done and gone.

17

I walked into an artist's mess. I tried not to show my surprise, but my smirk morphed into laughter. Clayton's apron was its own rainbow of colors.

Clayton gestured to the floor. "I told Charlie I'd paint the floor, but I don't think he understood that artists aren't worried about the mess they make as long as the painting gets done."

I nodded. I understood, of course. Clayton's medium was paint, mine was flowers, but we both could get lost creating a masterpiece.

"I'm still not very good using watercolors, but I'm better than when I started. You should have seen the mess then." His laughter rippled through the room.

The apartment, or studio, was filled with tables made out of wooden legs and flat sheets of plywood. Sketches and paintings covered most of the space. I walked over to one table to see what Clayton had done.

He picked up the painting of a daylily from the table. "I want you to have this one."

"This is beautiful. The flower looks so real. Just like those in Gram's garden."

"I went back to the farmhouse to get the proportions and details correct."

"You did?" That touched me. "It's even better than some of the real flowers, with all their imperfections."

"I've never painted flowers before. Well, maybe in school, but certainly not lately."

"Gram would have liked this." I held the painting at arm's length. He'd chosen the white lilies, and he painted them a perfect creamy ivory. The vibrant green leaves almost jumped off the paper.

I wanted to see all the paintings on the tables and was surprised when Clayton took my hand, put it in the bend of his arm, and pulled me to the table on our left.

"These are my first ones," he said, patting the table. "Well, not really. These are the first ones I thought were good enough to keep. I threw away most everything else. I'll be honest, though, I actually didn't know how to use the paints."

I looked at him, not understanding. "Are paints so different?"

"Absolutely," he said. "I painted landscapes and still life with acrylics before…" He waved his hand in the air. "…you know, before all the trouble. But the paints were too heavy for the delicate flowers. So I thought, if I have a new subject, I need a new technique. At least that's how it worked for me."

He chuckled, almost to himself, but turned me toward him. "I never imagined I would be using the grown-up version of a tin box with eight squares of paint and a fat brush. It's been a frustrating learning curve, but now I can do some pieces and see if they sell downstairs."

We traveled around his studio, stopping at various paintings for me to admire. I didn't tell him any white lies about his talent or the paintings. I didn't have to. Clayton was an exceptional artist. But would Wolf Creek have enough excitement for him to stay?

"Before you leave, I want to tell you that I've hired Heidi Fairmont to work in the gallery. Mom's been teaching her the basics of retail, like buzz words to describe a painting, how each painting is a one-of-a-kind work of art. That sort of thing. Mostly, it's to have a body in the gallery when shoppers come in."

He walked over to a drawing of a wild horse. So different than any of the paintings I'd seen so far. "Heidi did this. She has more raw talent than I've seen in a long time. And she wants to exchange some lesson time for working time. She's only in high school, so I'd like to channel her talent, help her develop it. But mostly, working here will let her be part of the art world. Selling art is one way to get her feet wet."

"And meanwhile, you'll be up here painting the floor and creating stock, as Gretchen called it." Neither of us could keep the laughter from coming out.

"Every day—or night—depending on what flows when."

"I get that," I said.

"I know you do," he said, the corners of his mouth turning up in a faint smile.

Our trip through the studio had circled to the door to go back downstairs. It was time for me to leave.

"Don't be a stranger, Megan. Call anytime. Come around when you can. I understand now how difficult it is for one person to run a business in this town." He leaned forward and held my face in his hands. "Stay well, my sweetheart." The kiss lasted longer than any of those before.

Instead of stepping back, he put his arms around me and I leaned into his embrace, returning it. It was time to tell Clayton how I felt about him with more than words.

The silence was magic.

I backed away and went down the stairs. No goodbyes or good nights. I simply left and carried the mood home with me.

The next morning, I danced around the shop, my spirit even brighter than the last few days. Busy, too. Sarah had texted about the three daytrip tours overlapping, making the Square extra busy for most of the day.

Before the madness started, I phoned Nora and we settled on an eight o'clock starting time the next day to begin her flowers. I asked her to bring the base of the Unity candle so I could be sure the flower boats around it would fit correctly. Her happy laughter wanted me to do the best for her even more.

I had a secret, one I'd share with Nora after the wedding. That meant I had to watch my words, so I didn't spoil the surprise.

The day unfolded just as Sarah knew it would. Steady traffic, few breaks, and a couple of hours where the Square looked like a crowded downtown street in Manhattan—at least the way I'd seen it in the movies. I yearned to hear Clayton describe it to me.

When I locked the door at the end of the day I gave the bell on the door a happy tap. Its jingle made me laugh. What a day. I already knew I needed to order more stock, especially the garden art and the pottery pieces.

All in all, the shoppers had been a patient group, but a few suggested that I find some help during peak hours. Little did they understand that our foot traffic changed all the time, even during the summer months. And I hadn't anticipated that the new shops, one on each side of mine, would increase my traffic flow to the degree they had. Now that I was here to stay, I wanted all the shoppers to visit my shop, and more were showing up on the Square every day.

The following morning at 8:00, Nora came in the unlocked front door, with an older woman following her in.

"Meet my sister, JoAnn Clark," Nora said, "my matron-of-honor."

Shaking my hand, JoAnn said, "I'm actually Nora's half-sister, but after years of making that distinction, we agreed to drop the half and just be sisters."

Nora explained that her sister had been with her during her late husband's illness. Then, after Nora's car accident, JoAnn and her husband, David, had been able to relocate to Green Bay to help her through the long recovery and rehab.

That about floored me. Imagine relocating just to help a relative. I tried to hide my shock at the story by making light of the whole idea of sisters. "A sister," I said with a sigh. "Some days I sure wish I had one. My two brothers can be smothering at times." Come to think of it, though, except for waving at me in Farmer Foods when I stopped to get groceries, I hadn't seen much of either one of them for several days. Apparently, they were busy, too.

"I'm not going to stay," JoAnn said, "but Nora wanted me to meet you before Saturday."

"I'm glad." I followed her to the front door and relocked it so we wouldn't be disturbed before opening time.

Nora took the base of the candle from its box and put it in the center of the table. I sat across from her, longing to ask how she and Matt had connected after being apart for so many years. Maybe as we worked and chatted, I'd find an opening to ask, or with any luck, she'd volunteer the information so I wouldn't have to be nosy.

"So, today we're choosing flowers for your sister's bouquet and the boutonnieres for the men. Right?"

"Including Matt's granddad. He's walking me down the aisle."

"Terrific. So three Bs," I said, speaking in my own shorthand language. "Three for the men. And then we'll need a bouquet for JoAnn. And then, there's the centerpiece to think about."

"And my bouquet," Nora said.

"I'll put that together Saturday morning," I said. "The stems need to be tightly pressed together so there are no spaces between the flowers. We'll talk about it before you leave today."

I went to the cooler and brought out two carnations for Nora to practice with before working with her roses. I gestured for her to come to the workbench, where I had the tools we needed. "If you prefer, you can use the stool rather than standing."

"Very thoughtful of you," she said with a grin.

Nora stashed her purse under the workbench and perched on the stool. Then she looked on as I cut the stem. I added a small sprig of greenery and twisted it all together with green florist tape. "We'll add the ribbon later," I said. "Now it's your turn."

Nora seemed hesitant at first, as if apprehensive to cut the stem of the flower. I stood back and watched her put the carnation next to my sample and then make a decisive cut. She debated less with the greenery. She did great, too, especially since this was her first attempt.

"Try one more sample," I said. "You know the technique now, so you'll get a professional looking lapel flower on your a second try. Guaranteed."

She gave me a bright smile and made the second cut and repeated the finishing process. "One for you and one for me," she said, taking a pin from the cushion and attaching the second carnation to my smock. She pinned the first practice piece to her own shirt.

I brought out three small white tea rose buds from the cooler and a new stem of greenery, putting wet toweling over the cut ends to prevent wilting. As soon as Nora finished with them, I'd put them back into the cooler. This time, Nora didn't hesitate and produced three boutonnieres in short order. When she finished, she arranged them on a tray in the cooler.

"Nice job. Let's create your sister's small bouquet." I opened the cooler door. "You pick the flowers yourself."

I stood back and watched as she chose five white roses, three pink tea roses, and two stems of Stephanotis. Then she changed her mind and added one more Stephanotis. She pulled out three different kinds of greenery, but then put one back.

She was a natural. I would have made identical selections.

We stood side-by-side while she shuffled the stems, bringing a pink rose forward and then putting the greens behind the flowers.

"That will be beautiful when it's put together," I said, "and like yours, I won't do that until Saturday morning." I added fresh water to a small container to keep the flowers she'd chosen separate. "There they are, ready and waiting for the ceremony."

"If it's okay with you I'll come Saturday morning and help. Sitting home the whole day with nothing to do will make me nervous."

"Don't you and JoAnn have appointments for makeup and hair…whatever."

Nora grinned. "Nah, we're not that kind of women. We like natural hair and not too much makeup. No sense paying for that. She'll help me dress and then she, David, and I will drive to the chapel. Matt and his Granddad will come themselves."

Family dynamics. They never failed to surprise me. Some families with much less in the way of financial resources sent four or five bridesmaids and the mothers of the bride and groom off to the salon for makeup, hair, nails, and for some, massages. But even with their money and status this family wasn't making a big deal out of wedding preparations.

"Of course you can come around on Saturday morning," I said. "How many brides can say they made their own bouquet?"

"Not many, I'd guess," Nora said, her grin smug.

"Oh, by the way, I ordered special ribbon for you." Handing her the box, I said, "If you don't like it, please say so. I can always use it for some other customer."

When she carefully opened the flaps, I snatched the invoice I'd forgotten to take out of the box. No need for her to think about the cost of anything.

She held up the spool and rolled a few inches of ribbon off. "Wow, Megan, it's gorgeous."

"That it is," I said. "Now flip it over. Look at the other side."

"Ha! Pink. To accent my dress. This is great. I haven't seen double-sided ribbon like this before. Where did you find it? It will make a beautiful bow."

She hadn't strung together so many words before. I guessed it was joy bubbling over.

"I thought so. I ordered different widths, so we can use it for the men's flowers, too." I picked up the medium width spool and looped a small bow around my fingers.

"Too big, too much," Nora said.

She was right. "Shall we use narrower ribbon or fewer loops?"

"Smaller ribbon," she said. "But what if we make a mistake?"

"Oh, I ordered plenty." I made a bow with the narrow ribbon. From experience I knew the smaller the ribbon the more difficult it was to make the bow. But I had nimble fingers from years of experience.

We kept experimenting, and after I opened the shop, customers wandered over to watch us, especially Nora's attempts to get all her fingers to hold the ribbon in the right places. Lots of laughter over that. The morning passed quickly in the light, almost airy and festive atmosphere in the shop.

After lunch, I called Melanie at Crossroads to let her know I'd be delivering the boats for the centerpiece right after closing at 3:00 on Saturday. Then I posted a sign to give shoppers fair warning that I'd be open fewer hours that day.

I also went through the box of supplies that went with me to every wedding. I planned to have my clothes and the flowers ready by noon on Saturday. My personal goal was to have every bride love her flowers so much she'd tell everyone they were from Rainbow Gardens. Everything needed to make that happen was scheduled to fall into place.

On Friday afternoon I spotted Lily Winters coming across the Square. It was near closing and traffic had thinned, leaving only small groups of two or three people window shopping.

Lily waved as I was about to lock the door, so I opened it wide and stepped out into the late afternoon sunshine.

"What brings you to this side of the Square?" I asked.

"Back at you. Haven't seen you at coffee in the morning lately."

"I…well…you know. Same conversation year after year."

"I get it. I'm not there much, either." She handed me the notebook of bridal arrangements I'd loaned to her Aunt Georgia. "Georgia and Elliot went through it and marked their favorites. Well, Georgia marked hers. Since Elliot fell asleep in the middle of the conversation, she asked me to help her decide."

"Hmm…sounds like my brother. He's been known to nod off at the most inopportune times," I said. "No matter. He won't be caught dozing when he sees Georgia. Come October, she'll be a beautiful bride. We can choose such strong, rich colors for the flowers that time of year."

"Lucky her," Lily said with a sigh. "Well, someday I'll get to choose my flowers."

"What kind of wedding do you want?"

Spontaneously, Lily twirled around, making her sundress billow in the breeze. "I want to be Cinderella."

I leaned toward her and wiggled my eyebrows up and down as if planning a conspiracy. "So what are you waiting for?"

She wrapped her arms around her waist. "It's my doing. Nathan keeps pestering me to pick a date."

"And?" I prodded.

She shrugged. "Organizing a wedding isn't easy, as if I needed to tell you that. With the shop and Toby and… and…"

I thrust both arms out to the side, as if embracing the whole Square. "You have a whole community to help. Not to mention your mom and your aunt."

Lily stared at the ground, or maybe she was focused on her bright yellow ballet flats. "Would you help?"

Fun idea. "Sure. I'll be your wedding planner," I said, bookending air quotes around "planner," since I knew only little pieces of what an actual professional wedding planner did. Sure, I'd had many calls from planners asking for quotes on flowers for weddings, from six to 600, and I had pages of arrangements on my website. In fact, I'd soon post photos of Nora and Matt's modest arrangements, especially the Unity candle.

"Yes! That's fantastic. Mom's already said she'd make my dress. Aunt Georgia is too busy with her own wedding, but Virgie will help, too. Maybe we can get Liz involved."

"Come inside. We'll look at my calendar." I flipped the page for July over. Two weddings were scheduled for August, both relatively small, but September only had Labor Day festivities marked. "If we start now we'd have two months to plan and prepare for a Saturday in September. That would still give me plenty of time for Georgia's wedding in October."

I held my breath. Was I taking on too much? When would I have time for myself? Or for Clayton? I shook that notion out of my head. Since my visit to his studio, he'd called once, and I'd invited him for a glass of wine one evening, and he'd begged off with some excuse about being busy framing pieces. The ball was in his court now. And what kind of message did he think he was sending? He'd sweet talk me one day, complete with passionate kisses, and all but ignore me the next.

That's when I decided I wasn't spending any more time trying to solve the puzzle that was Clayton Sommers. I'd be better off staying busy, and I had brides all over the place to distract me. Nora, Lily, Georgia…any bride would do!

Lily's expression suddenly turned serious. "I'm calling Nathan before I let myself dream it could really happen that fast."

I went to a circular display rack near the back of the shop to give her privacy with her call. But she didn't seem to care who heard the conversation.

"I love you. I love you so much. Tell Virgie you need that whole week off. Okay, Thursday and Friday. We need a guest list and…and. Bye."

When I approached her, she wrapped me in a huge hug. "I guess he said yes to a September date," I said.

"He sure did. So, now I need to call Mom and Georgia."

My heart raced. What had I signed up for? "Uh, well, first we need to get the group of us together one night next week. Oh, and order one of those wedding planning books for dummies or idiots or whatever. Fast."

"I'll order it online tonight. We've got free overnight shipping." She smiled at her phone, adding a note to herself. "I'm starting my to-do list."

"Be sure to share it with me. Email it to me." The glow on Lily's face reminded me of my first meeting with Nora. Yes, brides definitely had a special kind of glow about them.

18

On Saturday morning, Nora was sitting on the front step of the shop when I unlocked the door. Her wedding day. When she stood and turned to face me, I saw the contentment on her face. No visible evidence of bridal jitters.

"Come on in, Mrs. Nora Alexander...almost."

We laughed at my attempt at humor. I noticed she didn't use her cane when she came up the steps and followed me to the workbench.

I grabbed the small bucket of flowers from the cooler as we passed it, and we dove right in. Nora asked only a question or two as I showed her each step in making JoAnn's hand-held bouquet. But she watched so closely I was confident she could put her own together with little help from me.

I positioned the flowers and greenery to showcase the beauty of each flower, then cut them evenly across the bottom. The next step involved wrapping the stems tightly together without having any of the flowers move. I added a small gathering of tulle lace behind the greenery for fullness and balance. I quickly made a bow using a combination of the medium and narrow width ribbons. The combination of white and pink colors brought out the small tea roses nestled amongst the larger roses.

"Simple and elegant," she said. "That's been my motto for this day from the beginning."

I attached the bow securely and it was finished.

"Now for yours. No need to be skimpy with the flowers. It needs to be bigger than JoAnn's, but we don't want it enormous and overpowering either." I spread my arms wide, which finally brought a laugh from her.

As Nora worked on her bouquet, I busied myself with restocking and changing the water in the flower buckets. When she began humming the wedding march as she worked, I glanced her way and observed her lost in a dreamy world of her own creation.

Nora finished her bouquet by the time the first customer of the day came in. Acting like she worked in the shop every day, she put the bouquet in the cooler next to JoAnn's and then cleaned up the workbench and tools.

She touched my shoulder when she left. "See you at 4:00."

The hours passed quickly and pleasantly. Most shoppers were looking for summer bargains, the post Fourth of July sales, the time fall shopping began—in sweltering heat. Go figure.

At around 2:30, Art's son Alan came in. As usual, he addressed me using my initial—an odd verbal habit of his. "Hey, M. I heard a customer in our store telling her friend you were closing early today. Must be a wedding, huh?"

"That's right. Are you trying to shop for something before I close?"

Alan nodded, but didn't explain. "I need two white carnations and a yellow rose. Can you leave the stems long and put them in a box?"

"Sure." Curiosity got the better of me as I grabbed the flowers out of the cooler. "Do you mind if I ask if the flowers are for a special occasion?"

Whoa! His face and neck turned a rosy shade of red.

"I'm taking Rachel out for a special dinner tonight. It's her twentieth birthday. Dad and MA are taking care of Thomas for her—for us."

"Hey, that sounds like fun. And I know she'll love getting some flowers." I handed him the box tied with Rainbow Gardens ribbon. "Have fun and be safe and all that."

Good grief, I sounded like his mother. But Alan was like me. He'd lost his mother early in life, even earlier than I'd lost mine. As great a dad as Art was, a little fussing over Alan couldn't hurt.

"We will. Gotta run. Crazy with shoppers today." He held

the door open for another group entering Rainbow Gardens.

I waved as he passed the window and asked my new customers if they needed help. They quickly told me they were only browsing.

They scattered to different parts of the shop, and browse they did. As 3:15 rolled around, I turned the lights off in the windows and made a show of cleaning off the workbench, which was already spotlessly clean.

Finally, at 3:30 I needed them to leave or I'd never get changed and over to the chapel on time. "I'm sorry, ladies, but I have to close early today." I pointed to the sign I'd put out in the display area. "I'm delivering flowers for a wedding."

Unimpressed, they slowly filed out of the shop. What had I expected? Maybe catching the contagion of the moment? Didn't everyone love a wedding? Not that I cared, since my primary concern was closing up. I locked the door and flipped the sign. I was officially closed.

Time for a leisurely shower was gone. I practically threw on my clothes and dashed back downstairs. I carefully put the flowers in my van and took off, first to Crossroads and then to the Community Church and Chapel. Once underway, my mood lightened. I wasn't the first car in the parking lot, but I figured maybe the other one belonged to the minister. I took the box to the door of the chapel, prepared to knock. But an older man I didn't know opened it before I got there.

Looking at the box of flowers, he said, "I assume you're Megan. I'm David, JoAnn's other half."

I would have shaken hands with him, but I was carrying precious cargo. "Nice to meet you." I set the box on a small table in the entryway. "Where are the sisters?"

He pointed to a closed door off to the side. "Last minute preparations."

"Have you heard from Matt?" I'd witnessed one situation in which the bride had been forced to face the nightmare of the chapel alone—the groom had never shown or even called. A small twinge of fear had rippled through me over every wedding since. My face must have shown my concern.

"He'll be here. No worries about that," David said.

"Matt's a happy man in love. He's loved her for years, but family pressure kept them apart."

"Yes, so I've heard." I turned at the sound of the side door opening. First JoAnn stepped out, then Nora. JoAnn was beautiful, Nora, stunning.

"Hi, Megan. I see you've met David?" Nora sounded as calm as she looked, as if she were about to head to B and B for coffee. I marveled at her serene energy. And no cane. Maybe that was her wedding gift to herself. She'd never mentioned physical therapy or even a desire to walk without one. But I also noticed that JoAnn had her hand under her elbow.

"Has Matt called?" JoAnn asked.

David checked his phone and shook his head. "No message from him."

The minister walked down the aisle from the front of the chapel. "So, is everyone here?"

Nathan and Lily had come in and were standing with us. Like the other men, Nathan wore a black suit and white shirt. Lily, the youngest of the group, looked sophisticated in a bright paisley dress, its fitted halter top making her look like summer itself.

"Not yet, but we still have a few minutes yet." For the first time Nora looked a little uneasy.

Just then, David's phone beeped. "A text. They're pulling into the parking lot now."

We distributed the flowers and pinned David's boutonniere on his lapel, and by the time we were done, the door behind us opened and an elderly man walked in. At the same time, another door at the front of the chapel opened and Matt came in.

I sent David off with Matt's boutonniere and shooed away the women. "Make yourselves scarce. We don't want Matt to see Nora before the ceremony."

Then I held out my hand. "You must be Gustav Alexander."

He took my outstretched hand. "And you must be Megan. Call me Gus. All my friends do."

"Okay, Gus, hold still. I have a job to do." I stepped forward to pin his flowers on his suit. When he put his hand on my hip, I startled, nearly sticking him with the pin. Then he winked and laughed. "Gotcha."

I took the Unity candle to the front of the church, the last item to be put in place. Finally, the pianist started playing some pre-wedding march music. Matt and David were already in the front with the minister. And JoAnn and Nora came out of the room. After passing Nora's arm to Gus, she said, "Smile, honey. This is the beginning of a wonderful life for you."

I gave Nora her bouquet—a picture of perfection.

I felt dressed up and happy in my turquoise cocktail dress, sleeveless, and with a distinctive handkerchief hem. I'd not told Nora, because it was Matt's secret, but he'd invited me to join them for the ceremony and dinner.

Sending Nora off with Gus, I said, "You're radiant. Today is *yours*."

Nathan grinned and offered me his one arm. Lily already had hold of the other. Just like a big wedding, the three of us walked to the front of the chapel. We all took seats in the front pews. After Gus left Nora with Matt and the minister, he sat next to me.

The photographer intrigued me, primarily because she wore a totally black outfit, from shoes to jacket top. She blended in somehow, even with a small group of people. She never stood out or competed with anyone in the bridal party. Her digital camera never flashed or clicked, so she could take pictures of the ceremony without being at all intrusive. Before volunteering to help with Lily's wedding, I wouldn't have paid any attention, but I happened to have read an article in one of my trade journals that photographers made the top five list of things brides complained about after the fact.

I made a mental note to find out who she was and how well Nora and Matt knew her. From what I could see she managed to stay in the background of a wedding that had almost no guests, so she'd be good for a bigger affair—if her pictures were good, and we'd soon know.

About the time Matt and Nora exchanged their vows Gus reached over and squeezed my hand. He wore a huge smile.

I assumed he had waited a long time for his grandson to marry.

The wedding ended with a traditional kiss, and the rest of us quickly stood and clustered around the couple, knowing there wouldn't be a receiving line. Matt and Nora and the official witnesses went off to handle the paperwork with the minister and the rest of us left the chapel.

I picked up my flower box, the Unity candle, and other supplies and told the group I'd meet them at Crossroads.

"You'll do no such thing," Gus said, coming alongside me. "Matt has a limo for us. We'll pick up your van later. Nathan and Lily can do the same." Like Clayton had once done, Gus put my hand in the bend of his arm.

"Well, okay, but walk me to the van," I said. "I need to store these other supplies, but I can't leave the candle behind."

Gus hung on to the candle while I stored the boxes and grabbed my shawl off the front seat, just in case it was cool in the restaurant. Besides, Georgia had given it to me last Christmas and I was happy for a chance to use it. A classic triangle shape, it had specks of color through the crocheted chains of lace, and the most exquisite sparkling beads sewed on the edges.

Then, boxes dealt with, Gus and I approached the pristine white limo waiting to take us all of five blocks. The driver opened one of the rear doors.

"Let's get a seat before the good ones are taken," Gus said, laughing—and that wink was back. He stood apart from the group and waited for the three of us to climb inside.

"Quick, Megan. You sit next to Nathan and I'll stretch out across the back." Gus was enjoying his own antics. "Ha! The bride and groom can walk."

We could only play along.

When Nora and Matt approached the limo, Matt peeked in and saw his granddad's trick. In a wry tone, he said, "I see the ceremony wore you out."

"Getting you here on time took the starch out of me."

"I'll sit next to Granddad," Nora said.

Gus grinned and sat up, and Nora climbed in next to him.

205

"Poor girl, you married the wrong Alexander."

Nora laughed and then planted a kiss on the back of his hand.

"I guess I'll sit up with the driver," Matt said, playing along.

Gus moved on to his next target, JoAnn, as he switched seats to make room for Matt.

JoAnn laughed. "Hey, I'm hanging on to David for dear life. Looks like Megan is your partner for tonight."

He turned to me with a goofy smirk on his face. "You are?"

"Well, I've had worse dates, believe me," I said.

Having had enough, Matt took charge and told the driver to head to Crossroads.

The driver took a roundabout route to the Square, giving us more time to banter and providing Gus more opportunity to keep us laughing. Talk about a character.

Melanie greeted us at the side door of the Inn and took us to the small private dining room, where the server, Ron, would be right in.

The room was already aglow with lit standing candelabras. Ron and JoAnn took charge of the Unity candle and put it in the middle of the table. I nestled the flower boats close to the base. Then Ron lit the candle, the soft pink hue of the tablecloth adding just the right amount of color. In the far corner of the room a string quartet began to play.

Nora had created her simple and elegant wedding. Watching Lily, I knew she was tucking away impressions, just as I was. Granted, Lily had something else in mind for her big day, but so far, what Nora and Matt planned was working perfectly.

Playing host for the evening, Matt told us to go ahead and sit down while Ron poured the champagne. "I don't think any of us have eaten much today so we'll have them serve dinner soon."

With champagne poured, David picked up his glass first and began the toasts, with Nathan following. Both mentioned how long Matt and Nora had known each other, with Nathan talking about sharing his childhood with both of them. When Nathan raised his glass, he said, "I'm excited we're together again. That *you* are together."

Lily added her well wishes, as Ron topped off our glasses.

Gus pushed back his chair and stood, and the rest of us, except for Matt and Nora, joined him. "Well, now that you young folks have wished this couple good life and happiness, I want to add a few words, and of course, I wish you years of happiness and good health. We have a lot to accomplish in the years ahead and I'm excited to be part of the journey." He raised his glass. "Salute."

A great toast. And an equally great meal followed, with filet mignon as the main course.

Halfway through dinner and looking like she was about to burst, Lily finally made her announcement. "Nathan and I set a date. You're all invited to our wedding, the third weekend in September."

"Save a dance for me," Gus said to Lily.

I had a feeling Gus stayed in perpetual party mode.

The string quartet proved versatile and after we finished eating, Matt led Nora to an empty space between our table and the musicians. "Don't leave us out here alone," Matt said.

Nora seemed to have no trouble slow dancing, and one dance rolled into another and then a third. The rest of us switched partners and I danced with Gus and Nathan and finally, David. By the time we went back to the table, the plates were gone and a small wedding cake sat between Matt and Nora.

"Oh, isn't that lovely." Lily's eyes got big. She looked like she wanted to run her finger across the base and sneak a taste of the frosting. "Did they make it here at Crossroads?"

"Nope. Stephanie's sister, Cindy, makes cakes for every occasion," Nora said. "She also makes that toffee and peanut brittle Steph sells at B and B. She has a disabled son so she needs to work from her home."

"Is her kitchen certified?" Nathan asked.

Nora laughed. "There's a lawyer for you. Always asking about the details. And yes, she has a certified kitchen."

I made a note to remember her name, Cindy Baker. It

would be the first name on my list of wedding cake vendors. About the time Nora picked up the knife to cut the cake the photographer took several candid shots around the table. So far, a photographer and baker. Not bad after only one tiny wedding.

By the time I tasted it, I was a believer. With each mouthful I savored a delicious burst of lemon and almond.

Over coffee, Matt explained why he was *almost* late to the wedding. And the reason circled back to Wolf Creek. "Granddad and I didn't agree with Mom and Dad's decision not to fund the grant for renovating the Wolf Creek museum. But they were only interested in the requests for the larger projects, like a wing on the hospital or a new building for the homeless."

Gus waved his hand in the air. "Short-sighted, I say." He paused. "It's obvious, I suppose, that I don't agree with my son and daughter-in-law on every issue." He pointed to Matt and Nora. "My grandson is one lucky guy to get a woman like Nora to say yes. But all that aside, I have some ideas about the foundation grants, too. We need to preserve the history of the area. If it hadn't been for people fighting for this historic Square in the first place, we'd be sitting in some indoor mall and these historic buildings would all be gone."

Matt laughed. "Granddad's right on all accounts, so we decided to form a separate foundation for small projects, which will take nothing away from the big ones. We decided that the renovation money for the Wolf Creek museum will be our first grant."

I jumped right into his announcement. "Wow! Have you told Sarah yet?"

"Both she and Sadie Winston know," Matt said. "I called Sarah on the way to the ceremony. Sadie is being hired to sort and catalog."

"Who else knows?" Lily asked.

"No one else," Gus said. "We're still fooling with details in the document. So no spreading the word yet."

"This is a pretty big deal, Matt." Nathan leaned forward, his expression thoughtful and curious. "Gotta name for this venture?"

Matt laughed. "Oh, yeah. Granddad and I must have been tired because we came up with the Gus and Matt Foundation—GMF."

"Sounds like a morning TV show," Gus added. "I think we should switch it around and make it the Matt and Gus Foundation—MGF." He pointed across the table. "Besides, it was his idea."

"Whatever we call it, there's more. We've also decided to launch this venture in Wolf Creek."

Nora's eyes grew huge. "Really?" She looked over at me.

Maybe her dream to work in a flower shop was closer to reality.

Gus held up his cup for Matt to refill. "I bought the Sorenson house for us to live in."

"That old, broken down relic," I blurted. "It belonged to some old wheat baron decades ago."

"Precisely." Gus' eyes drilled into me. No humor in them, either.

Oops. They were willing to put their money into preserving the history of my hometown, and that included a falling down mansion.

"I'm sorry," I said, tapping Gus' hand. I sure didn't want to end the day with some kind of breach of etiquette. "I'm actually glad someone is finally doing something with the house. It's always been a bit of an eyesore, which is why I reacted." I paused, but not for long. Time for a change of subject.

"As a matter of fact, I also have a piece of news for Matt and Nora." I fidgeted with the edges of the napkin in my lap. "I'd like Nora to work regularly at Rainbow Gardens as soon as she can. The Square is much busier than any of us expected. With weddings and the festivals I can't do it alone anymore. We can always work out the number of days and hours as we go along."

"Are you sure?" Nora clapped her hands. "Oh, Matt, did you hear that? It's my dream come true." She gestured to me. "I can be there on Monday. Name the time."

The rest of us laughed, which was good for me and erased any leftover tension from my earlier remark about Gus' relic.

"No honeymoon?" Lily asked.

Nora rested her hand on Matt's. "We decided to wait and go somewhere warm in the winter."

"And since we need a lawyer on board," Matt said, "we're hoping you'll fill that need, Nathan."

"Of course," Nathan spoke with conviction, as if he'd been waiting to be asked anyway. "I'll make time."

Matt asked David to bring his accounting firm into the foundation board, and maybe consider opening a satellite office in Wolf Creek.

JoAnn laughed. "Since I want to be closer to Nora, maybe we can move to Wolf Creek, too."

David took JoAnn's hand in his and said, "Lots to consider."

"What role are you playing in this venture, Gus?" Nathan asked.

Gus tapped the table. "I'm glad you asked. I figure I can develop the oral history part of the project, you know, conducting interviews with long time residents. It's a big part of historical preservation these days. It started with tapes, but now most historical society projects have added videos. We need to get right on that for Wolf Creek. After all, nobody lasts forever."

Nathan added that his dad, Richard Connor, was busy putting together an online class about Wisconsin laws to help people set up trusts, write wills, and create leases. "Since he's working with the communication department at the university, maybe you'd want to talk to him about producing videos that are both entertaining and educational. Maybe you can get him involved. He sure likes talking to people."

Gus nodded, and jotted notes in a spiral pocket notebook he took from his inside pocket.

"I've got something to add," Lily said, beaming at Nora and Matt. "As a welcome to Wolf Creek and to celebrate your wedding, Nathan and I gave you the flowers as our gift to you. Megan's kept our secret."

Nora reached out to touch her bouquet. "Thank you. Coming from our friends, that's really special."

"By the way, Nora created her own bouquet," I said, "and she gave me the idea to offer that opportunity to other brides, not that everyone will want to take me up on that, but it's another item on my menu of services."

Ron came by with another carafe of coffee, and as a group we relaxed as the conversation became focused on the town and our businesses. Gus sat back in his chair and loosened his tie. As if following his lead, Matt, Nathan, and David did the same. We were winding down, but no one was quite ready to leave yet.

"So, here's another idea," Gus said. "I've known her all of a few hours, but I can already tell that Megan knows this community better than any of us. I think she should be on our board of directors. The museum is preserving the past, but the young women in town, like Megan and Lily, and many others, represent the future."

That was a stunner. "Me? But I know nothing about how a foundation runs."

"You'll learn. Please say yes." Nora was a radiant bride, but she was also a no-nonsense woman operating in persuasion mode. She looked like a younger version of Sarah.

"So, try it. Give us three months," Gus said, his eyes teasing me. "You look at us, and we'll look at you and see if it's a match."

I raised my hands in surrender. "Okay, okay."

There was a round of applause. But I had to ask myself if I could do everything I'd agreed to. Granted, Nora was already mostly trained, and she was a quick study anyway. But I'd taken on the role as Lily's wedding planner, and now I'd be sitting on a board of a new foundation. I laughed at myself. I'd always assumed people who served on boards were old and stodgy. And now *I* was one of them.

Yikes! I could just hear Eli's comment when he heard the news. And somehow, almost like a little voice in my head, step by step, I had committed more deeply to my hometown. Not winning the contest had given my decision finality, and now I was making good on the choice I'd made.

Sensing we'd soon be ready to call it a night, Matt asked

the quartet to play some dance music and we gathered on the dance floor and rotated partners until Matt and Nora ended up together again. We stepped back, laughing and clapping as the evening ended.

Matt and Nora thanked us for coming, and Gus faked a huge yawn and joked about it being way past his bedtime.

Nathan and David agreed to fetch the cars in the morning, and after handing over the key to my van, we drifted off in our separate directions.

As Nathan and Lily walked across the Square with me and we approached Rainbow Gardens, the three of us noticed bright lights shining in Clayton's studio.

"He's working hard to reestablish himself, isn't he?" Nathan asked. "I suppose it's pretty hard to make a comeback after being stripped of your pride and your career."

Nathan was cautious of his words, I noted, probably because both his own father, Richard Connor, and Lily, his bride-to-be, had burned a few bridges and caused a stir or two in years past. But Lily had forged ahead and was now on her own path to happiness. Richard had mended fences with Nathan, allowing the two to repair a badly broken bond.

Lily interrupted my thoughts. "I'll bring the wedding planner book over as soon as it comes in. Then we can set up a meeting on a night that works for everyone." She snuggled up to Nathan. "I've got the jitters already."

Nathan, calm and in fake lawyerly mode, rolled his eyes. Only I saw it. But I knew planning their wedding was going to be Fun, with a capital F.

"Well," I said, "the evening was more than a wedding. Nora, Matt, and Gus. They're bringing big changes to the Square with them."

"And a lot more work for each of us." Nathan chimed in. "I say, bring it on."

I waved and they continued down the Square. Meanwhile, I was tired, maybe dead tired, but definitely not ready to end the day. Before I'd even gone upstairs, I had an impulse and acted on it. I dialed Clayton.

"Hello." His crisp voice sent a shiver through me.

I wanted to be in his arms. "I saw your lights on when

I was coming back from Crossroads. Unlock the upstairs door. I'm on my way over." I disconnected before he could say no.

19

I went out the back and let the starlight guide me up the outside stairs that led to his studio apartment. I called out his name as I knocked.

He opened the door. Maybe I'd had too much champagne, but I laughed out loud. A big, hearty laugh, too. He looked like a clown. Paint covered his face, his hands, and definitely his shirt. And what was that black stuff on his fingers?

"Busy?" Now that he stood in front of me I didn't know what else to say. Finally I came up with, "You need a break." I stepped inside and kicked my heels off, conscious of him watching me.

I meandered over to the easel, where I noticed he'd highlighted the painted flower with black lines. The flower jumped off the paper. Not that his other paintings weren't good, but this one was dynamic. "Wow. Where'd you learn that trick?"

"From you. Remember the sketch you smudged with dirt when we were at the farmhouse? I didn't forget the impact that black had on my drawing. So I've added black ink accents to the paintings."

"Works for me, but what do I know about buyers and critics?"

"You're the first to see it." He put his brush in some kind of jar with murky looking fluid.

"Come here, Clayton. Sit with me and I'll tell you about the wonderful day I've had." I pulled him to the couch and pushed him into the corner. Boldly, brashly, I stretched out and put my head on his thigh. He picked up my hand and laced his fingers with mine.

I started at the beginning with Nora creating her own wedding flowers, and her suggestion about offering that experience to other women. I went on to tell him about Nora and Matt being childhood friends, now married and deeply in love. What joy I saw in their faces when they looked at each other.

I chattered on about Lily asking me to be her wedding planner, giggling when I admitted I had no idea what a wedding planner did.

"Trial by fire," Clayton said, managing to get in a few words when I stopped talking long enough to reposition myself.

"Yup. Trial by fire." I'd run out of steam, but was too comfortable to get up and go home. I'd wanted to be with Clayton and here I was.

The last thing I heard was, "Pleasant dreams, my love." I felt the soft wool of an afghan against my skin.

"Megan, time to wake up." Clayton's voice roused me.

Clayton?

I opened my eyes, then shut them tight against the bright sunlight filling the room. Where was I?

Then I remembered coming to his place and not going home. So, still dressed up for a fun party, I was stretched out on his couch. I hadn't slept that well in a long time, but my head rang like wedding bells.

"Maybe this will help." He held two tablets in his hand and a small glass of water in the other. "Works for me when I've had a little too much champagne."

I didn't object. "I smell coffee. What time is it?"

He grinned. "Early enough to get ready for another day of tourists tramping in and out of your shop."

I had a lovely thought and shared it. "I'm going to take a day off soon. I was dead sober when I asked Nora to work at Rainbow Gardens. And not just random days here and there, either, like she's been doing. We're going to schedule regular hours. It was my wedding gift to her."

Clayton frowned, obviously puzzled. "You gave her a job as a wedding gift?"

"Well, when you put it that way it does sound kind of odd, but I'll tell you about it another time."

By now I was on my feet—bare feet—and standing at the kitchen counter sipping delicious coffee. "My van is at the chapel, but Nathan is arranging to bring it to me. Did I mention the limo?"

He shook his head.

"My mind has finally kicked in, Clayton. I'll fill in the blanks eventually. But for now, I need to go home, change clothes, be ready for Nathan when he brings my van, and open my door to the world."

"Anything I can do to help?" he asked.

"Not a thing, except hope for a quiet day. Meanwhile, I need to move around and get my blood circulating. See you later." I gave him a quick kiss and grabbed my shoes on the way out.

❀ ❀ ❀

I managed to change my clothes before Nathan knocked on the back door to let me know he'd delivered my van. So, only Clayton would ever know I'd slept in my fancy turquoise dress. By the time I'd wolfed down a carton of yogurt and half a bagel, the Square was buzzing with people. But I took a few seconds to text Clayton: *Love the new painting.*

My first customer needed a funeral arrangement for Tuesday. Reality hit. Bummer. Not every day brought an upbeat, love-finds-a-way wedding. And so my work began.

My mood went back on the upswing when Georgia stopped in late in the morning and brought a box lunch for each of us.

"I took a chance you'd be free for a spur-of-the-moment lunch," she said.

"And I am. What a welcome break. I've got weddings on my mind constantly these days, so I'm happy to see a bride."

I set us up at the table in the back while we munched turkey sandwiches and homemade B and B chips and rehashed some of the town's news. Mostly, Georgia talked about working with her wedding planner, someone a Country Law client had recommended. But Georgia said she and the planner had a different concept for her wedding. Elliot was no help, since his position was to let Georgia handle the situation.

I listened without interrupting, filing away a tidbit here and an impression there. This was a sneak preview of my role as planner for Lily's wedding. I needed to listen to the bride, and groom, with a wide open mind. I was helping them put together their day, not mine.

Right. As if I'd ever be a bride.

Before Georgia left she asked me to come to the farmhouse after the shops closed. She had something to show me, and like the paralegal she was, always walking around with facts about things she couldn't share, she didn't give away so much as a tiny hint about what it was I'd see. Curious, I agreed.

"On second thought," she said. "No need to take two cars. I'll pick you up." As she approached the door to leave, she added, "And wear old clothes."

Now I was impatient, wondering what she was going to show me.

Georgia left through the front door just as a group of older women came in. They were already chatting amongst themselves, obviously women who knew each other well.

"Oh, look at this," one of the women said, holding up a ceramic owl.

I'd long ago relegated it to be in the basement forever because the owl's face had been designed to show an angry expression. That wasn't something I wanted in my shop, but I'd pulled it out for the yellow dot sale and hoped it would move out fast. Funny, whimsical, happy? Yes. But no angry owls.

"Looks like Brian," the woman holding the ceramic bird said loud enough for everyone to hear. Apparently, these women knew who Brian was and agreed the owl bore some kind of resemblance to him, most likely the expression. They all thought that reference was hysterically funny, so this Brian person must have been known as a grouch. One of the woman's companions held up another object and made comic remarks—or at least the other women reacted as if they were pretty funny comments.

Their playfulness boosted my spirits. I'd always enjoyed watching the camaraderie of groups of women, younger and older, out for the afternoon or the day. By the time they finished looking around at all the shelves and into the corners, each had an item for me to wrap and bag. That lifted my spirits even more.

Restocking the displays ate up a couple of additional hours. Tom's idea of removing the cupboard doors to highlight the vases and colorful pottery had worked out well. Using another of his suggestions, I kept a few spools of unusual ribbons scattered around the display area.

Business hours over, I heard Georgia's car horn beep from the back. I was almost finished tying my old sneakers, the ones I usually wore to weed the gardens. I frowned when I saw a hole in the toe of one shoe, but they had molded to my feet and were comfortable, way more important than style.

I locked the back door and slid into the passenger's seat. "Okay, mystery lady, drive on."

Georgia was going to be my sister-in-law, another woman in the family at last, and we'd already formed a bond of the kind only women understood. After six years of estrangement resulting from various family crises and secrets, Georgia had reunited with her sister, Beverly, and with Elliot.

During the short drive to the farmhouse she chatted about her wedding vision. "Just think, you're only a bride for one day," Georgia said with a nervous laugh. "Shouldn't that one day be perfect—no disasters to mar the memories?"

"So, you want to tell me the real problem?" I asked.

"I need to fire my wedding planner."

There, she said it. I didn't know about her, but I felt better hearing her come out with what had been weighing on her mind.

"There is no way *I'm* going to have the kind of wedding *she* wants for herself." She slapped the steering wheel. "Lily told me you're going to be her wedding planner. Would you be mine, too?"

We had pulled up next to the farmhouse by then, giving me no chance to think about or respond to what she asked.

She parked just beyond the gardens. "Come on. Let's go this way." She led me past the house and down the pathway to the barn.

I saw Elliot's truck parked there, but that wasn't unusual if he was helping the farmer that rented the barn load bales of hay. Then I heard a horse's whinny.

Georgia grinned, although she tried not to. When she took off running, I followed right behind. Two beautiful brown mares were penned at the far end of the barn.

"Aren't they something?" Georgia put her arms on the railing.

"When? How? Why?" I mirrored her and leaned on the fence.

"Elliot gave me a horse as a wedding gift." She snorted a short laugh. "Then he had to buy one for himself."

"I didn't know you liked to ride."

"We rode last summer when we went to Door County and haven't stopped talking about how much we enjoyed it. He probably thinks this is the best way to keep me quiet." She laughed again. "Wait 'til I keep after him to ride with me." She looked beyond the open doors across the pasture. "See those flags in the ground over there?"

I looked in the direction she pointed. "Yes, I see them."

"Our new house. Next spring." Another radiant smile crossed her face.

"Wow, big changes. I'm so happy for you and Elliot. It's still hard to believe it's taken so many years for you two to be together. But you're sure making the most of it."

"I look at it like wine. The best has aged the longest."

I nodded to the horses. "Have you ridden them?"

"We're letting them get acquainted with their new surroundings first. Maybe next week."

Georgia and I moved toward the sound of men's voices.

Elliot's laughter was distinct against the other man's voice.

"Hi, honey. Megan," Elliot said. "We just finished loading Bud's wagon." Georgia stood next to Elliot, and he lifted his arm to rest across her shoulders.

Bud Shillkey nodded to me and to Georgia. "Time for me to get going. I want to be home before dark. Hate driving these roads with a big load after sunset." He climbed into his truck and waved as he pulled away.

"Well, little sister, what do you think?" Elliot asked, beaming. "Lots of changes coming to the homestead now, and more in the spring."

"I'm happy for both of you. Horses and a house!" I tilted my head and flashed a phony disapproving look. "Whatever will the neighbors think?"

Mentioning the neighbors brought to mind the Peterson sisters. "Speaking of neighbors, have you seen or heard from Katie or Tracie since they opened their shop?" I asked.

Elliot brushed the hay off his jeans and shirt. "Almost every day they stop in to pick up supper from the deli just before we close. They're a nice addition to the Square." He gave Georgia a kiss and got into his truck. He offered us a ride, but Georgia said no.

"We've got girl talk to finish," Georgia said."

He eased ahead and pulled in next to Georgia's car. Then he bounded up the steps and into the house.

"You surprised me," I said, as we walked back to her car, "with both the horses and the house plans."

"I couldn't be happier, Megan. And you and Eli know I'll take good care of Elliot." She shrugged. "He'll do the same for me."

"I never doubted it. I'm not concerned about Elliot, not for a second. But I think Eli is already feeling a little lost. Probably like a part of him has gone missing. That might last a while."

"Well, he's welcome in our house anytime. You, too."

"Being Eli's little sister has had its challenges, but even though he grouches around all the time, he has a good heart."

She laughed in understanding. "Between you and me, I've had a few challenges with him myself." We stood on either side of her car talking over the roof. "I love Elliot. I always have."

"You're a very lucky lady."

She nodded. Georgia was nobody's fool. She knew exactly how fortunate she was to have worked things out with Elliot, and put old adolescent misunderstandings behind them. It was almost scary to think that they might have blown their chance and never known this kind of happiness.

Unbidden, and not particularly welcome, the image of Clayton drifted through my mind. His painting, his kiss, and his tender expression when he called me "Sweetheart." I pushed my confusing thoughts of him back and out of the way.

Our drive home was quick and easy. We exchanged stories about the increase in visitors on the Square and how even Nathan and Jack were surprised by the number of new clients at Country Law. She pulled in behind Rainbow Gardens to drop me off. "We wanted you to know about the horses and our house plans before word got out to everybody else on the Square."

"I'm glad you did. Otherwise I would have seemed unaware about what was up for the two of you if other people started talking about it." I got out and stepped back for her to leave.

"Megan?"

Sensing what was coming, I bent down to look at her through the open window.

"Will you consider being my wedding planner?"

I hesitated, searching for the right way to answer her. "I've got a lot on my plate at the moment, but I'm not saying no. Give me a few days to decide." It was hard to explain how busy my days were going to be very soon. Lily wasn't ready for her big announcement yet, and I wasn't free to talk about it.

"I understand," Georgia said. "Call me when you make up your mind."

Somehow I already knew my answer.

20

Mondays were slow days on the Square, even during the busy part of the summer, so I assumed it would be a great day for Nora to start. As I expected, she arrived at opening time, eager to learn everything in one day. But every time I started to explain this or that detail about the business, shoppers arrived.

Sarah stopped in around 11:00, breathless and with her phone at her ear. "Another bus?" She waved her hand as if debating her answer. "How can I say no?" She waited a beat, "Yes, right. I'll notify everyone that you're coming." She ended the call. "You heard. They're on their way and ready to shop."

I watched her leave and stop in the middle of the Square, presumably to send a text to the shops that another bus was arriving soon.

"Not much time to make you more familiar with the shop, today. Like my friend said, it'll be a trial by fire."

"I'll manage," Nora said. "It'll be fun."

And it was. Nora had an easy manner with the customers, laughing in all the right places, asking all the right questions. I quickly created some requested arrangements, and then we stood together watching as two women argued over the same elf statue.

"I had no idea that elves would be such in-demand garden art," Nora joked, busying her hands as she straightened the display area.

She stood back and pointed to the open spaces on many of the shelves. "Is there stock somewhere that I could put out?"

"Hmm… We don't want those holes," I agreed. "I'll bring some boxes up from the basement. This has been the summer of using up stock, some of it fairly old. I had some slow years and stashed some pieces away. But that will be our secret."

"My lips are sealed," she said with a grin.

I hurried to the basement and carried three boxes of assorted merchandise upstairs. With only a few boxes left downstairs I made a mental note to reorder more stock this week.

Back upstairs during a lull in traffic, Nora leafed through one of the books I'd used as samples for the floral contest. "Take that home if you'd like. Look through it, then put it back on the table if you don't want it."

"I will. Thanks."

"One of the perks of being an employee."

I showed Nora how I priced new stock and tracked it on the computer. She also made a few creative adjustments to a couple of displays. Once again, I noticed she was quick and efficient, much like Tom.

"I almost forgot something," I said, just before she left. "Tracie brought a bag of yarn for you and some books. Wait just a second and I'll run up and get it."

I remembered where I'd put it, so it took only a minute to grab the Fiber Barn bag and bring it downstairs.

I looked on as Nora, smiling broadly, pulled the yarn from the bag and put it into a Rainbow Gardens bag.

"A bag from this store won't arouse curiosity," she said. "This sweater I'm attempting is a big secret." She put her index finger over her lips and hurried out, the bell jingling as the door swung shut.

I locked up and flipped my sign. We were officially closed for the day.

Not quite home free, though. Once again, I spotted Lily running across the Square, calling out, "Megan, Megan. Wait."

I reopened the door.

"It came this afternoon." She handed me a book and told me it was known as the "quick study bible" for wedding planners. Her grin was more like that of a young girl than a woman about to be married. "And I brought this." She handed me an oversized book, an illustrated *Cinderella*. "You can study the pictures."

"I'll study both books before we meet next."

"Would Thursday evening be okay with you?" Lily asked.

I checked my calendar. For show. My dismal lack of a social life during these busy months left most every evening open. "Sure, Thursday night is open."

"Great. I'll let the others know. Will you come to my house?"

I nodded, tapping the cover of *Cinderella*. "I'll bring both books along."

Lily's phone rang and she waved good-bye. I locked the door a second time and went upstairs.

For the next three days Nora and I were swamped. Orders, shoppers—buyers, really—kept us moving from the time we opened until we closed. Given Nora's affinity for the work, I set her free to experiment with samples for the cooler. On her own, she reached the same conclusion I had about arrangements that hadn't moved after two days, and she set about taking them apart and redoing them with some changes, different flowers, a new container, or both.

"It's all about trial and error," I said. I heard Clayton's voice say, "Trial by fire." That, too. He hadn't been wrong.

Alone in my apartment in the evenings, I studied the wedding planner handbook, and dozed off after reading *Cinderella* as a bedtime story.

Meanwhile, I barely saw Clayton, but we exchanged texts two or three times a day. He was amazed at the tourist traffic, which gave me ample opportunity to tease him about how exciting life in a small town could be.

On Thursday, during a lull in traffic, Nora sat at the table sipping a bottle of water and grabbing a break when she could. "I never believed it would be so busy. And all day long!"

I'd wondered if standing for long stretches of time would be difficult, but she'd never mentioned needing a breather. "Be honest," I said. "Is there too much standing for you?" I rested my hip on the stool by the workbench to get a minute off my feet.

"Not really. Besides, it's so much fun hurrying around to help one customer and then running off to the next. I'm learning so much already."

I glanced around, double-checking that we were alone in the shop. "And more opportunities might be just around the corner." I paused. "This isn't public information yet, so I'd prefer you not to mention this to anyone, well, except Matt, I guess. I've agreed to be the wedding planner for Lily Winters and Georgia Winters." Not that I'd told Georgia yet, but I would, now that I'd said it out loud. "Lily is marrying Nathan in September and Georgia, Lily's aunt, is marrying my brother in October."

"Wow! You *will be* busy." She playfully shook her index finger at me. "Don't forget. Gus and Matt will be asking for some of your time, too."

I buried my face in my hands and shook my head back and forth.

"Back to the fun. What kind of weddings will they be?" Nora made circles on the table with her bottle.

"Lily wants a Cinderella wedding. I'm meeting her and her mom and Georgia tonight to begin planning it—I guess she'll have to define it for me first. I don't think I can come up with mice as footmen. Maybe a pumpkin coach, though." I grinned.

"Tonight? You're starting *tonight?* For September?" She let out a hoot of a laugh. "It's one thing to order dinner for eight, buy a dress, and order some flowers. I got that taken care of in no time. But a big extravaganza two months from now? You must be kidding."

"Oh, your skepticism is showing! But I know I can make it happen." I shrugged. "I'll move heaven and earth for that girl. Someday I'll tell you Lily's whole story."

"And Georgia? What kind of shindig does she want?"

"I don't really know. She's been working with a planner,

but they turned out to be incompatible for some reason. Georgia is cancelling that contract, and I've decided to go ahead and take over. She asked me on Sunday, and I'll let her know my answer later today."

"All I can say is, lucky for you I'm here to help."

I laughed at her wonderfully mocking tone. Then, as if on cue, the bell on the door jingled as it opened.

"There's Georgia now. I'll introduce you." I stood to greet her, but motioned for Nora to stay seated.

"Not so busy today?" Georgia asked.

"Just a much-needed lull. We've been crazy busy." I pointed back to Nora, who waved to Georgia, and then I introduced them. "Georgia Winters, Nora Alexander. Nora will be in the shop several days a week through the holidays."

"*Alexander?* Are you related to Matthew and Gustav?" Georgia asked.

Nora's face lit up. "My husband and grandfather-in-law."

"Their names are familiar, from Country Law business." She couldn't say more, but we all understood she was talking about the foundation.

"So, I was telling Nora I've agreed to be your wedding planner."

Georgia grinned and gave me a quick hug. "I had a feeling you'd say yes."

Nora stood and joined us at the workbench. "What *flavor* wedding are you having?"

Georgia laughed at the characterization. "Simple, fun, hometown. We want a big tent in the Square so everyone can come. Tables and chairs for an open-air dinner. Music handled by a DJ. Flowers from the gardens at the farmhouse."

"I should be writing all this down," I said.

"No need. I'll get you copies of the workbook I filled out for the other planner."

Workbook? I'd seen mention of that in the planners' book Lily gave me, but hadn't gotten to the sample pages yet.

Georgia glanced at her watch. "I need to get back to the office, but I stopped in to ask you if you could come for dinner tonight. Lily ordered chicken salad platters for us from Crossroads. We can throw out ideas while we eat."

"I won't have time to eat if I'm madly making notes about everything."

Georgia and Nora laughed, in that knowing way women have.

"You'll manage," Georgia said. "With all of us there nothing will be overlooked."

"Right," I said. "But isn't my job as the wedding planner to see that no details are missed?"

I never got a response, because a cluster of people filed in, and Georgia quickly left. Rainbow Gardens was quickly back into the business of being one of the busiest shops on Wolf Creek Square.

The afternoon flew by. We packaged up sales, replenished displays, and answered questions. All the while, Nora hummed along with whatever music I'd loaded into the CD player.

"You're welcome to change the music," I said. "I've heard it so often that I don't realize it's on. Thank goodness it shuts itself off."

"It's new to me so I'm enjoying it." She stepped forward to greet a new customer.

"I'm going to the basement, Nora. We need more stock." I chuckled to myself, thinking of how often I'd needed to restock shelves in the last few weeks.

Most of the time I managed to quash thoughts of Clayton, although I enjoyed our texts—it was almost as if we had a secret relationship. Still, I made heroic efforts to characterize us as nothing more than casual business friends. A few texts and a quick dinner now and then, a handful of visits. Too bad my efforts weren't working.

True, the way we communicated had shifted slightly since the night of Nora's wedding. Things seemed a little easier between us, even though we'd had few face-to-face conversations. It was clear he wasn't willing to get any closer. As much as he was on my mind, I wouldn't push myself onto someone not ready, or willing, to reciprocate my feelings.

All this was going through my mind as I brought up a couple of additional boxes for Nora to unpack. I made yet another mental note to place another order. And fast. My odd procrastination would cost me money with the extra charge for Express shipping if I didn't act soon. But the big boost in business on the Square, the surge in tourist traffic, seemed almost too good to be true and held me back. I needed to get over my fear of over-ordering, though, if I was going to wring every ounce of profit out of this busy season. And pay Nora's salary.

Nora was like a child in a Christmas toy-land when she opened the boxes I stacked up on the table. More elves, more frogs, another grouchy owl. Had I really ordered two? She also unpacked three pottery bowls shaped and colored to look like pumpkins.

"Is it too early to put out fall items?" Nora asked.

Tilting my head back and forth, I said, "I'm not sure. In the past I waited for August, but at Quilts Galore, Marianna is running a Christmas in July sale all month."

"Why don't I put them out and we'll see if they sell."

"Works for me." I managed to grab my phone when it rang and balanced the box on my knee.

"Hi, Megan." Clayton's voice was upbeat and energized. "Sorry I didn't respond to your last text. I've been talking business with Gretchen all morning. Uh, was there something special you needed?"

I need you to say you love me.

"Oh, I was just updating you on what we're doing over here. I'm working with Lily this evening. We'll be planning her wedding."

"How'd you get involved in that, besides doing the flowers, I mean?"

"Well, that's my news. I agreed to be her wedding planner."

"Big job, Megan," he said, without a hint of surprise, "but you'll do an ace job."

I heard a beep on his phone.

"Another call. Gotta go."

That was that. Our call was disconnected before I could

say good-bye. I made a face at my phone, feeling slighted by the quick brush off.

Seriously? Wasn't I being a little high schoolish? He was rebuilding his career and running a gallery. Only last week, I'd cut short a call from him myself.

By the time the last customers left, it was 5:30. Nora made an attempt to straighten the display areas, but stopped. "Why don't I come in early tomorrow and put the new stock out as I make some order of this." Her arms arched around the room.

"If you'd like, but I don't expect you to work more than you agreed to."

She smiled. "Putting things to right helps me learn what's in the shop. And that makes it easier to help the customers."

"Sure, but we won't make a habit of early hours. Next week, though, I will want you to meet me at B and B early so I can introduce you to the other shopkeepers on the Square. A regular group of owners and employees gather there before the shops open."

"I'd like that, especially since we'll be official members of the community soon." She laughed. "Matt wants to move now. Like yesterday. He's all wrapped up in the museum project and being involved with the renovation. Foundations usually just provide the money."

"I think Wolf Creek is the real benefactor."

She waved when she pulled the door closed. And the bell made its happy sound.

I finished closing up and ran upstairs to change into light-weight pants and a cool cotton blouse. Then I gathered the books and a notebook in a Rainbow Gardens tote bag and hurried out.

Georgia had inherited her uncle's home last year after his death, and when she convinced Lily to return to Wolf Creek, she offered her a place to stay. The house was only two blocks off the Square so I decided to walk. Working in the shop on my feet all day wasn't the same as stretching my legs. Even breathing the fresh air during the short walk felt good.

Lily met me at the door before I rang the bell. Her

appearance shocked me, though. Rather than a happy bride, she looked like she might burst into tears.

Skipping past a greeting, I said, "What's the matter?"

"There's not going to be a wedding." Tears welled in her eyes and she turned and stalked away.

21

I stepped into Georgia's house. Since two cars were in the driveway and one was parked on the street, I assumed Georgia was home and Beverly had already arrived. I walked toward the voices, which took me through the living room and past a large table in the dining room. Lily sat down between Beverly and Georgia at the small table in the kitchen.

Georgia offered iced tea, and I said yes, simply to break the silence and have something to do. I took the last open chair and bought some time taking the books out of the tote and putting them on the floor next to my chair. Georgia came back with the tea and I used up another few seconds taking a couple of gulps.

In a shaky voice, Lily said, "I'm sorry to waste your time, Megan, but there will be no wedding."

My mind tangled with all the reasons weddings were cancelled, and came up with the obvious. The bride or groom called the whole thing off. But that didn't ring true. I assumed this had something to do with Toby and a complicated past. The little boy was Lily's birth son, and Nathan's brother and sister-in-law had adopted him. Not long after, the couple had been killed, and Nathan was awarded guardianship. Nathan left his father's law firm to become a partner at Country Law and Lily returned home to Wolf Creek. It seemed like a miracle that Lily was able to donate one of her kidneys to Toby, but when Nathan and Lily fell in love, we had our own magical story on the Square.

"So, I'm at a loss here, Lily," I said. "Are you going to

tell me what happened?"

A short burst of laughter followed. "There's no place in town for us to be married. We only have a couple of ministers in town who could marry us, and they're busy every weekend in September. Then Melanie broke the news that the private rooms at Crossroads are booked through New Year's Day." She used hers finger to countdown her points.

"Is that all?" My heart beat in relief. "I thought you and Nathan…or Toby."

Lily looked shocked. "Oh, no, nothing like that. We're good. But Toby wanted to carry the rings and now he'll be disappointed. How will I explain a delay to him?"

"Not so fast," I said. Acting as if I knew what I was doing, I added, "I agreed to be your wedding planner. That means it's my job to make lemonade out of lemons."

That brought a laugh, of sorts, from everyone, and released the tension that had built with Lily's overly dramatic attitude.

I reached down and grabbed the planner book and my notebook and put them on the table, where we could see them. I spread out photocopied pages from the calendar for July, August, and September.

I grabbed my phone and speed-dialed Sarah. "Are you busy right now?" I asked, pausing to wait for her answer. "Come to Georgia's house as fast as you can. We're in wedding disaster management and need your help."

Hearing that Sarah was joining us, Georgia went about creating a fifth chicken salad platter by taking a spoonful from each of four she already had. Pretty ingenious. Beverly moved the place settings and basket of breadsticks to the dining room table where we'd have more room to spread out. Staying busy eliminated the need to make conversation.

A few minutes later, Beverly let Sarah in and explained the dilemma. "So, as it stands, they want to get married in September, but we don't have a minister or reception site available until January. And they want the wedding here in Wolf Creek."

"Busy little town we've created," Sarah observed.

"Too busy," Lily whispered under her breath.

"Let's eat," Georgia said, "while Sarah digests all these various pieces of the problem."

Sarah groaned at Georgia's pun, which immediately lightened the atmosphere.

"So, how many guests?" Sarah asked.

Lily frowned, looking uncertain. "We can't be precise, but family, the shopkeepers and employees on the Square, plus Nathan's friends and associates add up to close to 100, maybe a few more."

A large number, and not at all what I'd assumed. That was about the limit at Crossroads, anyway.

Sarah chewed another bite of salad, holding her fork poised in the air. When she put the fork down, she picked up her phone and began scrolling.' "Okay, the only place I can think of is the Community Center."

"Yuck! That old building."

Well, Lily, tell us what you really think.

Sarah raised her hand in defeat, but her body language said she was still in the game. "According to my calendar, on the date you prefer, the middle-school has it reserved until 2:00."

I quickly opened the Cinderella book to the wedding illustration showing arches and garden gates as the backdrop. "What if we could make the center look like this?" I turned the book to show everyone. "Remember the Harvest Festival last year? Didn't look like a big, old building to me."

"How can I forget?" Lily blushed, apparently a little embarrassed. "It was beautiful."

Nathan had proposed to her that evening, and in front of half of the town.

"Have you thought about an evening wedding?" I asked. "If the school is out by 2:00, we can have it ready by 5:00."

A smile crossed Lily's face. She was back in planning mode. "Wedding at 6:00. I can see the men in their gray tuxes and tails. Lots of fairy lights." She stretched her arm to point to the prince in his long coat.

I stepped into my role as planner. "Let me call the minister you want. If he has objections, I'm sure Nathan or Richard knows a justice or judge who would be willing to officiate."

"Your dress?" With her authoritative tone, Sarah had moved into planning committee demeanor now, and as we all knew, Sarah was familiar with being in charge. Then she grinned at me. "Oops, sorry." She grabbed a breadstick and took a big bite, effectively relinquishing the lead.

Beverly pointed to the Cinderella book. "Virgie and I are making the dress. We'll need to borrow that book for the design."

"Oh, Mom, you don't need to copy it out of a book—you and Virgie can do your own design."

Beverly laughed. "Never in a million years did I believe I'd be making your wedding dress." She reached across the table and squeezed Lily's hand.

They were close now, but for years, Lily and Beverly had been estranged. It had taken Toby's health crisis and Lily donating a kidney to bring about their reconciliation, but at least it happened. Later that night, Elliot asked Georgia to marry him. Yes, it had been quite a festival.

Before I became completely lost in the magical memories of the previous fall, I had to get us back on track. "And what about food?"

Shrugging shoulders, shaking heads. "Okay, I'll check on that." I made a note to talk to Lily about a finger food buffet instead of a sit down dinner for over 100 people.

I checked my list of topics for this evening's meeting.

"Invitations, Lily?" I asked. "How soon can you finalize your list? Once we nail down the location, you can get them ready."

Lily didn't answer, but instead, frowned at Beverly before saying anything. "Speaking of the invitations, are you okay with being included on them with Richard Connor?"

Beverly nodded. "Sure. We're friends now."

That was another complicated family situation, which had apparently been hashed through.

We moved on to the issue of attendants, and by the time we were done, it was decided Georgia would be the only bridesmaid, and Beverly would enjoy being the mother-of-the-bride.

"If it hadn't been for Georgia, I wouldn't be in Wolf Creek with my son—or Nathan." Lily reached over and squeezed Georgia's hand.

Lily explained that Nathan was asking his law partner, Jack Pearson, to be his groomsman, and that she wanted Richard, as Nathan's dad, to walk her down the aisle.

Wrapping things up, I told Lily to pull together her guest list, and made a note to ask her if children would attending the wedding.

The wedding book described handling children's activities before, during, and after the wedding. An especially daunting challenge. But it could wait. I made a note to talk to Lily about it all later.

"So, Toby will carry the rings." I wanted to confirm every detail.

"He'll stand with us, so he'll need a tux," Lily said. "We're already a family, not just a couple."

I suddenly realized with a kind of overwhelming certainty that Lily was the luckiest woman I knew. She'd been given a second chance to be with her child, and she herself had given her child a second chance to live. And she got a really great guy to boot. Who could ask for more than that?

"You've been quiet tonight, Georgia," I said.

"Maybe I never allowed myself to believe this day would come for my family. I'm happy for all of us."

I got a kick out of knowing she'd have the wedding of her dreams, too. If we could pull it off.

Feeling overwhelmed by paper and lists, I needed to get home and make sure I was organizing everything correctly. I understood the value of the workbook pages now, and they'd allow me to keep Lily and Georgia, and their differing fantasies, separate and distinct in my mind.

The next morning, Nora wanted to know all about the meeting. I hesitated to talk about it until I reiterated some ground rules about watching our words in the shop.

Protective of both Lily and Georgia, I didn't want news about their weddings to become fodder for casual banter on the Square.

"Well, Megan, prepare yourself to be even busier. Matt's going to call you today. I asked him to wait to start the foundation business, but once he gets an idea in his head, there's no slowing him down."

"Guess I need to get another notebook," I joked. "With so much going on, my organizational skills will be put to the test." Many years of running a successful business reinforced my confidence in my skills, but I'd also done things my own way, and had been known to turn my back on a mess in my shop at night. Then I'd rush around madly the next morning to get the place ready for customers. That's what I almost pulled off the morning I met Clayton. Too bad I overslept.

Sure enough, Nora and I were in the middle of reorganizing a display when Matt texted with news of the meeting he scheduled at the museum: *Sunday at 7:00. Short. Home before midnight—promise.*

"I see your new husband is quite the comedian," I said. I read the text back to her and remarked, "A five hour meeting…sounds like fun." I didn't tell Nora I hadn't been out past midnight in many months.

I texted back confirming I'd be there. I reminded myself that I was trying this out for three months, and they were trying me out, too, although I had a feeling that staying with it would be my decision. The more I thought about it, the more I wanted to be part of the foundation that was preserving my town's history. In a matter of only a few days, it had become very important to me.

I planned to call Sarah to ask about the inner workings of foundations, including the buzz words I'd probably hear from Matt. I decided to make the call the next morning, right after I placed some new orders to boost the inventory. Studying the growing list of items online, I realized I was moving forward again with my whole heart. And it felt good, real good.

Sarah beat me to it, her call coming in right after I

unlocked the front door. But at least it eliminated one item on my to-do list. She was eager to talk about the meeting, her excitement over the grant still alive and fresh.

"Sunday night is an odd time to hold a board meeting, though," I said, walking to the back of the store. "You have to admit that." It puzzled me. I'd served on committees for the Square and other things, and we somehow managed not to mess up Sunday nights.

"True enough," Sarah said, "but…but…"

"But what?"

"Well, it's still a professional meeting. I don't know why Matt would schedule it for such an odd time. But this project, the grant, well, it's a very big deal."

A little bell rang inside my head. I had told Sarah a little more than I should have about the conversation at the wedding dinner. "I think I get it, Sarah." I chuckled. "You want me to watch my mouth a little. You know, maybe not refer to old rich guys' houses as broken down piles of bricks."

Sarah groaned. "You caught me. And I'm way out of line. Sorry. But it's just such a big development."

"Yet another in a long line of things you've managed to bring to the Square," I said. "But don't worry. I won't embarrass you in front of the hometown crowd. Besides, you know what I really meant. That old Victorian is wonderful, but it's an eyesore—has been for years." I paused. "To tell you the truth, though, I'm going to need your guidance about this. Being on a foundation board is not the same as chairing the Square's Sidewalk Sale committee."

"You've done a lot more than that to help out around here," Sarah said with a laugh, "but I know exactly what you mean. You can count on me to fill in some blanks for you. I've made about every mistake possible in dealing with both the private and public sector in my search for money to fund Wolf Creek projects. I can't give you insight from the inside as a board member, but I know what it's like to approach these various foundations."

"I'll be honest, I'm nervous."

"Sadie said the same thing." Sarah lowered her voice when

she added, "But after what she's been through, I'm surprised she doesn't shy away from this kind of involvement."

"I'm not surprised at all," I said. "She knows exactly how important this project is to the Square, and to you."

I looked across the store at Nora helping a customer at the shelves where we'd just put out new pieces a local potter had delivered. She'd been on her own and doing fine. I might get a day off, after all.

"Oh, by the way, Megan, if Lily wants the Community Center she has to let me know soon. We always have a lot of people inquiring about it. I want her to reserve it first."

"Okay, thanks for letting me know. I'll get back to you." My wedding planner hat firmly on my head, I made a mental note to contact Lily.

Sarah, like Clayton, disconnected before I could say a polite goodbye. Were we all so rushed we couldn't be polite? Or had the definition of polite changed? I decided it was the latter.

My mind drifted back to what I would wear to the foundation meeting on Sunday. Why would I mull over such a trivial decision? I couldn't have said. But with a smock covering my clothes every day, I rarely got to wear some of my favorite things. I liked how I'd felt in the slacks and pinstripe jacket I'd worn to that first dinner with Clayton and Sadie. Maybe I'd wear that to the meeting. It was definitely not stodgy, but then, neither was I. In fact, running down the list of individuals I knew who were involved with this project, they were all serious people, but not at all stuffy. Not Nathan, Matt, or even Gus—especially not Gus.

Picking out clothes and settling on a favorite outfit made me realize that two months had passed since my dinner with Clayton and Sadie. Yet, it seemed much longer ago. The days and weeks had raced by. I reminded myself of Mom, who often talked about how quickly time passed, especially when she was having fun and staying busy. I wondered what she would say about her daughter branching out from florist to wedding planner and now, foundation board member.

By the time the meeting day rolled around, I was celebrating one of the best weekends I'd ever had.

Throngs of people crowded onto the Square. Nora had reorganized many shelves, because most of the yellow dot sale merchandise had sold. She ended up grouping those remaining closer to the sale table.

While she shaped up the shop, I placed yet another order for additional fall and holiday items. We'd soon shift the focus from summer to fall, and the three pumpkin bowls we'd put out were sold shortly after Nora priced them. What did that tell me? Get more stock in through the back door and move it out in shopping bags through the front.

Later, the temperature on the hot day kept rising, prompting Nora to comment that she'd reminded Matt to bring cold bottles of water or iced tea to the meeting. "It's going to be hot inside that old building."

Yikes! She was right. I'd forgotten the museum was not air-conditioned. It was one of a handful of buildings on the Square yet to be renovated and modernized. I laughed at myself as I mentally made another quick clothing switch. A camisole under a light summer jacket. A much better choice.

After locking up, downing a quick sandwich, and changing clothes, I walked to the museum. Matt and Sadie were already there and had moved a hodge-podge of chairs into a circle, with a name tag, a file folder, a notebook, and a pen on each seat.

The name tag seemed a bit much, but a couple of minutes later, I found myself introducing Sadie to David Clark. Gus was in fine form, telling everyone I was his date for the evening. Since there wasn't much to be done about his old-man humor, I had to simply go with it.

"I would be honored if you would sit next to me," Gus said, swooping his arm across his body and exaggerating a bow.

"I don't know, Gus," I said, "Matt had our seats arranged already, including our name tags."

"No problem. As the eldest here, I can move my chair anywhere I like."

He sounded funny, but it wasn't much of a stretch to imagine him chairing a meeting with an air of authority or calling someone to task over a mistake. I had a feeling his humor could vanish in a split second. I'd been on the receiving end of his disapproving glare and would try to avoid that again.

Matt looked at his watch. He wanted to get started, but Nathan hadn't arrived, and neither had Sarah. The reason for the name tags became clearer when Charlie Crawford arrived and I realized not everyone knew him, either. When Sarah and Nathan came in together, Matt got the meeting underway.

Gus shifted the arrangement again to suit himself, this time putting Sarah on his other side. Like me, she kept quiet.

From the minute Matt started down the items on the agenda, his long experience with this kind of grant and project spoke for itself. Our file folders had a detailed timeline for each phase of the project, plus the steps needed to make the museum an entertaining attraction for the town. My enthusiasm grew by the minute. We were going way beyond rows of historical objects with nameplates. Matt was casting a wide net for bids from museum design firms who could create the interactive exhibits to attract children and adults, local people and tourists.

Charlie would oversee building renovations, and calls for bids would go out, but he was recommending two cousins of his who just completed the reconstruction and renovation of one of the historical buildings at Heritage Hill Park in Green Bay. "Reed and Nolan are top carpenters and experienced in historic renovation," he said. "Not that many firms around here are, so this would be a good project for them."

I would help Sadie with the genealogy of Wolf Creek's founding families, and those whose roots went back 100 years or more. Of course, Sarah would be our primary resource for that. Sadie was going to need an entire wall just for Sarah's family, the Hutchinsons and Crawfords, the original founding families.

"Megan is a long time resident of the town," Gus said, "so I'd like her to introduce me to members of the community for the video interviews. Maybe she could come along on some of them to pave the way. We don't know if older residents will want to talk to me. I'm still a stranger."

He was right. I saw myself heading away for an hour here and two hours there, leaving Nora in charge. Somehow, in a matter of an hour or so, phase one of the grant was launched. Now I wondered if I could keep up?

After asking for confidentiality for a little while longer, Matt laid out the next steps, including speaking at the next business owners' association meeting and at a town-hall meeting. So far, only a few people knew about the grant. "We need to make sure we don't have speculation and misinformation spreading around town," he said. "Gus and I have always been transparent with our primary foundation's projects, and we'll operate the same way with these smaller grants."

"Isn't this exciting?" Sadie leaned forward past Gus and Sarah, and touched my arm. "I'll be needing lots of help."

"Just ask when the time comes." So, far, there was nothing intimidating about any of it. What a waste of energy! I'd been nervous for nothing.

AUGUST
22

With Nora at my side, I turned the calendar to August one day early, which gave us a chance to do a quick rundown on the orders ahead and to inventory arrangements on hand and ready for purchase. As the days passed, we were almost like partners in the shop; she'd honed her skills as a florist and also became popular with the repeat customers. Unfortunately, August sales, while still good, came in a notch under the record-breaking July we'd had on the Square.

When the shop was empty and we worked side-by-side, Nora talked about her new life with Matt, including her move to Wolf Creek. They had already begun packing, but the move to Wolf Creek was still some weeks—or even months—away. As I had tactlessly put it, the old mansion was still a wreck.

Meanwhile, the wedding planning went on at full speed, along with working with Gus to set up interviews. He'd taken charge of hiring a videographer, who hired interns from the community college to work on local not-for-profit projects. A perfect partnership for us. He ended all his emails and calls by saying, "I'll call when I need your help."

One morning, Georgia dropped off the work sheets produced by her first wedding planner. Before she left, she jabbed her finger at the top of one page. "Look, she didn't even spell my name right." She turned on her heel and out the door she went.

When I had a few minutes, I looked through the checklist

and Georgia's notes, apprehension stabbing at my gut. More wasted energy. I soon realized Georgia's wedding would need much less time to pull together than Lily's.

During lunch I brought the calendar to the small table, where Nora and I ate our B and B salads.

"Ah, the calendar," Nora said. "I'm not surprised. You're doing so many things all the time, that's one way to keep track of everything. It must be tiring."

I took a swig of water. "Honestly, it's more frightening than tiring. The shop is special to me, but so is the museum, and Georgia and Lily mean the world to me, too. I don't want to fail them."

"You won't." She stabbed at the greens and tuna in her salad. "The thing is, every bride is important to you. That's why Rainbow Gardens has become the go-to place for wedding flowers. Your side business as a wedding planner will just keep growing, too."

"I remember my first wedding. I was so nervous I stuck myself with the pins and dripped blood on the groom's shoes." I laughed at the memory. Then I pointed to the calendar. "August is a transition month for the Square. It's usually hot and dry around here for days and weeks at a time."

Nora confirmed with a nod.

"The school supply lists are out, too. Extra money goes into back-to-school expenses. And many people are home from the vacations. So that usually means less activity on the Square."

Was I trying to convince myself I didn't need Nora in the shop every day? Not really. Nora had stepped in when I most needed her. No longer could Rainbow Gardens be a one-person shop.

"That means fewer tour buses, too, doesn't it?" Nora asked. "At least until the leaf tours." She took a bite of a chocolate chip cookie. "Mmm, these are good."

"Steph makes the best." I fiddled with my pencil. "Have you seen pictures from your wedding yet?" I needed to contract with a photographer for both Lily and Georgia, and soon.

"Yes, and they're fabulous. I was waiting to show them until we settled on what proofs we're using. But I downloaded the file to my iPad."

"So, you really like her? Do you have her name and number?"

"Absolutely. I'm putting a testimonial on her website as soon as I have the final prints."

I scrunched my face. "I hope I haven't waited too long. She could be booked solid for the fall by now. But I'll give her a try. See if she has the time."

"Lily and Georgia will be happy with her. I'm sure of it," Nora said.

"Before I get side-tracked with that, I want you to schedule some days off." I grinned slyly. "I never expected you to work like you own the place."

"I wish I did."

I heard wistfulness in her voice, but the thought of selling Rainbow Gardens stopped me cold. I was here to stay.

"There's a wedding this Saturday morning, and another later in the month, here." I pointed to the days on the calendar. "If you could be here on those days I'd be covered."

"Consider it done." She ran her finger across a three-day span, mid-week and mid-month in August. "I need to be gone these three days." She grinned. "We're moving."

"Moving? Already? I mean, that old house can't be ready yet."

She laughed. "No, but we're eager to get to Wolf Creek, so we rented a duplex in the new subdivision south of town. One side for us, the other for Gus. Matt doesn't want to move without him, and you know Gus. He's telling everyone he's not letting us leave him behind."

"Ooh, the subdivision. You wouldn't know this, of course, but you might say there was a *heated* debate over taking what was once rich farmland and building houses on it."

Nora sighed. "I suppose that's a normal response."

"Some people objected to having their country views changed," I said, "and others thought the new places wouldn't sell and the vacant houses would be an additional eyesore. But young families seemed to flock to get in line to buy the new places."

"'You won't need more than three days to close up Gus's house and yours?" I asked.

"That's what moving companies are for," she said with a laugh. "They'll pack, unpack, and I'll tell them where to put everything. Naturally, Gus wants to settle himself in." She rolled her eyes. "He thinks that if Matt and I take charge, he won't know where anything is."

"That sounds like Gus," I said, "but he'll be glad for the movers. Trust me. He's so busy with the history project he won't want to bother with arranging his closet."

Nora glanced toward the door. "Did you want to see the proofs of the wedding pictures before the crowd picks up?"

"You have your iPad with you?" For some reason that hadn't occurred to me.

"Sure. It doesn't take up any room." She pulled her purse out from under the workbench and within seconds had the dozens and dozens of shots of her wedding for me to see.

"Wow, these are all gorgeous. How will you choose?"

"It hasn't been easy." She clicked on the thumbnail of an image and enlarged it. "Some days I think this one is my favorite," she said, pointing to a close-up of her snuggled close to Matt, both smiling ear to ear. "We look so happy in it."

"I'll say. You're radiant, Nora, and he's a guy who's gone nuts over his wife."

Nora kept clicking, showing me one stunning photo after another—she had the perfect feminine figure for a sheath dress. The rest of us appeared relaxed and in our top form. "JoAnn and David looked almost as happy as you and Matt," I remarked, a curious longing in me taking over.

I suppressed a sigh. I'd soon watch my brother marry Georgia, and Lily and Nathan were getting their happy ending. Nora and Matt made as attractive a couple as anyone could imagine. I was involved with the six of them in various ways, yet on the periphery of their lives. And still alone.

The photos were so much more than a mere record of an event. They expressed emotion, the joy surrounding the

245

marriage. I noted the photographer's website. I wanted her for Lily and Georgia.

"Monrow?" I asked. "That's her name?"

"Artistic, huh?"

"And interesting," I said. "It struck me that she was dressed all in black, and like the men do at any wedding, blended into the background. She wasn't the least bit obtrusive, even with a wedding party of eight."

"I noticed that, too." She patted the calendar, still open in front of us. "So, those three days are okay?"

"Fine. And I'm glad you won't be far away."

We cleared away the remains of lunch as the bell jingled. A foursome of young women came in, each carrying a bag from Styles.

"I'm going upstairs to call Monrow. Holler if you need help."

"Sure thing," said Nora.

Minutes later I heard the bell jingle again so I came downstairs and saw an empty shop. "The women are already gone?"

"They stopped in for information about flowers for a baby shower. I told them we could custom design any arrangement they needed. They took your card and said they'd call."

Maybe they'd call, maybe not. I shrugged it off. "Well, I have the best news. And it's thanks to you." I put my notebook on the table. "Monrow is available for both weddings. When I mentioned your name, she didn't hesitate to commit."

"Word of mouth advertising is the best," Nora said, as she began rearranging the circular display rack, putting a few fall items that had arrived at eye level. Another marketing technique she favored.

As the next few days passed, I focused on Lily's wedding, spending time on the phone and over coffee with Lily after the shop closed. Nora took on more responsibilities and became increasingly familiar with the day-to-day workings of Rainbow Gardens. She even took on the window display, a project I'd all but forgotten in my preoccupation with the upcoming weddings, including the two for which I was providing only the flowers.

I showed Nora where I stored the boxes of display supplies in the basement, but she shooed me away, declining my offer to carry them upstairs.

"My leg is much stronger now. I think being active, standing and walking around, has helped it heal." She flashed her characteristic dazzling smile. "And it's been so much more fun than physical therapy."

"My good fortune." I slapped my hand over my mouth. "Sorry, bad wording, but you know what I mean."

She waved me off.

Speaking of good fortune, I needed to tell Clayton that I considered meeting him, by chance through the contest, my good fortune. Somehow, since I didn't want to say that in a text, it hadn't been said at all.

Every time I checked my to-do list for Lily's wedding I was amazed how easily things were coming together. Too good to be true, maybe? The little flutters in my stomach reminded me not to get overconfident. A disaster, large or small, could have Cinderella sitting next to a pumpkin instead of in a carriage with white horses.

Seriously? A little over dramatic here?

With Nora waiting on customers, I was able to head upstairs to finalize delivery of the arches and garden gates to the community center. The flutters in my stomach became a whirlwind when the owner of the accessories shop sounded flustered, soon admitting she'd marked the wrong date on her calendar. On the day of Lily's wedding, the pieces I requested would be decorating someone else's backyard.

My mind went into overdrive. I took a few deep breaths and thought of Sarah and how often she'd told me stories of circumventing disasters on the Square.

"When are the pieces being returned?" My hand shook as I opened my notebook to a blank page to make notes.

"Not until the following Monday." Her flat tone told me

she was not willing to dig in and solve the problem.

"Monday? That's not acceptable. I need your help here to correct the mistake. Give me the name of the client. I'll call her myself."

With a little more coaxing, she relented and gave me both the woman's name and number.

After a few more calming breaths, I called the bride, who answered on the second ring. Against all odds, she immediately empathized and explained that the decorations would only be needed for the morning backyard wedding. The reception was in another town.

"So, they'll just be left in my parents' yard anyway," she said, "and I'd have thought the company would have wanted to get them back. I'm not sure why they scheduled a Monday pickup."

Another mistake, perhaps? I suspected as much.

It took two more calls, plus a third from the bride, to finalize the arrangements for the decorations. I only needed to arrange for the pickup and delivery myself. I could figure that out.

I laughed to myself. Granted, it was a nervous reaction. One day, after the wedding was long over, I'd tell Lily about the close call with the arches and garden gates. For now, it was my secret. Well, mine and Nora's, but I could trust her to keep my secret.

Thank goodness for an evening wedding! Crisis number 1? Averted. Well, almost.

Later that afternoon, when I brought my trash to the recycle bins in the back, I saw Tracie and Katie working with three men about their age. The women were directing the placement of the shelving the men were moving into The Fiber Barn. Hadn't they said something about a veterans' group that helped carry stock into the store for their opening?

I walked over and followed the men into the store.

"Looks like you're here to stay," I said to Tracie and Katie, both of whom were directing the men as they set up the shelving.

"Come in and see," Tracie said. "Lots of changes since

you were in last."

I stepped inside and, yes, the shop was totally different. It was more inviting now, with a table where customers could sit and browse through patterns and other books on fiber arts. Katie introduced me to the men, who were friendly and pleasant, as well as strong.

"I'm going to be bold here and ask for what I need," I said. "I'm looking to hire some strong guys to do a pickup and delivery for me." I described the particulars of the wedding, including the location of the decorations and the exact timeframe I was working with for it. "And I'll throw in invitations to the wedding. We've got plenty of room, and you can bring a date for the evening."

One of the three men was unavailable for the evening, but the other two jumped at the chance. I laughed when they turned to Katie and Tracie and suggested a foursome.

That was a tidy finish to what could have been a messy problem. I got a delivery and four people got dates. I was surrounded by couples. I didn't allow myself to dwell on that. I was much too busy.

The men left before I did, and without warning, I second-guessed myself. I turned to Katie. "Uh, let me ask you something? Are these guys responsible? I mean, they won't forget the day and the details, will they?"

"Let me put it this way, Megan, I'd trust my life with either one of them," Katie said, not hiding her impatience with the question. Tracie nodded.

"Good to know," I said, embarrassed that I'd unintentionally hurt their feelings. My problem solved, I walked into Rainbow Gardens through the back door.

Into chaos.

"Glad you're back," Nora said. "A tour bus, detoured by road construction, stopped in town." She was interrupted by a woman trying to balance an armful of pottery.

I noticed one was a bright orange pumpkin bowl. I'd come to think of them as Nora's favorites.

"I'll help her." I stuck my notebooks under the workbench. With the amount of information they contained I needed to guard them. I would never admit to it, but I took them to bed with me.

"You're a lively group," I said to the group of four clustered around the garden art.

"We're bonding," one woman said. "Can't you tell?"

I must have looked puzzled because a man around my age quickly explained that they were teachers from a nearby district on a pre-back-to-school field trip, teachers only.

"Looks to me like you're bonding over whimsical garden pieces," I said, grinning.

"The administration planned a different day, but lucky for us, road construction got in the way and we get to shop instead." The woman who spoke was eyeing the garden reflecting ball.

"That's my last one," I said, putting a playful warning tone in my voice.

"I love it," she said. "I'm going to get it for my classroom. It can sit in the corner—the kids will love it."

"I'll help you carry it to the bus," the man offered.

"Now that's some teacher bonding," I quipped, pleased with the sale.

A few minutes later, the ball and the stand were paid for and packaged, and the two carried it across the Square and onto the path to the parking area reserved for buses.

Meanwhile, Nora was running credit cards and fielding questions.

I stood back as the teachers came and went, most carrying bags with logos from the different shops on the Square. I saw many from The Fiber Barn and Quilts Galore, and plenty from Styles. Farmer Foods often attracted shoppers, too, because of the local jams and honey they stocked. We all benefitted from the detour.

"Next time call me for help," I told Nora when the last customer left and we could breathe again.

"You told me I'd learn this business…" She stopped to think. "I believe your exact words were 'trial by fire.' I wanted to see how much fire I could handle."

"One customer at a time." That had been another saying my wise dad used often.

"And a few calls for you." She handed me a list.

"None for you?" I laughed when her eyes got huge.

"I'm sure my voice mailbox will be full soon. Gus is debating what he should pack for moving. He calls all the time, even after I told him I was working, but…" She put her hands in the air. "So, what was I to do? I turned my phone off."

Together, we straightened the display area, and with closing time only minutes away, I ran the totals for the day. Wow, teachers were big spenders. Well, not really. But considering they were gearing up for the school year, they'd obviously had some fun.

"Oh, by the way, one of those calls is from someone in that group from the other day that asked about flowers for a baby shower."

"Good deal…I'll call her back."

She shut the door and the bell filled the room with a happy sound of jingling.

23

My happy spirit made me less concerned about what was happening—or not happening—between Clayton and me. The summer was drawing to a close, but with the wedding business opening up a new path in my life, I was content for the time being to have an easy going friendship with him. We texted a couple of times a day, called back and forth now and then, and waved to each other at morning coffee at B and B, where even the established couples on the Square drifted to the women's and men's tables. We were both busy, on the run, and finding our way in our new ventures.

One evening after closing, I sent a text inviting him to meet me for a drink at Sid's Corner Pub, a small restaurant a couple of blocks off the Square. Another night, he called me to join him and Art and Marianna for pie and coffee at Crossroads. These interludes kept us connected through the hectic summer days.

Although the days—and evenings—were hot and sultry, the calendar didn't lie and the last of the summer tour bus visits made the days fly by. I managed to convince Gus to wait until after Lily's wedding to begin his series of interviews, but that didn't keep him from stopping by the shop at closing time to invite me to Crossroads for dinner.

He grinned when I checked my calendar, but a few days before, I'd gone out for pizza with Clayton, completely forgetting about a meeting with Lily. It was a great evening, too, but that was hardly the point. Missing a meeting was not the best way to calm a bride's anxiety over the details of her wedding!

"I'm good to go," I said, flipping my calendar closed.

I grabbed my purse and followed him out, and as I turned to lock the door, I noticed something shiny in the window. I looked closer. Nora had changed the window displays, but had never said a word.

"Something wrong?" Gus asked. "You look shocked about something."

"I'm so embarrassed." I pointed to the window. "Nora changed the display, but I didn't notice it until now."

"Hmm…well, Nora mentioned you're busy all the time these days, almost like you're running away."

Running away? "I might have considered literally doing that a while ago, but not now. Wolf Creek is the place for me." I wanted to stay longer and look at the displays, which I could see had a Labor Day theme. The sun bounced off a large cutout of a silver star that covered the floor. But Gus tugged at my arm.

"You can study those later. We need to get a move on," Gus said, "or all the window tables will be taken."

I grinned. "Yes, sir."

During our dinner, which we ate at the last available window table, Gus told me stories of himself as a young man earning a fortune trading in gold and silver, only to lose it, gain it back and then lose it again, before he figured out how to make money grow. At that point, he started his own financial consulting firm.

"After I lost so much money, but then figured out how to rebuild, I was certain I could help others avoid making the same mistakes."

"You need to share your story, Gus, so others can benefit from it."

He waved his hand at me. "Nah, no one will listen to an old man."

"Oh, yes, they will. You know a lot, and you're funny, and you spin a good yarn. I know some people who would love to hear you speak." Those young mothers who had gathered at Quilts Galore needed exactly the kind of schooling on money and life that Gus could offer.

Over coffee, Gus confided his disappointment with the

Alexander Foundation under the direction of his son and daughter-in-law. I also sensed an ongoing sadness about what seemed like a rejection of Matt and Nora's marriage. Gus seemed to push that aside, though, and I immediately saw it was an off-limits topic. He quickly perked up when the subject turned to Matt and their *new* foundation.

"Needless to say, I'm a fan of the new foundation coming to Wolf Creek," I said.

"It's a unique place," Gus said. "Lots of history here, and interest in the future."

My sentiments exactly.

Dusk had arrived before Gus and I finished dinner. After he left me at the door and crossed the Square to his car, I stepped back outside to look at the front windows. Nora had put out a variety of patriotic bowls, some filled with carnations, some left empty. Others were stacked two or three high. She'd found old bunting I used years ago for Memorial Day and wove it around the edges of the window and across the back, ending at a hand-lettered sign: *Labor Day—Support the Workers of America.*

I had one word for Nora's efforts. *Extraordinary.*

I smiled when I saw the theme in the other window. A small desk was placed off to the side, a large bowl of artificial apples sat next to it on the floor. Among my old supplies of decorations, she'd found a flower container with "Teacher" painted across the front and had used zinnias, mums, and greenery to form a simple arrangement.

Other than using the abundance of wild flowers that filled the fields and bordered our local roads, finding suitable back-to-school and Labor Day decorations were tricky for many shops on the Square, including mine. But Nora had combined both with a light hand. And it was her first attempt. Some tension I hadn't even been aware of melted away. I no longer had to come up with *every* idea to stay fresh twelve months a year. I'd be pleased to tell Nora the window displays between now and the end of the year were hers if she wanted to take them on. Imagine what she'd come up with for December... I couldn't wait to see.

I planned to apologize for my lack of attention. Good

thing Nora was a self-starter. But then, I'd given her little choice.

If late August slowed down a bit, it was only to give us a chance to rev up for Labor Day weekend, the high point of September. The vendors would be back to sell their wares within the Square itself, with some due to return in early fall with the Harvest Festival and Halloween.

Busy with Farmer Foods, Eli hadn't been in my shop lately, so I was surprised when he requested my help with the vendors. Since I couldn't remember the last time Eli had asked me for help in recent years, I said yes without checking the schedule.

The trucks cleared out of the Square shortly before the shops opened on Friday morning, but with so many vendors, their canopies nearly overlapped. I helped Eli put the placards for the tents in order and was about to ask what else he needed when a tall, willowy woman about Eli's age spoke just before I did. "Mr. Reynolds." She reached out and put her fingertips on his arm.

He jumped back, startled by her touch. "Yes."

"My name is Zoe Miller and I've reserved a vendor booth for the weekend."

Eli checked his list. "Yes, you're on my list. I have assigned you a table farther down the row, across from Country Law." He pointed to the other end of the Square.

"I'll take this booth." She pointed to the one nearest us, the first one on the corner in front of Farmer Foods.

"Uh, this one is for Farmer Foods, you see, and uh, we've had this space for years."

I stared at my brother. He was nearly tongue-tied. A strange and new phenomenon. Usually, he blurted whatever thought popped into his head.

I took a closer look at Zoe Miller, with her huge brown eyes and hair, the color of rich sable, hanging free to her waist. As tall as she was, she had the advantage of being eye to eye with Eli.

I tried hard to suppress a smile, but failed. Giving me a sidelong glance, Eli saw I was amused and frowned. He likely expected me to jump in and help. I moved closer, but I wasn't going to rescue him. This was much too entertaining.

"Like I said, Ms. Miller, your booth is farther down the row."

"But, Mr. Reynolds—may I call you Eli?—the energy is the strongest here. I need to be in *this* booth." She touched his arm again and sent the most radiant smile his way.

Eli bought a little time fumbling with the signs until he found hers.

"Well, all right," he said, stealing a quick look at her, "I uh, suppose we could move everyone down one booth." He gave the placards to me. "Here, you take care of these."

Well, well, Madam Zoe had made quick work of my tall, grouchy brother. I couldn't wait to tell Clayton. I pulled out my phone and sent him a text.

SEPTEMBER
24

Memorial Day was one bookend, and Labor Day its pair. The success of both holiday weekends depended on Wisconsin weather, so when bright sunlight filled my bedroom I started the morning energized and happy. I wanted a busy Square with lots of customers, and since Nora planned to work all three days, I'd be free to leave my shop now and then to take a quick walk around to the other stores and visit the vendors. I was eager to see what they offered, because I often did some early Christmas shopping over Labor Day weekend. This year I'd added Georgia and Nora to my list—and Gus.

By the time I unlocked the front door, most of the vendors had filled their tents and groups of people were wandering from booth to booth. And music. Sarah had mentioned that various bands would be performing in the bandstand during the day and into the evenings, but at 10:00 AM on Saturday? Apparently.

Nora arrived with three shopping bags. She put them just inside the door and said, "I'll be right back. A vendor's holding more bags for me."

She was back in a matter of minutes. Talk about power shopping. This lady had the technique down pat.

"Have you seen Madam Zoe?" she asked, stashing her purse and donning her apron before taking a breath. "Everyone was talking at coffee the other morning about a fortune teller coming this weekend, so I had to have a reading."

I waved my hands in the air. "Wait, wait. You've been to morning coffee?"

"You've been so busy, I figured I'd go over one morning and see what was up. Georgia recognized me and introduced me to the others." She finished tying her apron and went to look at herself in the mirror of the cooler. She smoothed her hair and straightened her apron. "Actually, everyone was happy to meet me and invited me to visit their shops."

I was happy. And angry, no, *disappointed* in myself. Happy that Nora had forged ahead to meet the group on the Square. And disappointed that I hadn't followed through on my promise to introduce her. Nora didn't seem to mind, but that was beside the point. I hadn't kept my word and that got me down.

There was nothing I could do until after Lily and Georgia's weddings to ease my time commitments, but, then, how busy did I want to be? I was too busy to keep a promise to Nora, and barely managed a quick drink or pizza dinner with Clayton. Texts and calls were fine, but they didn't make a relationship.

"So what did Madam Zoe tell you about your future?" I asked, interested.

"The usual: good life, happy times, and…here's the best news…*changes* in the family." Her radiant smile appeared. "Maybe that means my in-laws will come around and accept me. Matt doesn't talk about it, but I know that would make him happy."

Her frown told me she had more on her mind, but she was saved by the jingling bell. She switched to business mode fast when a family came in. Rainbow Gardens wasn't geared for small children, and I'd learned to keep a watchful eye when they entered.

This family handled the situation themselves. Quietly and without fanfare, Dad herded the three kids back outside. Mom roamed the shop alone. Disaster averted. But the woman slipped out empty-handed at the same time a large group came in.

By closing time, Nora and I were giddy from fatigue and nonstop talking to an endless stream of customers. We tried to fill the empty spaces on the shelves during the day, but laughed when shoppers took the items out of our hands before we could display them.

I didn't want to open the shop without stock available, so I worked until midnight bringing inventory upstairs and reorganizing the tables and shelves. Before I went upstairs I shuffled through a drawer next to the workbench where I stashed stray notes and business cards. I always meant to organize them, but somehow never got around to it. I sorted through the cards until I found the one I was looking for. In the morning, I'd call the teacher I'd spoken to back in May, and if he was still interested, set up a time to speak to his science classes at the middle school. With Nora available to take care of the shop, it was time for me to pass on some of what my two wonderful mentors had taught me about flowers.

I slept well knowing my shop and I were ready for another day.

By late Monday afternoon, Madam Zoe dominated the buzz on the Square, mostly because she had a steady stream of customers waiting in line. Eli had stopped in during the day, proud as a peacock for the way he'd managed the vendors.

"Guess you'll help Sarah next year, huh?" I observed.

"Don't see why not. It's not a hard job."

"And Ms. Zoe?"

"She's a fake. We all know that, but people enjoying having her here."

I shook my head. Eli's people skills left a lot to be desired. He'd have to change his ways if he was going to be in charge of the vendors every year.

I wanted to tackle the mess in my shop on Tuesday morning, when I'd be alone for the first time in several days. The new flower delivery needed immediate attention, and in unpacking and storing the flowers in the cooler, I had a chance to reflect on the previous days. All the shops and vendors had finished a successful summer season with a blowout Labor Day weekend. Next month would begin the holiday celebrations and we'd sail along to the end of another year. Could be some rough waters—including fall and early winter storms—along the way, but they were always exciting months.

I unlocked the door and let in my first customer. She glanced around, but in a disinterested sort of way. "Sorry to bother you, but there's a sign in Clayton's window saying the shop is closed until further notice. Do you know when that might be?"

"Closed?" He'd never mentioned closing during our numerous texts over the weekend or during any of our recent evenings out. I ran next door and confirmed the lady's message. "Why? When?" I asked the air, not believing Clayton could, or would, walk away from Wolf Creek. *From me.*

The woman left with no more information than she had before she came in.

I pulled out my phone and tried calling Clayton. The call went to voice mail, so I texted him. I waited a few minutes. No reply.

I tried Sadie next. "I'm sorry, Megan, but this is something Clayton needs to explain to you. He's taking care of something from his past." She was quick to end the call.

Sarah didn't know much more, only that he'd closed his shop and left town. At least that was all she was willing to say.

I was desperate and kept searching my mind for something that might provide an answer. Art was no help, either. He was as surprised as I was that the shop was closed.

Heidi. Heidi Fairmont, the young student Clayton hired. He must have told her, although she'd be going back to school soon. During a couple of free moments, I grabbed the phone book I kept under the counter and saw three Fairmonts listed.

Later that morning, I dialed each number and asked for Heidi or left a message. A couple of hours later, Heidi called back, and when I asked her about Clayton, she said she hadn't worked in his shop for over a week.

A week? That meant he'd handled Labor Day without Heidi's help.

Clayton was hiding something from me. That hurt. Over the few months I'd known him, I'd given him my heart. Maybe he didn't know that, but I did.

I turned my attention to the flowers. They brought me back to my real life, a life I could see and touch, not some fantasy with Clayton. I prepared the arrangements to fill the orders and sorted the few older flowers in the cooler. I'd sold most of my flower supply over the weekend.

When I cleaned the mirror in the cooler I took a minute to look at myself. I saw the same person who had entered the Bartholomew contest. Maybe I was the same on the outside, but inside my world had tilted, and I didn't know if I could right myself.

The day dragged by, and with few people on the Square, I locked the door early and went upstairs. I couldn't hide myself the way Clayton did. I had Lily's Cinderella wedding to focus on. She had a flesh and blood prince to marry, and it was my job to make it a fairytale. Oh, boy, lucky me.

I spent many nervous moments anticipating possible problems that would turn Nathan and Lily's wedding into a train wreck. My worst nightmare. But using local suppliers helped ease my fears. Lily and Nathan's story was well enough known that most people wished them the best and were happy to be included in the wedding plans.

In a matter of an hour, the arches and garden gates had been delivered from a backyard to the community center, transforming it into a garden complete with trees decorated with fairy lights. At the front, the arches and garden gates we loaded with flowers.

"I don't care what kinds of flowers we have," Lily had said when it was time to place her large order. "But I want lots of colors. Everything doesn't need to be white."

As planned, at 6:00 in the evening, Toby held a small cushion with the matching wedding rings attached and took careful steps to the front where he joined Nathan and Jack. Then the lights dimmed and Lily walked down the white carpet on the arm of Richard Connor. She smiled at Nathan and he moved into place next to her. And so began what Lily believed to be her Cinderella life. For the moment, everyone present caught the fairytale fever, and if there were dry eyes in the house, I couldn't spot them.

As the ceremony progressed, Monrow ducked in and out of corners and between people to get her pictures. Meanwhile, the videographer, who was also the instructor at the college, was surreptitiously recording the ceremony. Before the reception began I had checked my notes one more time, but stayed in the background as wedding planners and photographers are supposed to. Meanwhile, Clayton's absence was noted. By me. Others had been curious, but no one else felt his disappearance as a personal loss.

After a full day of rushing and worrying, I stuck myself at a corner table to take a breather. Ahh, it felt good to sit.

I grabbed my phone when it beeped an incoming text. Since I'd given up on hearing from Clayton, his text with a selfie came as a surprise. The twinkle in his eyes and his smile sent jitters through my body, head to toe. Another text quickly followed, with a picture of a program from a gallery opening that showcased Clayton's flower paintings.

I took in a quick breath, but my heart raced ahead. The name of the exhibit was *Megan's Garden*, with his painting of the white lily he'd shown me when it was still an illustration.

He'd taken his paintings captured from the farmhouse to New York. A third text with another photo came in, this one of Clayton with Gretchen, who showed a thumbs up to the camera. That said it all.

I tried to hold back the tears when the final text came: *Home for E n G wedding. I lv U.*

Yearning to hear his voice, I called him once, and then again, but all I got was his voice mail.

I went to find Sadie to see if she knew about "Megan's Garden," but Sarah said she'd already left.

The wedding ended with Nathan and Lily getting into

their white carriage—a limo—for their honeymoon in Door County. That was my signal to begin to gather my boxes and bags. The caterers were cleaning up, the rental company would pick up the infamous arches and gates in the morning, and the flowers would be sent home with various guests.

Every cell tingled, and I so wanted to be alone with my thoughts and feelings about Clayton…and *Megan's Garden.* When I finally got home, I read the texts again and again, then smiled back at the photo of Clayton smiling at me.

❀   ❀   ❀

It was my secret, and I enjoyed every minute of it. Clayton had called every day about his return to New York and sometimes we talked late into the night. And I kept our conversations to myself.

I waited until a week after the wedding to finally show Nora the picture of the exhibit brochure. She responded by giving me a big hug. Nora had started out as an employee, but she had now become my friend.

One morning near the end of the month, Lily, back from her honeymoon, ran into the shop, apparently on a mission. "Oh, Megan. You did it. Everything was perfect. Just like my life." She twirled around, then stopped and wrapped me in a tight hug.

"Did you hear about Georgia's gift?"

I shook my head. I didn't know what she was talking about.

"She gave us her house! The family home. And it has a big backyard for Toby."

"Oh, Lily, how wonderful. Your life just keeps getting better and better."

Like mine, but I'll never tell…not until the moment is perfect.

"And I want to do something special for Georgia, but I have no idea."

"Something for their house or maybe for the horses?" I asked.

"Horses?" Megan frowned. "They have horses?"

263

"Yup, she and Elliot each have one."

"Okay, thanks for the idea." She left as fast as she'd come in.

Since Elliot and Georgia's wedding was approaching fast, my focus was on them and on Clayton's return. Oh, yeah, and Rainbow Gardens. After a couple of phone calls and a quick discussion with Nora, I'd scheduled a trip to the Howard-Suamico middle school in late October. What had once seemed impossible was now a firm date on my calendar. Steadily, one development at a time, life was feeling fuller—and I liked it that way.

OCTOBER
25

Almost overnight, the Square had changed from summer decorations to scarecrows and mums and marigolds in brilliant colors of rust, gold, and burgundy. Bales of straw, stacked in groups of twos and threes were embellished with pumpkins and gourds and the brilliant orange leaves on the maple trees sparkled in the sunlight.

In childish fashion, as one day ended, I marked it with a big X. Each X meant Clayton was one day closer to returning to Wolf Creek. *To me*. Our conversations were sprinkled with talk of "when I get back," and "next year we'll…" We had dreams, but even better, we had plans.

Sometimes, Clayton would wryly repeat one of the comments from friends, who were astonished about his move to Wolf Creek. "They call it the boonies, or if someone is being extra polite, they tell me how charming the 'Heartland' can be."

Maybe at one time I'd have been offended, but now I only laughed. Soon he'd be back in the Heartland, where he'd won my heart.

Considering that Clayton was always on my mind, it seemed almost odd to go out to the farm alone one evening. But I wanted to check on the pumpkins I'd planted in the spring. I also needed to look at the array of flowers in the gardens so I could see what we could cut for Georgia's wedding. As long as the flowers came from the garden, she was happy. The garden was as strong a link to our family as the house itself.

A few years back, I'd found a popular niche with my artistically carved pumpkins I sold only in October, when demand was high enough to justify the labor intensive job of making each one unique. They were great fun to create, though. That evening, I found six that were ready for picking, enough to keep me busy the rest of the week. I'd carve many more later...after the wedding.

Fortunately, Georgia's original wedding planner had secured the large tent that would sit in the middle of the Square, along with the rented tables and chairs for the open air meal. It seemed fitting that since the Reynolds, Owens, and Winters families helped establish this community, their descendants would want everyone to be part of their hometown celebration.

Elliot had arranged for the veterans' group to grill the hamburgers and hot dogs, served with Stephanie's famous potato salad and gourmet baked beans. She managed to offer something for everyone, including raw vegetable and fruit platters, and large bowls of pasta in marinara sauce. With Steph acting as caterer and Elliot managing logistics, I never gave the food another thought.

Well, maybe a couple of thoughts, primarily because the noon wedding was the peak time on the Square. Georgia had planned it that way and assured me she was prepared to supply enough food for all comers. Was that possible? I had my doubts, but Step and Elliot were confident they'd calculated for the maximum number of guests. Time would tell.

"I want to help you cut the flowers at the farmhouse for the tables," Georgia said a few days before the wedding. "I found old canning jars in the basement we can use for vases."

"Maybe we can put a red checkered napkin under the jars. That would add a little color," I suggested.

Georgia beamed. "Oh, I like that idea."

I smiled inside. I'd managed to find the easiest-to-please

bride in all of Wisconsin. Georgia had a vision, and it turned out to be pretty easy to create.

A DJ would handle the music, the same guy who was at last year's Harvest Festival. Meanwhile, Cindy Baker checked in with me about the bride's and groom's cakes. Lily couldn't have been happier with hers, and now a public wedding would spread the word about Cindy's wedding cake business. "Just make sure you allow plenty of table space," Cindy had said.

I added a note to my list, and over the next few days I checked off one item after another.

Then their day finally arrived. When the music started on a golden fall day, the Square was alive with shop owners, employees, and visitors, who stood and watched Beverly and Eli take their places, ready to walk the length of the tent. Virgie had designed a rust colored dress for Beverly—she looked wonderful. And my brother, well, Eli looked like no one had told him a suit was required. Still, he was handsome in the crisp white shirt and black suit.

Relaxed as always, Elliot stood with the minister. He'd waited a long time, but now he was finally marrying the love of his life. I couldn't resist waving at him from the back and his subtle nod let me know he'd seen me.

Georgia had asked me about being an attendant, but while not saying no outright, I explained I couldn't be both the planner and a member of the wedding party. She was fine with that. She didn't want a big glitzy scene like Lily's fairytale anyway. It wasn't so much the age difference as it was Georgia's quieter personality.

Watching Georgia now made me think about my brother's incredible luck. No starry-eyed bride for him. Elliot and Georgia were true life partners. I bubbled with joy for my brother, and carried a secret wish Eli would one day look as happy as his twin.

Beverly and Virgie had made Georgia's dress, a soft burgundy silk, with three-quarter sleeves and a handkerchief hem. To go over her dress, Virgie had fashioned a length of paisley print fabric, rich in fall colors, into a long vest styled like a shawl. As planned, Georgia carried flowers from the gardens at the farm.

On the arm of Jack Pearson, her boss at Country Law, Georgia's dress swished as she walked the length of the tent toward Elliot.

Meanwhile, Monrow, gorgeous in her black pantsuit, moved around, as if in a dance, bending, leaning in, leaning back, raising, and lowering the camera as she shot numerous pictures. I was likely the only one who paid any attention to her.

The ceremony, short but poignant, made me think about marriage, the partnership that was formalized, and the kind of joyful event it could be. Their kiss at the end was greeted with hoots and whistles and loud applause.

Let the party begin.

Except for me, although I was careful to conceal my disappointment. I wasn't about to ruin my brother's day by revealing how sad I was that Clayton hadn't showed up. With both of us rushed and busy, we hadn't spoken in two days. But one of the last things he'd said was that he'd be back in Wolf Creek in time for the wedding.

I'd put my faith in his promise, which had set me up to be disappointed. And I was.

I avoided small talk and focused on the men at the grill who began turning out a steady supply of hot dogs and burgers. I moved in and out of the tent, pretending to efficiently assess what was going on, although we hadn't encountered anything close to a glitch. The more the people lined up for food, the faster Steph and her crew moved to supply it.

I stood back for the traditional cake cutting, which made for lots of laughter when Elliot put frosting on Georgia's nose and then kissed it off. Sure enough, Monrow was there to capture the moment.

I sighed to myself, wishing the day would pass more quickly.

When my phone pinged, my stomach flipped. Maybe, maybe…

There it was. *"Delayed, mechanical. NY. Didn't want to interrupt ceremony. Sorry."*

I moved to the tent and took a few photos of the newlyweds and sent them to him, texting, *"Wish U were here."*

Then he wrote back, *"Wait 4 me."*

My spirits again soared. I'd have saved myself many angst-filled moments if I'd known of his troubles earlier.

And with a message now and then and the wonders of the electronic age, he was in Wolf Creek at the wedding in spirit.

Later in the evening, tables had been moved aside and a wooden dance floor assembled. This was a party that would last into the night, maybe into morning. Neither Elliot nor Georgia looked like they would leave early.

When the DJ announced that the traditional bride and groom's dance would begin, I looked at the crowd gathered to be part of yet another change to Wolf Creek Square. Newer shop owners, like Marianna Spencer rested her head on Art Carlson's shoulder. His son, Alan, stood with his arm around Rachel Spencer, Marianna's step-daughter.

Liz Pearson, Jack's wife, buzzed about the crowd in her usual animated way, always visible in her signature look, a silk geometric jacket. Sarah and Sadie sat together at one table, and Richard Connor had joined them. I watched Gus Alexander head their way.

Nathan and Lily spent most of their time on the dance floor, and Katie and Tracie seemed to have lucked out with their dates, who were pretty smooth dancers.

If I'd made my presence more obvious, I could have taken a few turns on the floor myself. Gus would have been only too happy to shuffle me around, and Matt and Elliot each would have done his duty and coaxed me to dance. I spotted Eli as he ducked out of the tent. And I also was ready to slip off quietly. Georgia had wanted a hometown wedding and that's exactly what she got. As her wedding planner, I'd done very little.

I was about to leave when another text from Clayton arrived: *"Dance with me."*

I must have said yes out loud because I heard him laugh. I spun around and rushed to him, flinging my arms around him, not caring who saw me kiss him.

We danced through the next song the DJ chose and the one after that. But the music didn't matter. We were locked inside our own world, making our own music.

"Can you leave soon?" he said, his mouth against my ear.

"Any time now. My job is done for today."

I linked my arm in his as we walked under a starry sky toward his gallery, listening to the rustle of leaves blowing across the Square.

He unlocked his door and with the light from the antique street lights we navigated through the empty display walls to the steps leading to his studio. A few lengthy kisses slowed our progress.

He turned on the light switch and the room filled with soft light. One spotlight shone on his easel, the painting resting on it covered by a soft cloth. He stood behind me, his hand on my shoulders.

"Megan, my love. I fell in love with you the first day we met. You in your old baggy jeans and paint-spattered shirt. But I couldn't let my feelings show until I proved to myself I had a future to offer you."

I tried to turn toward him, but he resisted, keeping his hands on top of my shoulders as I still faced the easel.

"Because of you," he continued, "what you saw in me, and your belief in my talent, I'm here to stay." He reached around me and lifted the cloth.

I gasped. Tears pooled in my eyes. He'd painted my three contest entries using his new technique of watercolor and ink.

I had no words, but the gasp communicated everything. I didn't move, so he came around to face me. "You like it?"

"Oh, Clayton. I don't know what to say. I'm speechless."

"You don't need words." His arms brought me to him. "I love you, Megan."

And the words finally came, the only ones I needed. "I love you back."

Clayton took my hand and led me to the window, where we stood looking down on the Square. "Your home, and now mine, too," he said.

I smiled at the scene below, some couples still dancing,

but the crowd slowly thinning as the evening drew to a close.

He reached into his pocket and brought out a blue Art&Son box. When he opened it, I saw a twinkle in his eyes. "I know a great wedding planner."

"You don't say? I hope she's available." I laughed as I wrapped my arms around him. My mystery man had come to life. Best of all, he'd come to me. I hadn't needed to walk away from everyone and everything I loved. Now, we were both home.

If you enjoyed reading about Megan's story in Rainbow Gardens, you may enjoy these other books by Wisconsin authors— Virginia McCullough, Lily Silver, and Nancy Sweetland...

Praise for The Jacks of Her Heart by Virginia McCullough:

"Such a romantic book... loved the main characters so much! I was starry-eyed right with them."
—Audrey Greenwell

Virginia McCullough

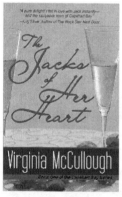

The Jacks of Her Heart

Lorna Lindstrom and Jack Young just got married in the tropics—and their grownup kids don't like it one bit...

Mere acquaintances in their hometown of Capehart Bay, Wisconsin, Jack and Lorna turn up on the same Caribbean cruise. They soon fall victim to moonlight, champagne, and dancing—and that leads to an impulsive wedding. But now they're back home, feeling like a couple of fools. Both agree a quick divorce is their best way out of this embarrassing predicament. Lorna's two kids and Jack's daughter are all for that, but their meddling prompts the stubborn newlyweds to rethink their plan.

A professional organizer, Lorna is a little *too* proud of her spotless home. She fell in love with Jack's generous heart, but must he rescue every abandoned dog in town? The owner of a popular '60s nostalgia café, Jack feels right at home in Lorna's bedroom, but he might as well be a stranger everywhere else in her perfect house. Suspicions that Lorna's up-and-coming professor son-in-law is a womanizer soon pushes Jack into a different kind of rescue mission. Meanwhile, Lorna steps up and organizes her elderly father-in-law's move and offers her support to Jack's daughter in a crisis with baby Joanie. Too bad those classic "irreconcilable differences" appear to doom the pair, even as their kids are beginning to warm to the marriage.

Maybe sharing a couple of romantic dances on the night Jack launches his Blue Sky Nostalgia Music Festival can bring this "opposites attract duo" together again. Will Jack and Lorna decide they can find a way to make peace with their dueling quirks and have some fun with their second-chance romance?

Before she began writing novels, Virginia McCullough was a ghostwriter for doctors, therapists, lawyers, professional speakers, and many others, and she produced over 100 nonfiction books for her clients. Her award-winning novels that have Wisconsin as the setting include *Greta's Grace, Amber Light, The Chapels on the Hill*, and *Island Healing*. Asked about the themes of her fiction, she says her stories always come down to hope, healing, and plenty of second chances.

Praise for Gallant Rogue
by Lily Silver:

Lily Silver

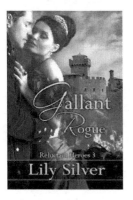

Gallant Rogue

*She's determined to escape her past
and change her future...*

Chloe O'Donovan decides to take charge of her destiny and
begin anew in a place where no one knows she is the love
child of a plantation steward and a slave. She sets off for
Spain in the hope of finding the love and acceptance with her
father's family. The only obstacle is the dashing sea captain
who kindles desires she believed were buried forever with
her beloved husband. Captain Jack Rawlings represents her
past—a past rife with scandal, rejection and heartache. Can
she ignore her feelings for Jack to embrace a brighter future?

He's reluctant to let go of the past and embrace the future...

Captain Jack Rawlings lost everything years ago; his fiancée, his wealth, even his self-respect. Could it be a change in the wind when Jack is given the task of escorting a beautiful widow across the sea to Spain? Jack must protect the woman he once fancied and might have wed years ago. His attraction to Chloe interferes with his tasks as they make the journey from the West Indies to a country struggling to break free of Napoleon's iron grasp. As they travel through the dangerous Spanish countryside, Jack will do whatever it takes to protect Chloe from French soldiers, but he's not certain he can protect her from his own desires.

This is Book Three of Reluctant Heroes; Bold Men, Independent Women...finding true love was never in their plans!

Lily Silver lives in Northeastern Wisconsin near the shores of Green Bay. She loves history and romance so it seems natural to blend the two in her writing. When not writing she enjoys working in her art studio and enjoying nature photography.

Praise for **The House On the Dunes**
by Nancy Sweetland:

Nancy Sweetland

The House On the Dunes

Will learning the truth cost Olivia the only life she's ever known?

Surprised by inheriting spectacular emeralds and a lavish home on Lake Michigan, Olivia Hobart is compelled to uncover the secrets of her late mother's past. Ignoring her controlling husband's wishes, she moves into Dunes House to learn what has been concealed. But her efforts are complicated by dangerous incidents and withheld information. Is the old caretaker really blameless or the possessor of long-held secrets? Is her handsome neighbor romantically interested in her or only attempting to gain access to what has he sees as his rightful estate? Dunes

House holds the answers…but will learning the truth bring to light an affair that could cost Olivia the only life she has ever known?

Along with mysteries (*The Spa Murders* and *The Virgin Murders*) and romance novels (*The Door to Love* and *Wannabe*) set in small Wisconsin towns, Nancy Sweetland has published articles, award-winning short stories and juvenile picture books. Her Midwestern characters reveal the hopes, dreams and problems of ordinary people living sometimes extraordinary lives.

Acknowledgements

No book is created without the help and support of many people, usually too many to name individually. However, I do want to mention a few.

First, and always, my family. My husband, Gary, understands that sometimes characters become real people I've invited to dinner. In male understanding, he shakes his head. Mom has supported all of my dreams, and is the reason I write. I love you both.

I would like to thank Lily S., author and artist, for sharing her knowledge of watercolor painting and ink work. Your suggestions added realism and texture to my story. Thank you.

Also, florist Bridget E. who offered continued support for this story, and generously shared her knowledge of flowers. Your talent brings happiness to many.

There are special friends, critique partners through the years who lend an understanding ear when I struggle to get the words right. Kate Bowman, Shirley Cayer, Virginia McCullough, and Barb Raffin have been with me from the beginning. Oh, what a ride it has been.

To members of the Greater Green Bay Area of the Wisconsin Romance Writers of America. Thank you for the support each of you has given me.

Brittiany Koren and the production team at Written Dreams transform my words into a book. Your work makes my story a joy to hold. Thank you.

About the Author

Gini Athey grew up in a house of readers, so much so it wasn't unusual for members of her family to sit around the table and read while they were eating. But early on, she showed limited interest in the pastime. In fact, on one trip to the library to pick out a book for a book report, she recalls telling the librarian, "I want books with *thick* pages and big print."

Eventually that all changed. Today, Gini usually reads three or four books at the same time, and her to-be-read pile towers next to her favorite chair. She reads widely in many genres, but her favorite books focus on families, with all their various challenges and rewards.

For many years, Gini has been a member of the Wisconsin chapter (WisRWA) of the Romance Writers of America and has served in a variety of administrative positions.

Avid travelers, Gini and her husband live in a rural area west of Green Bay, Wisconsin.

Rainbow Gardens is the third book in her Wolf Creek Square Series; *Quilts Galore* is book one, and *Country Law*, book two. For information about Gini and her series, visit her website at www.giniathey.com.